DAPHNE'S GHOST

D L BAYLIS

First published in Great Britain in 2019 by Master Crest Books

First published in paperback in 2019

Copyright © D L Baylis 2019

D L Baylis asserts the moral right under the Copyright, Designs and
Patents Act 1988 to be identified as the author of this work.

*This is a work of fiction. Names, places, events and incidents are either the
products of the author's imagination or used fictitiously. Any resemblance to
actual persons, living or dead, or actual events is purely coincidental.*

A CIP catalogue record for this title is available from the
British Library.

ISBN-13: 978-1-913085-00-1 (paperback edition)
ISBN-13: 978-1-913085-02-5 (hardback edition)
ISBN-13: 978-1-913085-01-8 (e-book edition)

Cover design by
Matt Buckett
www.ink-pot-graphics.com

FOR LOELIA

CHAPTER ONE

A coastal wind sent strands of hair whipping across Selby's face. She fiddled with the electric button to close the car window before remembering it was broken. "Turn left," the Sat Nav called out as she raced down a narrow lane. By the time she arrived at Menabilly, she was already late. She parked and hurried up the path to the two-storey, Georgian mansion. Tickets sold for today's luncheon and garden tour would benefit a Cornish charity, but everyone was in fact there to see inside the house where Daphne du Maurier had lived for twenty-five years.

Voices echoed from the back of the house where the crowd was already seated in the dining room. She passed a mirror on the wall and noticed her hair was a tangled mess. "Get the blasted car window fixed, so you don't always arrive at every place looking a sight," she said.

Arrows on a sign marked "Ladies" led her to the floor above. The bathroom was down at the end of a dark corridor. She pushed the door closed and quickly repaired lipstick and hair before making a final appraisal. The pale violet shirt emphasised the blue of her eyes, and the brown fitted jacket showed off her waist. "Selby Lyons, you look fine. Try to relax."

She turned the doorknob to leave, and it came off in her hands. The other half fell to the floor with a thud on the other side. "How bloody boring," she muttered, sitting down on the rim of the bathtub to think. The window's security bolts prevented her calling for help. Someone may come up to use the facilities, but when? She thought of ringing Menabilly, but that would embarrass her. Should she ring the police? Neither idea appealed; she pulled out her mobile anyway. There was no signal. Now uncomfortable, Selby realised she was locked in this room, and no one knew she was here. There was no option but to alert the crowd. She began shouting and pounding on the door.

"Could you stop that noise," a woman's voice called out.

"Hello. I'm locked in the bathroom. The other half of the doorknob must be on your side. It should have the spindle attached. Could you put it back in, so I can get out? So grateful you came up."

Selby waited for the door to open, but nothing happened. Silence, until she heard a repetitive and increasingly loud tapping sound. It was echoing from a vent in the wall above the cistern. She called up in its direction. "Was it you just now? Can you hear me?"

"Yes. I can. They can't downstairs. So, there's no point shouting. Now shush."

"Shush? What do you mean shush?" Selby was annoyed at the brusque remark. It wasn't much to ask someone to turn a doorknob. She listened carefully to the constant tapping and intermittent pings of a bell, like those old-fashioned typewriters. "Who still uses those things," she murmured before taking a deep breath to have another go. "Not sure you heard what I said? I'm locked in this room. Need your help to get out." When no reply came, she stood on the loo on tiptoes, so she could bellow directly into the vent. "Why don't you answer? I'm trapped in here."

"We're all trapped, one way or another."

Selby shouted back, "Why won't you open this door?"

She heard laughter and recoiled. The woman must be demented. What reason could there be to keep her locked in? Although she knew someone would find her eventually, patience was not Selby Lyons's strong suit – especially when she was working on a book. These past few weeks, her pace of writing was slower than usual. The flyer at the post office had offered a break from the laptop.

Luncheon and Garden Tour at Menabilly
To Benefit the Cornish Churches Trust
By Kind Permission of Simon Rashleigh

Her plan had been to see the house and garden, then leave. Now trapped in a room at the top of the house with a stranger cruelly ignoring her, Selby thought of du Maurier's most famous book, *Rebecca*: the tale of a brutal murder and an evil housekeeper.

3

The haunting stare of Mrs Danvers came flying into her mind.

By late afternoon, the sun had come around to the other side of the house making the bathroom stuffy and hot. Selby cupped her hands under the tap to drink. Whatever reason the woman had for ignoring her, it was now clear she had no intention of opening the door. The rhythmic tapping of the old typewriter echoing relentlessly through the vent made her feel drowsy. Grabbing a magazine from a basket, she slumped to the floor, pushing her back against the wall. An article on the good and the great of Cornwall was spread over four pages. The Rashleighs were mentioned in the middle section as landowners since the sixteenth century.

Her own family had been newcomers to Cornwall the year before her birth, moving from a one-bedroom flat in London to a house near the beach with two art studios: one for her father, John Lyons, abstract painter; the other for her mother, Celia Lyons, sculptor. Closing her eyes, she saw herself as a child running down the beach with her mother and sitting at her father's feet while he worked at his easel. These memories belonged to better times before the hurt and pain of abandonment.

Success at a biennale art exhibition in Venice had changed everything. European art dealers began selling her father's paintings. The family moved to an artist's colony set in the grounds of a Tuscan Castle when Selby was seven. John and Celia were quickly accepted. They made a striking couple: Celia, six feet tall, green eyes, high cheekbones, waist-length dark hair; and John, towering over his wife, athletic-build, intense blue eyes. Dinners for the community were raucous affairs in the courtyard with wine and music lasting late into the night. Selby saw less of her parents, and more of Viviana, a local woman hired to look after her. Home from their studios at the end of the day, they patted their daughter's head before rushing off again. Desperate to catch their attention, she called out to them, but it didn't matter. They were always in a hurry to get onto the next project, the next social event. She was invisible, except to Viviana.

Selby thought back to the day when life had suddenly become bearable. "We going to cook," Viviana had announced one evening. "You going to learn cooking everything mama teach me. Meat sauce, *delizioso* desserts. *Tutto*. Then, you going to teach your little girl. *Carissima*, one day wonderful man going to love you. He going to see your beautiful soul." Taking the edge of her apron to wipe tears from Selby's face, she had held her chin gently as she whispered, "*Si, bellezza, e vero*, but first we put music. Music is happy thing like cooking. We going to cook our way to happiness." The Latin rumbas and sambas of Viviana's music mixed with laughter had saved her. Though the heartache remained, the cooking had been lovingly shared.

Thinking about Viviana's food made Selby's stomach growl. She focused back on the absurd situation of her bathroom prison, calculating that the luncheon could go on until three thirty. Her bottom was numb from sitting on the floor. Gathering up hand towels and a small rug, she flung them into the bath as a buffer and climbed in.

5

She thought about Raphe. Had he found someone else? Their broken relationship no longer dominated her thoughts, but it was impossible to ignore five years. CC, her godfather, had tried to persuade her not to leave London. Though no fan of Raphe Wentrope, moving to Cornwall was not going to solve things, he had insisted.

What would she have done without CC after that Christmas holiday in Italy with her parents? He was there at Heathrow to drive her back to boarding school. Bursting into tears, she had hidden her face against his coat while describing the conversation she had overheard.

"University? A job? It's all a mystery," her mother had said. "Always so many decisions about the child. Perhaps we shouldn't have been parents."

It had broken Selby to hear this. Second place after their work, she had accepted, but to hear they may have wished she had never been born was too much to bear. CC had done his best to comfort her. They had sat in an airport café discussing the self-centred nature of artists. He didn't condone their behaviour, but nor could he change John and Celia Lyons. Before driving her back to school, he had bought notebooks and biros. "Take these," he had said. "Fill them with your feelings and emotions. Get them out. Don't hold them in to fester. Re-read old bits from time to time."

That night, when she returned to her dorm, she had written down her thoughts for the first time, unloading the hurt and loneliness. Dumping the anger and feelings of abandonment had been liberating. Writing offered freedom from the burden of truth she had carried for so long: neither her mother nor her father had time for her; she was a stone around their necks.

The following year, she had won first prize in an English writing competition at school. Recognition for something she had written boosted her self-confidence. CC had brought the family to take her for Sunday lunch to celebrate. She began spending holidays with them except for Christmas when she flew home. For one day, she had her parents' attention. The rest of the holiday, the house was full of people. She remained invisible. "All right, love?" her father had asked if he happened to bump into her. She had been happier in the kitchen with Viviana.

Dear CC, she thought, it would not have been possible to survive without him and his loving family – the kind she had hoped to have with Raphe. How had she got it so wrong? There had been an instant attraction to Raphe when they had first met. A writer like herself, he was well dressed and quick-witted. Silver hair topped a distinguished face. CC described him as self-absorbed, competitive, and lacking a sense of humour after meeting him six months later for dinner. He warned her the next day on the phone: "He's twenty years older than you are, Selby. Don't go looking for a father figure."

Tapping a file on her mobile, which held her private diary, she searched for the last entry made six months before in London.

Raphe becoming more difficult since poor reviews of his latest book. Daily repartee: short, curt remarks. Wearing me down.

Came back to flat after lunch – my teenage diaries scat-

7

tered all over the floor. Raphe had read all of them. Incredulous that he could think it okay to read my most private thoughts. Horrified. Angry. Unable to think of words. To scream – you beast, pig. How could you?

Him – now I see why you write about these pathetic characters, read by more pathetic women like you, emotional cripples – dominated by men who are just bored out of their minds, like I am.

Me – then why did you stick around for so long if I was so boring, so pathetic?

Him – because I thought you had potential

Me – for what? To be your lap dog?

Said nothing when asked how he could invade my privacy. Just snickered.

Him – and that pathetic shorthand speech when you're stressed – yes, I noticed. Everyone notices.

Never said sorry once for any of it. Told him to go. Kicked him out of flat.

Ended up in heap on floor when he left.

Five years together, and he packed within the hour. No goodbye. Was it so easy for him? Was he longing to get away, bored all this time, purposely letting me discover he'd read the diaries to force an end to things? Did he feel neglected? Had I given enough? Love given freely as child, ignored. Wasted effort. Hurt. Pain.

Not sure I loved him. Living with someone – I'd longed for that when I met him – wanted the closeness – feeling of belonging to someone.

Morning

Exhausted. Wrung out. Can't cry any more. Unsure if I'm crying for him or myself. Decided to live on my own –

some place quiet. Write in peace. Not be bothered by having to look after someone else or worry if they're happy. My happiness? Good things: Viviana. Cooking. CC and his family. Writing.

She thought Raphe had been especially cruel to mention her speech. The child psychologist that CC had arranged for her to see while at boarding school had been helpful, but her words still got tangled up sometimes even as a grown woman.

Waking suddenly from a sharp, back pain, Selby realised she had nodded off and noticed the mobile in her hand. "God, why did I read all that? Fed up. Want out of this claustrophobic space." Slumping down in the bath, she put her feet up on the edge, and went back to reading the magazine. A printed email, addressed to Simon Rashleigh, fell onto her lap.

Dear Simon,

In answer to your recent email, sales of Arabian Desert Journal have been ticking along, but I fear they will not match your most recently published book which incorporates descriptions and recipes of native cuisine. We have perhaps pulled in readers of cookbooks though I do not mean to diminish the unique observations, comments and style which incorporate the other aspects of foreign cultures about which you write. As a friend, I have a definite preference for books like ADJ. However, as your publisher, I confirm that the team has agreed the outline for the

Cameroon is fine if you beef up the number of recipes – no pun intended.

Best wishes,
Julia

Bossy woman, Selby thought. Turning the page of the magazine, a photo of a man leaning on a shepherd's crook made her smile. CC had sent five Soay sheep as a housewarming present when she had taken possession of Rose Cottage. "Something to tend apart from a broken heart," the accompanying note had said. Cornwall was further than she had meant to move, but the sales brochure had looked interesting enough to warrant the four-hour drive from London. It had not been difficult to make up her mind. Three bedrooms, some with sea views, a large sitting room, a study, and a big old-fashioned kitchen were more than adequate for her needs. Cornish palm trees and mature plants filled the lush garden. A further two fields across the road were also included. Since the move six months before, she had not regretted the decision.

Floorboards creaking made her spring up out of the bath to sprint for the door.

"Hello? Hello?"

A woman replied. "Hello?"

"Locked in here since before lunch."

"Oh dear, poor you. I'll get someone."

She was about to scream "no, don't go away again" but then she calmed herself. This was a different voice; she was sure of it. A few minutes later, a group of men arrived.

They were all talking at once. One of them called out to her. "Hello in there. Haven't you got the spindle? It's a long skinny thing. It fits inside the knob."

As tempting as it was to lash out and say that any moron could have opened the door if they'd had the spindle, she simply replied no.

"Right-o, then," a man shouted to her. "I doubt you'd get the old bolts off this big door even if there was room to slide a screwdriver under to you. It will have to be a ladder job. We'll find Simon." The group trudged back down the corridor.

"Honestly. Men. They do say the most simplistic things sometimes. Of course, you must go down the ladder. Done it myself lots of times." It was the voice of the woman who had ignored her pleas for help.

Selby hopped straight up on top of the loo seat, so she could yell directly into the vent as loudly as possible. "When I'm out of this room, I shall find you. I've heard you typing the entire time I've been stuck in here. It's driven me mad. Heartless to have left me in here."

"Not heartless," a woman said in a petulant voice.

"Makes no sense. Ridiculous – you ignored my predicament. Trapped in here all afternoon like a caged animal. You could have got off your backside and found someone to help, but you didn't. Why?"

Selby had ranted at the voice until a knocking at the window interrupted the vitriol. A man on a ladder with a hammer in his hand was waving and urging her back. He smashed the glass in one of the small panes. Reaching his hand through, he offered a key. "Unlock the security bolts on the central rail. Then, raise the window."

Glass crunched under foot as she unscrewed the lock and heaved the frame up to the top. She took a breath of fresh air.

"I'm truly sorry about all this." Red blushed up from his neck to his cheeks. "I gather you've been stuck in there all afternoon. I was in a rush to get things finished for today. This door – it's just been painted, you see, and the decorators must've stuck back on any old doorknob. Is that your mobile there on the sink?" He turned his head as he spoke out of the side of his mouth, looking down at the floor. "Sorry, the WI-FI is out. I need a new router."

What a shambles the man is, she thought.

"I'm Simon Rashleigh."

She didn't give a toss who he was as long as he had a plan to get her out. "Selby Lyons," she said impatiently.

Offering his hand to help her on to the ladder, he cautioned, "Come down above me slowly, and if you don't mind my saying it – you would be more sure-footed in bare feet."

She had been in the mood to give someone a tongue-lashing, but the thought of baring her teeth at the handsome man on the ladder kept the lid on her temper. "Look out. Shoes coming," she yelled to people gathered below.

"Visiting someone local?" he called up.

"No. Bought Rose Cottage." She concentrated on moving down the ladder. "Grateful – finally found," she added. Her teeth were now chattering. She was cold, hungry, and exhausted from the last three hours. "Didn't mean to sound ungrateful. Thank you for bringing the ladder. Woman in the next room spoke to me. Heard her through the vent in the wall – wouldn't help – constant tapping noise, and an annoying bell."

The ladder lurched to the left. People below gasped. Thinking she was going down, Selby screamed. She clung to the trellis on the wall in front of her, the balls of her feet barely in contact with the ladder.

Simon grabbed the trellis and worked his way back to an upright position. "It's okay," he yelled up. "Let's just get you down, shall we? Slowly now. Not much further."

When her feet touched the ground, the crowd that had gathered gave a little cheer and patted her back. Someone handed her the shoes she had thrown down. She put them on, and searched for Simon Rashleigh to thank, but he had disappeared.

Too rattled to find the woman who had ignored her pleas for help, she fled for the field where she had parked her car earlier in the day. At the end of the path, she turned to look back. Sun beat down on Menabilly, reflecting soft hues of gold-flecked Cornish granite. Pale pink roses covering the facade were pruned around bay windows – a romantic setting, she thought, for such a nightmare of an afternoon.

"A mean-spirited woman – no earthly reason for refusing to help in a situation like that."

When everyone had left Menabilly, Simon Rashleigh walked to the end of the drive to chain and padlock the gates. It was a bore to remember to do it, but it was also necessary if he wanted privacy. Sometimes he wished the wretched woman had never lived in his house, but Daphne du Maurier was now as much a part of its history as his ancestors. Not even her death, thirty years before, had erased the allure of the author.

Once back in the house, he raced up the stairs and along the corridor into the linen cupboard and through another door. "You promised there would be no trouble if I didn't touch anything in this room – if I didn't tell Pa about you after Mother died. You promised."

"She interrupted my train of thought," a voice said.

"Don't you think I have enough problems trying to keep people from roaming all over this place? I lock things up, but it still doesn't keep them from walking across fields to snoop. How do you think I could contain things if word got out? It's bad enough I can't have friends over. Forty years old and no social life."

"The reason for that is debatable, but then you don't like it when I give you opinions on you. You're exaggerating," the voice said. "That girl doesn't know anything. She's telling herself right now she imagined the whole thing. Calm yourself before you get that rash again." The voice began to giggle. "Ha ha, rash got Rashleigh."

"My skin rashes are none of your business. If you can't keep to the deal we made, I'm getting a conjurer here to get rid of you. I want a different life. I'm fed up with this crazy arrangement. And stop smoking. Mrs Taylor mentioned it again last week. She knows I don't smoke."

"I think you mean an exorcist, dear boy."

"Yes, and the Bishop of Truro if I must. How stupid do you think I felt today, letting the ladder slip off to one side when she mentioned hearing the typing? She said someone heard her calling out and did nothing. What rational explanation should I have offered, I'd like to know?"

"One would've made oneself scarce, as I suspect you did when you got off the ladder."

His temper was rising. "You know very well I did. If she'd stayed for the garden tour, I wouldn't have been able to avoid seeing her, would I? I want a change in our arrangements, and I don't mean in your own good time."

"Humph, if you feel like that, but you may come to regret it." The door slammed, sending a rush of cool air whirling about the room.

"Come back here," he shouted. "We haven't finished this conversation."

It was no good his protesting now that she had gone into one of her sulks. They could last for days. Simon Rashleigh took a series of short, shallow breaths which were followed by hiccups. He always gulped air during a quarrel with the ghost of Daphne du Maurier.

CHAPTER TWO

Finding herself in the middle of a pretty room, Daphne floated along to look further. Down the hall should be a kitchen, she thought. Watching in an invisible state while the girl had made her way down the ladder at Menabilly, she had heard mention of Rose Cottage. The name meant something, causing Daphne to picture a different time and setting. Was this the place? In the sitting room, two long sofas were positioned to view herbaceous borders in the garden. French doors opened to a stone terrace with large terracotta pots filled with purple agapanthus. Across the room, a pair of over-sized armchairs at right angles to a smaller sofa made a cosy place to sit in front of the fire.

"Very smart," she said, moving to the bookshelves to read the titles. Three were by the same author and tied in blue ribbons. "By Selby Lyons – oh yes, that's her. She told Simon her name in the bathroom. What kind of name is Selby for a girl?" On the shelf above was a collection of birds' nests. Some were woven of horsehair; others twirled around with thin strands of grass, the largest a mixture of dried hay and dark twigs. "I like that."

She wandered up the stairs to the floor above. "Now, let's see. Which one shall be mine?"

At the end of the hallway, there was a bedroom with windows on three sides looking out to sea as if on a prow of a ship. Memories of being in this room during her lifetime began to emerge. She had lived here at Rose Cottage, she decided, though not in such well-appointed décor. The floral chintz in red and green, which festooned the windows, repeated on the bedcover and small sofa. A rocking chair was positioned for the best view of green fields and the sea beyond. "No desk, however," she said. "One does need a desk and a typewriter. How to get them from Menabilly, that's the question. Couldn't possibly ask Simon. What a bate he was in when I left. Serves him right. Let him wonder where I've gone, taking me for granted all this time. Strange to be in a different place though after all the years at my beloved Menabilly."

It had been so easy. She had simply said the name, Rose Cottage, reappearing moments later in this house. Unable to go to anywhere besides the Rashleigh farmhouse and Menabilly, this was an exciting new adventure. Thankfully, she had also been able to walk over moors and beaches. She could not have done without walks along clifftops like the ones enjoyed during her lifetime.

"A view of the sea – one always needs a view of the sea. Yes, this will most certainly do."

Settling down into the rocking chair, Daphne kicked

off with her feet. She felt at peace. But would the girl have her here?

When she returned to Rose Cottage, Selby layered masses of ham, cheese, lettuce, and tomato between pieces of granary bread lathered with mayo. She wolfed the sandwiches down in the garden. Thorns from the climbing rose she had grabbed on the wall at Menabilly were still lodged under her nails. They throbbed while she held a hot mug of tea.

Ridiculous waste of an afternoon, she thought when finally sitting at her desk later that evening. She was looking over recently written chapters of her book when she suddenly stopped to sniff the air. "Cigarette smoke?" she asked before answering her own question. "Your imagination. You quit when you met Raphe. He'd insisted. Control over me, the bully. Didn't stop his friends stinking up my flat with massive cigars at dinner parties."

She wondered if he was with anyone now. Maybe that redhead who ran the gallery on Cork Street had finally caught his eye. Doubt he'll stay alone for long. Is he working on a new book? When she glanced at the clock, she had been staring into space for half an hour.

"Grr – why am I sitting here daydreaming about someone I no longer care about," she said aloud.

"Loneliness," someone whispered.

Selby turned quickly to look around the room, knowing there was no one there. "Tired," she said, closing the laptop. "Fresher in the morning. Need a soak in a hot bath anyway. Get these rose thorns out. Not surprised I'm hearing voices after being locked in that stupid bathroom. Exhausting." The lights dimmed low for a second before surging back. She flicked them off. A rush of chilly air flew past her when she opened the door. "Going down that ladder." She tapped on the glass of a barometer on the wall. "Might've broken my neck. And that woman," she called out as the wind rattled the sash windows. "Good riddance to that witch on the other side of the wall."

Simon could no longer ignore the morning sunlight across his face. He got up, had a shower, and went down for breakfast. While making coffee, he remembered the exchange with Daphne. Running back up the stairs and into the linen cupboard to her bedroom, he called out.

"Daphne?" Silence. He waited, considering whether she was still there, but invisible. A good baiting had done the trick in the past; he chose the prickliest of subjects.

"Good. You're gone, aren't you? Peace for me. Peace for my house. Yes – my house. You were only a tenant here. Anyway, then you died, so anything after that doesn't count. I shall talk aloud to myself now if I wish without someone answering me back all the time."

When there was still no answer, he returned to the kitchen to luxuriate in having the house to himself. He glanced at a list: Fix fence posts with Trevor. Rewire front of chicken coop. See farrier. Then, he would settle down to work. Editing a travel journal for his current book had taken most of last week with the remaining days allocated to getting things ready for the charity luncheon. It wasn't that the house was a mess. Mrs Taylor came twice a week to clean and tidy, but Daphne had been relentless.

"When people one doesn't know are coming to one's house, one wants to have things looking their best," is how she had phrased it.

Then he had listened for the umpteenth time to her story about when royalty had come to Menabilly when her husband had been Treasurer to the Duke of Edinburgh.

Daphne had continued, "Tommy was in an awful state, running around looking for the best cutlery, the best plates and glasses. I told him he should stop fussing, that HRH would just have to take us as he found us, but Tommy insisted on rooting around for the silver polish, cleaning to perfection anything destined for the luncheon table. I thought it all looked good enough, but in the end, I pitched in as he had a point. It wasn't every day one had royalty in one's house. So, Simon, my boy, get busy – one's house reflects one's personality."

"One's house." Who was he kidding? Whilst his own family history was filled with ancestors of note, the reality was that there was still an unquenchable thirst for anything to do with the author who had let Menabilly for twenty-five years. He couldn't see how that short interim compared to his own family's tenure and status. They had been powerful merchants during the reign of Henry VIII and Elizabeth I. "Not unimpressive," Simon insisted. Yet pages on the writer would forever dominate a search on Google of his family seat.

He loved Daphne's books just as much as the next

person did. That the most prolific time of her life had coincided with the years she lived at Menabilly was hardly her fault. It was that other wretched book he blamed; the one published four years after her death. That summer, tourists had poured up the drive, wanting to see the house, causing his father to lop a chain over the gate. *Letters from Menabilly*, a collection of correspondence between Oriel Malet and Daphne du Maurier, had been an instant success. The letters spoke of Daphne's passion for Menabilly, describing walks she took, the hut where she wrote, and her deep love of Cornwall. It was a private correspondence on her life, friends, and family.

I wouldn't want my innermost broodings to be read by all and sundry, he thought. Yet, complete strangers did write to him with questions to which they expected personal replies. They didn't get any. Most post he received, envelopes marked, 'Rashleigh', were obsessed with two of Daphne's books – *Rebecca* and *The King's General*. They wanted to know – was there really a tunnel to the summerhouse; and did he ever see the ghost of the Cavalier? A Rashleigh relation had told Daphne the story of a skeleton found walled-up behind a buttress in the house during an early restoration. Clothing entombed with the bones was attributed to a Cavalier from the mid-seventeenth century. She pounced on the tale and madly researched Cavalier-Roundhead local history during the English Civil War. The result was a tale of love, betrayal, and murder for *The King's General*. Nothing, however, compared to the number of letters received about her most famous book. The haunting opening of *Rebecca* had transfixed even Simon when he had read it as a teenager.

The scene describing a mysterious house called Manderley had stayed with him and everyone else who had read the book. Forever more, strangers would intrude to gaze upon Menabilly, looking for Manderley. Alas, too true, dear boy, Daphne might've said had she been standing there.

Without warning, a cloudburst sent rain pelting against the windows. Black clouds approaching from the west hung low in the sky. He suddenly felt quite flat. Turning to the middle section of the paper, he read a few columns, and stopped.

"It's all so different. So quiet. So alone," he said under his breath.

Imaginary scenes from her books had prevented a decent night's sleep. From *Brushed Together*, Jackson Pollock had slashed Lee Krasner's paintings; from her second book, Marianne North had been locked in a tower by her father; and from the one she was writing now, Mary Hemingway had been thrown to a lion by her husband, Ernest.

Selby opened her eyes. Raphe's phrase about the women in her books repeated in her head. Were they pathetic? American artist, Lee Krasner, had subjugated her own work so that her husband's painting could flourish. Marianne North had given up her youth to travel the world as companion to her widowed father. Did these selfless acts make these women pathetic?

"Why are you obsessing with this now?" she asked. "Get up. Dress. Coffee. Emails. Work."

While she got into jeans and a T-shirt, she noticed the state of the room. It was a mess. Piles of laundry and dust balls went unnoticed when she was working on a book. Routines were rigidly followed: mornings in her study writing, break for lunch, more writing until supper at six, and then back to the laptop until eleven if things were flowing.

What she absolutely had to guard against was roaming around the house to admire her new home. It was perfect in her eyes. The sale of her Kensington flat had provided more than enough money to buy Rose Cottage. Soon after she had taken possession, CC's middle daughter, Joanna, had come for the weekend, bringing masses of fabric samples. Selby had asked for help to create a distinctive look; different from the style of the London flat which Raphe had arranged to suit his taste. Joanna's interior design company had organised the making and delivery of curtains, headboards, and bed skirts. Furnishings and paintings had come from CC. When she objected, saying she couldn't accept such a generous offer, he had insisted.

"Dear girl, you know I downsized from the Primrose Hill house to a flat," he had explained. "The girls have all taken what they want. Why shouldn't you have the pleasure of these things when you need them? Just come up and go through the storage facility where they're kept and take what suits. No arguments."

As she caressed the bow-fronted dressing table that had belonged to CC's mother, she felt a daughter's love for her godfather and his family. Was it the closest she would come to giving love freely and having it cherished and returned? Looking out on the beautiful views from her bedroom window, she wished CC could visit Rose Cottage, but he was now in his late nineties and too frail for such a journey.

The rain falling steadily meant no temptations. Sunny days on the beach were still a novelty since moving to Cornwall. They were hard to resist if she wasn't writing a mile a minute. After breakfast and with a large mug of coffee, she went into her study to begin work. When she turned on the light, she let out a shriek. Her manuscript no longer sat in a neat pile on the desk where she had left it the night before. Instead, the papers lay scattered over the floor at her feet. Bits of char from the grate in the fireplace were mixed in amongst the mess. Had birds come down the chimney? Or worse, rats – in the queue at Tesco's last week, she had heard someone talking about rodents. They said rats burrow in anything from piles of blankets and car seats to the stuffing of sofas. The thought of rats breeding in the house made her skin crawl.

While collecting pages from the floor, she realised big chunks of the manuscript were missing. This was serious – it was the copy with hand-written edits which she had not transposed yet to the Word document on the laptop. It would take ages to re-read the entire thing and reconfigure sentences and text. Frantically searching under the desk and chairs, she panicked when nothing else turned up. Had rats taken the pages to use as nesting material? She hadn't used the fireplace in the study yet. Did they live in the chimney or use it as an escape route? Feeling queasy from the idea of a rat infestation, she wasn't brave enough to check all the rooms for evidence. The local farmer came to mind. Soon after Selby moved into the cottage, he had arrived with his wife who had brought a cake. They dispensed local gossip and gathered information on her to pass along to the village. "Ring," he had said, "if you need help with anything. We're only across a few fields." She looked up his number. The full-time rat-catcher he employed would be there within the hour, he promised. "If they're there, he'll find them."

"Damnation," she yelled, after switching off the phone. "This will add days of work before I can get back to writing new stuff."

Before moving to Menabilly, Simon and his family lived at a farmhouse on the other side of the estate. It was there he first noticed what his father called, 'Mother's quiet times'. They were interludes lasting for hours. As a boy he watched from his bedroom window as she walked around the garden. He could see her lips moving as if she were speaking to someone. He knew grown-ups sometimes talked to themselves. Then, for some reason, everything changed after living at Menabilly for a year. She didn't keep to herself as much. It was a cure, his father insisted. Up on the hill, he reckoned the sea air blew away the cobwebs in her mind. Simon still saw her talking to herself, but where there had been brooding conversations, she now seemed to laugh aloud.

It wasn't until his mother died, when he was seven, that he met Daphne. Alone in his room, wishing his mother was still there, he heard someone crying. Getting up to peer into his father's room, he found him sleeping soundly. Yet, Simon could still hear the whimpering. Tracing the sound to the linen cupboard, he opened the door. Shelves from the back wall had been removed and lay stacked to the side, revealing another door. He pushed on it. It gave way to a room with furniture. Shelves filled with books lined the walls. A lamp on a table cast a yellow glow on faded, moth-eaten curtains hanging at the windows. The weeping stopped.

"You can come in. Don't be afraid," a voice said.

Too startled to hang about to discover who had spoken, he ran back to bed, pulling the covers over his head. There he remained until morning when his father went downstairs for breakfast. Then, he crept back to the linen cupboard, and entered the room hidden behind the second door. He had not imagined it.

"Oh good, I'm glad you came back. I was afraid you'd be some silly scaredy-cat and go blab to your father about my room," the voice said.

Fear gripped him as he turned slowly. Standing in the corner of the room, a woman dressed in baggy trousers, floral shirt, and a beige cardigan was smoking a cigarette.

"I'm Daphne," she said. "No need to run away. I was your mother's friend. I miss her. That's why I was crying. I imagine you miss her too. I used to live here. Though no longer living, I'm not sure what I am. I seem to go back and forth between being something and being nothing. Your mother kept my secret. I hope you will too, and that we can be great friends. So much jollier that way, isn't it? Before she died, she must've taken the shelves down from the wall in the linen cupboard, hoping you would find me one day. I went away for a while, you see, so I'm not sure."

Simon slowly inched a few steps back, sitting when his legs hit a chair. He stared at the lady, not knowing what to say.

"Don't try to figure it out. Your mother and I often talked about why I'm here. We decided it was just meant to be. She went to see a medium about it once. They said I would be here for as long as I was supposed to be."

Feeling reassured at the mention of his mother, Simon asked if she ever went downstairs.

"Yes, I do, but no one except your mother seemed to be able to see and hear me."

"So how come I can?"

"That, my boy, is a question for the sages. I've absolutely no idea. Promise you won't tell?"

He had never kept anything from his father. He needed time to think about it. How would he explain a ghost who claimed she had been speaking to his mother all these years and was now speaking to him?

The rat-catcher arrived at Selby's house at midday. When he walked through the door, the stench from his clothing was a mixture of decay and chemicals. Images of what he had been handling all morning made her feel ill.

"Thanks for coming so quickly. Show you what I found this morning. Distressing. Rats in the house," she explained.

They stood in her study looking at the floor while

Selby described how the papers of the manuscript had been scattered amongst bits of char. The rat-catcher went over to the fireplace. Leaning in to investigate the chimney, he pulled a torch from the pocket of his coveralls and flicked the light on and off. Grunting, he left the room to search the house. He checked the attic, bottoms of cupboards on every floor, air ducts of the kitchen fan, under the fridge and ovens, under sofas and all the furniture in the sitting room. It had taken ages. She had checked in drawers, amongst the wood stacked near the boiler room, and any other place that seemed a hospitable place for rats to breed.

"I can't find nothin', Miss. This nose knows rats, so I'd say there ain't none here. May be birds that done it," he said before leaving.

His strong smell was still in the air. Selby flung open windows throughout the house. It will take hours to air, she thought. No peace. No writing. No rats – good news, but if no rats, where are the missing pages? She really had no idea what had happened in her study during the night. "Come on. What's the plan?" she asked, drumming her fingers on her chin. Opened windows made it too chilly to sit in the study to begin the re-editing she was dreading. No sun – no beach. The antsier she got, the more obvious the answer. After changing the sheets on her bed and towels in the bathroom, she moved on to dusting and hoovering. When the bathroom was clean, the large pile of laundry went on the wash cycle. By six o'clock, she had hoovered the entire house. Her back ached, but the house smelled fresh again. She lit a fire to warm the sitting room before snuggling down on the sofa and pulling a wool shawl up over her legs. Her eyes closed easily until a loud crack forced them open. Wood in the grate, now fully ablaze, had spat embers on to the carpeting. The smell of singed wool made her jump up. She chucked the coals back onto the fire and poured a bit of water over the spot for insurance. Reaching down to lift the metal fire screen across the opening, she groaned. Perhaps she had over-done the cleaning bit; her back was killing her. A long, hot soak was what she needed. Tomorrow, she could print the manuscript. She hoped rats or whatever had made the mess in her study would not return during the night.

It was just too quiet. The peace Simon thought he wanted was now downright annoying. He was accustomed to Daphne's presence; used to knowing she was about. Had she really disturbed him? She kept to herself, working most days at her typewriter until suppertime. Then, she would saunter in, and chatter away while he ate. Her absence now highlighted how pathetic his life had become. Had he used her as an excuse for the lack of a social life? Perhaps Daphne had filled the gap he had not wanted to think about.

There had been girlfriends when he lived in London, but no relationship lasted very long. Average complaints from women either had to do with how much time he spent writing, or how much time he travelled so that he could write. His travel books sold well enough with a surge in sales around Christmas – probably due to stocking fillers, his publisher had suggested. His third book had the added-bonus of a girl who had followed him home from Cameroon. They had lived together for six months before she went off with a poet who recited in the local pub at the weekends. The note she left said she was sorry to leave, "but you are often preoccupied with other things besides me." Then, there had been a few years with a painter, but her hours were worse than his. When she finished a painting, he was in the middle of writing a book or vice versa.

He had finally moved back to Cornwall to his beloved Menabilly. Daphne and he had worked on redecoration needed in the house to get things looking smart again. "But to what end?" he asked. "For whom? Not even Daphne is here to enjoy it. What a rotter you are, Simon Rashleigh."

CHAPTER THREE

Someone banging the door knocker woke her. Opening the window, she shouted down, "Who's that? Reason for waking me at half dawn?"

"Selby, it's George. Your sheep have gotten out. It's not the first time I've been on this errand. They're all mixed in with mine again. I don't know what the rams have done to your ewes. I warned you this could happen if you didn't fix the rotten posts in the fence line."

"Be right there," she called down. "Bloody sheep," she muttered, going into the bathroom to look in the mirror. "Circles under eyes, hair matted down, spot front and centre on chin. Don't like that. Not sure I like George Renfold. No other man knocking at the door, asking me out. So why are you encouraging him? Have I?"

They had met three months earlier when he had banged on the door, yelling in a furious voice that her Soay sheep had mixed in with his prized flock of Herdwicks. When she had opened the door, he had stopped ranting. He had not been expecting the pretty brunette with hair to the middle of her back. He had grabbed the flat cap from his head, ran his hand through his hair, and wiped the sweat from his face with his forearm.

"Sorry for making such a noise. I'm George Renfold. I've got the fields marching on yours. Some Soay sheep are running through my ram field. The farmhand told me they were yours. Is that right? If you need help getting them back in, I'd be glad to lend a hand."

"Feel stupid. Sheep were present from godfather. No idea what to do with them. Been a city girl most of my life," she explained. "Sorry they got out. Put them in the field when they arrived. He said they just need grazing. They're all girls, so no problem there. Said they were easy to keep."

"Mostly right," he replied. "*Ovis aries* – they're descended from a feral population from the Western Isles of Scotland. I studied them at Ag' college. Why anyone would want to keep them is a mystery though. They're not good for anything. Their meat tastes awful – very gamey. True, they don't need dipping, nor do their feet need tending. They shed their wool naturally. The most important thing if you're not planning to breed them, and from what you say, I take it you're not?"

"Not. No. Absolutely. No breeding. Five is enough," she added quickly.

"Right, in that case, keep them contained, and away from rams – no rams, no lambs. I'll go back and round them up and put them into their field. By the way, you need new posts and new fencing wire. Mole Valley Farmers has both." He had said goodbye and had flipped his cap back onto his head before hopping back into the Land Rover he had left running.

The following weekend, Selby had made him dinner as a thank you. Since then, they had met up from time to time. She wasn't looking for romance so soon after Raphe. True, she was lonely sometimes, but not for the mess of a relationship. Plus, there were moments with George when she wasn't quite sure what else to say. She knew nothing about farming.

Focusing back on the image in the mirror, she threw water on her face. Then, she dressed and hurried downstairs.

"Too angry for a cup of tea?" she asked, opening the door.

George hung his coat over the back of a chair in the kitchen before starting on his favourite lecture. "I just can't figure out why you can't have normal sheep like the rest of folk around here. Those Soays are wild things needing a gaucho to round them up. It exhausted my sheepdog, but we got them back into your field. You should've returned them to sender."

Selby put two mugs of tea down on the table and sat opposite. "I like the wildness of the Soays. Not like other sheep you see in fields. Couldn't send them back anyway. News about your rams is not good."

"Don't look at me like it's their fault. It's down to you entirely. If fence posts rot, wind and rain soften the ground enough so that when sheep push against them, they loosen. Sheep push against them if there's lush grass on the other side. They get out. The rams find the ewes. Nature takes its course. It's not rocket science."

"I get busy writing. Forget things like fence posts."

"You need a man around here," George said with an emphasis on 'man'.

She changed the subject. "Went to a luncheon for the Cornish Churches Trust yesterday at Menabilly. Got locked in the bathroom all afternoon – big pain in the arse. Waste of time."

"Yah, I knew Simon as a boy. We were both at the local school. Even though he's got that big estate, he doesn't have any interest in farming. When his Pa died, he sold the dairy herd. The land is let to a man who does contract work. Rashleigh – he's a writer type."

"Writer type? That how you describe me?"

Not missing a beat, he replied, "No, strawberries and cream and the smell of fresh hay in the sun." Embarrassed, he looked away before asking if she had given his invitation to the Royal Cornwall Show any more thought.

"Oh, George, a day away from writing – not easy, and birds got down the chimney yesterday. Manuscript was all over the room. It will take ages to figure out what's missing. Rat man came. Found nothing. Says must've been birds. Was thinking of putting ladder up to the roof to look down the chimney?"

Stuck back on the sentence about her not going to the RCS with him, George didn't hear the rest. He was counting on showing her off, having a nice day out, and watching the livestock competitions.

"Ladder up to roof? What do you think?" she asked.

Draining the rest of his mug, George stood up to put on his coat. He opened the door to leave, but stuck his head back around for one last remark. "I've got too much work of my own to keep fetching your sheep back where they belong. You need a man around here. That's what I think."

Her temper flared the minute he closed the door. "I don't need anything," she said, banging a pot down on the counter. "Most especially a bloody, bossy man telling me what I need."

A door slamming in the corridor made her jump. Walking down to investigate, she found an opened window banging back and forth against the wall in her study. "Stupid idiot, you've got to remember to close up. Probably how birds or rats got in. Foul humour – no good for writing. Need coffee." She made her way back to the kitchen.

As steam from the boiling water passed through the grinds of the Italian espresso maker on the hob, the aroma made Selby think of Viviana. It was the first scent of the morning, which wafted up to the alcove where she had slept at weekends as a child, reminding her she was with someone who loved her. Her smile faded. Always, along with the good memories, were the bad ones – she had only been with Viviana because her parents couldn't be bothered with her. The sinking feeling threatened to take hold.

"No wallowing in self-pity," she insisted. Food would fortify and take her mind off wretched feelings crowding in. Grabbing an avocado from the fridge, she scooped it out of its skin, pouring olive oil over it and a squeeze of lime juice. She diced a tomato and red onion for a salsa. While she waited for the coffee to finish, George's comment about needing a man continued to annoy.

Of course, she would like someone in her life, but writing took up all her time. Her new life had just the right rhythm, and the necessary quiet. Walks in the countryside resuscitated her after long sessions at the laptop. How she would feel when this book was finished would be the real test. It was always a satisfying feeling, but also anti-climactic until the next book idea emerged. Decorating the cottage remained, of course, but she would eventually complete these tasks. The unanswered question she had just posed would still be there: was she lonely? Yes, she decided. There were times she was lonely, but filling that space with a man just to avoid the feeling was nonsense. Anyway, one could feel alone in a relationship as well. There had been plenty of times with Raphe when she had felt isolated and friendless. "Too much brooding on self. Get cracking on the bloody re-editing job."

It was the one part of writing she disliked. To make the same edits twice was an abominable waste of time. By six o'clock, her intolerably bad mood forced a switch – she began writing new material until hunger demanded food. She inhaled a small sandwich at the kitchen table, and quickly returned to the laptop, anxious to restructure a scene she had thought about while eating.

"Where have you got to?" she said. Scrolling down further, she searched for the text. It wasn't there. She clicked on 'undo' but that also failed to work. She moved back up the page again to double-check, but the chapters she expected to find had vanished. Standing up, she paced the room, and thought back to what she had written before breaking for supper.

"African trip and funeral of best friend – that's right. Then, Cuban section – yes, I'm sure of it."

She looked again, but all the work from the previous three hours had disappeared. Had she just thought it out? Writing it in her head, but not typed it? There had been times she had thought through various scenes in bed before falling asleep at night, looking for them on the computer next morning until realising, but this was different. She had only just worked on these chapters. Where were they?

Stepping over to a small drinks table, she poured a generous amount of cognac into a glass. She walked back and forth, muttering. "I actually remember writing it. How could I have imagined it? Living in my own little world? Working too hard?" She poured more cognac, sipping while she paced again, thinking about her state of mind lately. Other things forgotten: the fences, sheep out again, window open in study, letting birds or rats in. "Absent-mindedness," she said in her defence. Taking a big gulp of cognac, she rushed back to the screen with an idea. She searched and could not believe her eyes. 'Auto-Save' was turned off.

"But this is not believable. I would never have done that." Over and over, she considered the possibilities. "No memory of having done it, but clearly I must have," she admitted, and downed the remainder in the glass. "Working too hard, too late at night? Up at dawn, more writing – perhaps it's exhaustion. I'm confused. What's going on with me?" she wailed.

"Oh, now don't be a silly girl. It's not that bad," a voice said. Sitting in the chair opposite was a woman with her hands folded over her chest "Stop that. What's all the fuss anyway? You wrote the stuff, didn't you? Surely you can write it again. I may have touched a few wrong buttons on that thing when I tried typing something."

"Drunk – too much cognac, you idiot. Hallucinating. Putting glass down. Going to bed." Weaving her way back to the laptop, Selby slammed the lid shut. "Enough of this. Better in the morning."

"It won't be any different tomorrow," the voice said. "I should face the demons tonight if I were you. How I wish I were you. I'd love a bit of that tipple you've been knocking back."

Selby pointed her finger at the apparition in the chair in the corner of the room.

"You – figment of imagination. Me – going through rough patch. Nervous breakdown – not incurable. Will come through this."

"I'm Daphne du Maurier, and most certainly not a figment of anyone's imagination. We met the other day in a manner of speaking. Don't ask too many questions. I'm not frightfully keen on them, especially if they concern me. It wears one out trying to explain, you see. I must've liked the idea of your being a writer. Nothing complicated – I won't cause any trouble."

"Not here. Not happening. Dead. Can't exist."

"I assure you, my girl, I can, and I do. I might be a ghost. I couldn't say precisely what that constitutes. I'm not frightfully keen on the word in any case. Don't analyse it like you seem to do about everything. Just accept it. Anyway, I like you and your writing. It's a good book on that machine, by the way. A few problems I've spotted, but nothing that can't be sorted, don't you know. Why do you think Mary Hemingway put up with it all?"

Walking sideways across the floor to the desk, Selby slurred her words. "Love. Makes you do stupid things." Her mouth hung open at the depth of her hallucination. She was now having a conversation with a phantom. "Serious, big trouble. Call doctor. Tomorrow." She lay down on the sofa. "Walls going round," she whispered. Her shoes slipped off, falling to the floor. She passed out.

"Good Lord, rather a dramatic thing, isn't she," Daphne said, staring down at the girl. "I certainly didn't mean to cause such upset. I just wanted to see how that machine worked. Mind you, I'd have been raging if anyone touched my typewriter when I was in the middle of a book."

The cotton-wool mouth and headache were bad the next morning. Selby sat at the table in the kitchen, nursing the hangover, and drinking a large mug of coffee. Her mind swirled from the absurdity of it all – the missing chapters, the failure to recognise 'Auto-Save' had been turned off, no memory of having done it, and the cognac. CC had warned her not to spend too much time alone. "You're isolated there. Be around people. Make new friends your own age," he had advised.

"Happy here. Love cottage. Just the way I like it."

But the hallucination? That was a whole different kettle of fish; possibly symptoms of a deep-seated psychosis. That she had conversed with 'It' was the most disturbing memory.

"Head pounding. Can't think. Few days away." She felt too fragile to show up at CC's door, and she certainly couldn't tell him what she had seen in her study last night. There was no one else except Viviana. Was she up to driving to Bristol? "No," resounded through the headache. "Go to bed." It was the only thing she felt capable of doing. She chucked the remaining coffee down the sink and guzzled a jug of water before dragging herself back up the stairs to her bedroom where she pulled the curtains closed and got under the duvet.

In the darkened room, she lay perfectly still, forbidding any thoughts of the night before, but her mind was swirling with self-doubt. The hangover was self-inflicted, but what had caused the spectre she had imagined in her study? A feeling of helplessness filled her being. Breathing exercises had worked in the past when she was frazzled. She inhaled through the nose to the count of four, and exhaled to the count of six, repeating the sequence until eventually drifting off to sleep.

When Selby woke, she drank the remains of a bottle of water on the bedside table, and walked into the hallway. It was dark. She turned on the light to see her watch. She had slept seven hours. The head was better. The brain fog had disappeared, but the desire to see Viviana was strong. She went online to book a ticket to Tuscany.

"Train to Bristol Airport. Rent car at other end. No parents. Stay with Viviana. Just weekend. Sleep. Talk with someone who knows you're not crazy. Get head together." Tomorrow she would pack.

CHAPTER FOUR

S evere weather over the English Channel had grounded Selby's flight in Bristol the next day, getting her to Tuscany after ten that night. When she had finished the second helping of cannelloni at Viviana's kitchen table, the housekeeper took her hand. "*Adesso, carissima,*" she said. "*Qual è il problema? Dimmi.*"

Selby put her head in her hands and began to weep quietly. Where to begin? After a few minutes, she let Viviana led her up to her old weekend sanctuary in the alcove on the floor above.

"You need sleep. *Domani,* we talk," Viviana said before going downstairs. It had been a long time since she had seen Selby in this state. As a child, she had suffered plenty of heartache and lots of tears. Viviana had lavished all the love she would have given her own daughter if she and Carlo had not been childless. How she cried when Signor and Signora Lyons sent Selby to boarding school. Her husband said they were jealous, especially the mother. The Lyons couple explained that children in the UK go to boarding school at a certain age. She counted the days until her Selby was home for holidays. They had not seen so much of her since she began living with that man who had broken her heart. Was it another man problem?

Selby woke in the night. Tuscan summer temperatures mixed with heat rising from the kitchen below had made the alcove stifling hot. "Need cool air," she gasped, reaching for the water bottle in her handbag. Dressing quietly, so as not to wake Viviana and Carlo in the room below, she slipped out into the courtyard to walk to the small village square. The fountain splashing in the basin echoed in the open space. She dipped her hands into the pool and sat on the edge of the marble surround, staring into the water until scuffling across the cobblestones made her look up. A man weaving his way across the courtyard looked very drunk. She felt panic. He was at the fountain when she considered running away.

"Thought I was hallucinating," he said while catching water up in his big hands and throwing it on his face. "You, here? Didn't know."

"Father, I –"

"Been with some friends at a party in the village," he said. "A bit too much vino. Been doing that a lot lately. Your mother's taken up residence with another man. Yup, left your ole dad. Can't blame her. Not the best of husbands possibly. Not the best father either, huh?" He threw more water on his face. "Staying with Viviana?

Good woman. Came home to her instead of us. Speaks volumes. Doesn't surprise me."

Selby didn't know what to say. No, she hadn't told them she was coming. Yes, Viviana was a good woman – the person who had had time for her as a child, the one who had given her love.

"Your mother. Confused. Figured out she's getting older. You know. Got used to being the most beautiful woman in the room all these years."

"Beauty and the little beast," Selby said under her breath.

He sat down beside her, reeking of cheap wine. "No, no, no, no," he repeated as his head fell forward. He slapped his lap and stared at his shoes. "You're the image of your mother when I met her – uncanny, the resemblance. Expect she's always seen it – your youthful face, a reminder of the passing of time. Not a vain person, but she's used her beauty to get what she wanted all her life. No longer queen bee, that's the problem. Younger beauties around here now." He looked up, squinting, trying to focus on his daughter's face.

"Found nice flat, huh. Charles said it was a sound investment."

"It's fine. Thank you for making it possible. Haven't told you that I…"

"*Coscienza sporca*," he bellowed.

There would have been no need for a guilty conscience, she thought, if you had only shared yourselves with me, even a little. They sat in silence for a few moments.

"Cornwall was good," he suddenly said. "Had good

times there, didn't we? It all got crazy when we moved to Tuscany – late nights, competition, be the smartest, the best, the wittiest in the group. Done well for our work though. My dealers sell the things before the paint is dry. Your mother had a major show in Rome a few months ago. Did you know that?"

How would she? They never rang. Never emailed. She knew CC had written to them while she had been at boarding school to give them news of her. They never replied. A monthly allowance to a trust account for her expenses and the school fees were the only communication.

"Yup, Rome, it's where she met this chap. He's a painter too. Don't like his stuff. Clichéd, pretentious – probably not his work she's interested in."

Selby fidgeted, feeling uncomfortable discussing what was probably her mother's sex life.

"Need money? Got enough? How's that writer fellow?"

"Not together anymore," she replied.

"Ah, men problems – why you're here. We're all bums. May be a few good ones out there. Grab him if you ever come across one. Must be lots of them hounding you. And take it from me, Sweet Pea – you look so like your mother, it's like looking at a photograph twenty years ago. Thought you knew that – prettier maybe. Must be my contribution. Least I gave you something worthwhile." He laughed.

"Sold flat. Bought cottage in Cornwall. Good place to write."

"Read your book on Lee Krasner. Very good." He slapped his knee again after a few minutes. "Cornwall? Really? Went back there? Remember when I first saw you.

45

Brought you and Celia home from the hospital to that house near the beach. You were a tiny thing." He got up and went around the corner down a lane.

She considered escaping, but a moment later, he weaved his way back to where she was sitting.

"Tiny hands, tiny feet, pink bows for lips – a real little sweet pea, yup. That's when I started calling you that," he said. "Did some sketches in pencil of you as an infant."

That was more than she could take. "Heard you and Mother talking one Christmas holiday, wondering if you should have been parents. Little late to reinvent the past with flowery descriptions of bow-shaped lips."

Swaying from left to right, he stood. "What's got into you? Never said such a thing. Celia can be dramatic. Says and does things she doesn't mean. Like this chap she's gone off with. Know she'll be home when she tires of his youthful grins."

"Does everything have to be about you – about Mother?" she cried out. "Nothing has got into me. I am the offspring of two people who ignored their child for most of her life. The person in front of you. Damaged. Lack of affection. Nothing more. Did you really think you could have a child and then that would be the end of it? A child needs nurturing, love, attention, time – time neither of you was willing to spare away from your work. Would it have been too much trouble for you to save weekends? To take a walk with me? For Mother to take me shopping occasionally, instead of just handing Viviana money to buy something I needed? How do you think I got through nights at boarding school, crying myself to sleep after listening to other girls talk of what they'd done at home for holidays with loving families? Go to the cinema together? No, but Viviana took me. Viviana fed me. Held me when I cried. Gave me love even though she was only the hired help. CC provided the rest. Only right decision you ever made for me was to make him my godfather and guardian."

She hadn't mentioned that CC had taken her to a psychologist in her teens to get help with her depression. The school had written to say they were concerned about her speech pattern.

Her godfather had noticed it, but when Selby was with him or his family, she used full sentences. It was only when she got stressed or when she was around strangers that she reverted to a shorthand way of speaking. He found someone local to her school whom she saw one afternoon a week. CC had not sent the initial diagnosis to John and Celia, but he had shown it to Selby after university.

As a child, Selby Lyons saw her parents for only a few minutes each day. During these times, she spoke quickly in a series of short phrases to get their attention before they left the room. This abbreviated vocabulary developed into her everyday speech pattern. I have observed that the more stress she feels, the shorter the sentences become, deleting verbs, and connecting words.

Her school mentions that when she writes her assignments, she does so with full sentences. This is because she's in control of the pace at which she's expressing herself, and feels no pressure to get the words out quickly.

Because her parents offered little love and attention,

Selby feels isolated and suffers from bouts of depression. I suggest weekly sessions with a qualified child psychologist who can help Selby develop a sense of herself in order to cope with the neglect she endured from her parents.

Tears rolled down Selby's cheeks as she thought of her childhood. She felt exhausted from having finally wrenched up from the bottom of her soul all the anguish she felt towards her parents from years of neglect.

John Lyons sat down again, letting his elbows sink into his stomach for support so he could hold his swaying head. "What are you saying? That you hate us? Believe me, we love you. Just stink at being parents. Yah, we put our work first. Probably what you heard Celia speaking about – our guilt for doing that. Thought you were happy with Viviana, happy at that school. Don't know what to say. Need Celia. Need to speak to her. Not feeling strong just now."

Selby had imagined this scene over and over; fantasised telling her parents what she had suffered. Now she wanted to scream, "No absolution." She had long ago given up trying to rationalise their neglect. Realising it was not her fault had been a turning point in sessions with the psychologist. All this now, all in the past, she decided.

He moved several feet away from her to stretch out on the cool stone of the pool's surround. "Just going to take a nap for a bit – too much *vino veritas*."

Hearing her father's snores, Selby got up to walk back to Viviana's. Tonight, for the first time in her life, she had noticed his abbreviated way of speaking. Had she copied him, hoping he would notice his signature in his daughter's speech? Whatever the reason, she was closing the door on this pain tonight.

He suddenly bellowed across the square, "Sweet Pea, we do love you."

"Too late," she whispered.

In the morning, when Selby woke a good night's sleep had produced a clear head. She went downstairs for a shower. After the steam cleared, she looked in the mirror. Did she look like her mother? The unexpected meeting with her father had been traumatic. Yet, somehow, having come through it, she felt liberated. Crawling into bed last night, the realisation she had not spoken in abbreviated speech during the entire rant had made her sob. She cried for the little girl who had felt obliged to get the words out quickly. So many times as a child, she had hoped to say something that would spark interest, something that would cause them to sit down next to her for a while. In the end, a drunken stupor, and the incapacity to walk had provided the captive audience she had craved for years.

"*Buongiorno, amore, come stai?*" Viviana asked when Selby came into the kitchen.

"Much better." She gave Viviana a hug before sitting down at the table.

"*Si, e vero.* And the face? Let's see. Much better – back to the pretty girl we all love."

There's that word again, she thought. Pretty. Never thought of myself that way – never as beautiful as Mother. People said things to be kind. Made things up in drunken stupors. She decided last night, before falling asleep, that she didn't want to be at Viviana's if her father sobered up and came looking for her. Or was that still wishful thinking?

"Viviana, I'm going back to London on the evening plane. I know that sounds mad, but I overreacted to a situation. Been working too hard lately on a book. Had too much to drink night before last. Think it pushed me over the line. Felt I couldn't go on. Thought I was hallucinating – all silly stuff. Sorry for just appearing so late last night. I hope I didn't disturb Carlo? I'm feeling so much better. I don't know what all the fuss was about."

"Not like you to drink too much. Not like all those up there at the castle. Every night, Carlo tells me he finishes the music, most of them walking sideways back to their villas." Viviana stopped speaking. Her husband had described in great detail how he had seen John Lyons staggering home after watching his wife dance in a suggestive manner with a younger man. Rumour was that Mrs Lyons had run off with the man last week. Since then, Selby's father had been drunk most nights. She would not mention this to his daughter.

"Oh, this is truly delicious," Selby said.

"Eat. Eat. It's all for you. Carlo had his before work. All your favourites are there – *caffe latte, fette biscottate, brioche con marmellata et con crema.* Just like I always made for you."

"How nice it is to hear Italian."

"You must not forget it. You must use it."

"I'd have to talk to myself. There's no one where I live who speaks it."

"Talk to yourself, then. We all do it." She laughed

"I'd like to go shopping with you before I leave if you have time today. First thing on the list is coffee beans to take back. How I've missed good coffee, but not as much as I've missed you, dear Viviana."

"Of course, I have time – for you, always. You know you can come here, don't you? Any time is good for us. Worried you working too hard. Work all the time is bad. Food is most important – no problem about the cooking. You learned from the best." She winked at Selby. "Sleeping is next important thing. Wish you living here. I could bring dinners. Wish you staying longer, but I understand, and Christmas not too far away. You stay with us at Christmas if you want."

Would Selby come back for Christmas after last night's episode with her father? She didn't know. Today, she would spend the day catching up with Viviana, and find something nice for her.

When they finally left the house, it was scorching hot. They shopped in the market place, then stopped to drink something cooling. She hoped her father's hangover was bad enough that they wouldn't run into him in the village square. Selby loaded up on *parmigiano reggiano, prosciutto crudo* and as many bags of coffee beans as would fit in her overnight case.

When it was time for her to leave for the airport, Viviana handed her a small bundle, wrapped in brown paper, tied with string. "It's got all your favourites inside the *panino*. For the airplane," she explained before taking Selby's hand. "*Et allora, ascoltami.* Go home and make new plan. Whatever it was. Whoever it was, don't run away.

Begin again. *Come se niente fosse.* Remember, you know who you are – a beautiful, wonderful girl with a loving spirit. You going to find someone who sees this. He going to love you. When you give him your love, most wonderful thing will happen. You going to be happy. Believe what I'm saying, *carissima.*"

Selby threw her arms around Viviana. "Your love is so important to me. I miss you and Carlo. I want you to see my cottage. Next Easter, or summer, or whenever you want. Just say when, and I'll send the tickets. I want you and Carlo to come to Cornwall."

This is what he liked doing best – sitting on top of his mare, Almond, and breathing the fresh sea air. "Surveying the policies," his father used to call it. Simon wasn't interested in doing the farming himself, but he knew the land needed to be managed. When it became obvious Simon's passion for travel and writing could earn him a living, his father had broached the subject. "I've been a weekend farmer the last part of my life," he had said. "The law practise has taken up most of my time, so I understand the conflict. Contract out to someone you trust and keep a steady eye on things. Don't just look at the paper. Go out and get on the land to see what needs doing, and what's been done." The contract farmer engaged after his father's death was a safe pair of hands.

Rounding the corner of a field at the southernmost tip of the estate, Almond came to a halt. A small group of Soay sheep grazed in front of her. "Not again," Simon said, under his breath. The farmer had mentioned his new neighbour kept this breed; that they had escaped into his planted fields a few times. Left where they were, they would trample some of the crop. He pushed Almond forward and whistled. The sheep looked up. Slowly, Simon urged them to the other side of the hedge and out on to the public road. The high hedges would keep them walking in the direction he thought they belonged. Twenty minutes down the road, he saw a gap in some fencing. Moving the Soays ahead, he dismounted to pull the gate open. The sheep ran through. Coloured twine hanging from one of the posts had been used to secure the fencing in disrepair. He wound it tightly into a knot. Getting back on Almond, he continued down the road until he came to a cottage at the end. Tying his mare to a low-hanging branch, he went through the gate and banged the door knocker a few times. After several minutes, a face peered out looking half-asleep.

"Hello. I seem to be in rescue mode again," he said when he recognised the woman he had helped down the ladder at Menabilly. "I think I've just returned your sheep. Do you keep Soays?"

Having arrived into Heathrow from Italy in the middle of the night, it had been only a few hours since Selby had crawled into bed. "Yes. Soays. Mine. Sorry. Just back from Italy. Early this morning."

"Look, I don't want to intrude. Just wanted to let you know about the sheep. I had to bring them home before they made a mess in the planted-up field. It's not something farmers take gracefully. Compensation for crop damage can be expensive."

"Bit weary today," she explained. "I only –"

Simon interrupted, realising he had obviously got her out of bed. He retreated down the path. "Sorry I woke you," he called over his shoulder. "I've pushed them back into your field, the one with red twine holding the gate shut. I'm afraid you can count on them escaping again, if someone doesn't repair it."

He was already out of earshot when she said thank you. "Nice of him to bring the Soays back. Handsome." She went back to bed.

Simon mounted up to make his way home. He had forgotten she mentioned buying this place when he helped her down the ladder at Menabilly. "And only a half-hour hack away."

In an invisible state, Daphne had been listening to the brief conversation between Simon and Selby. The girl needed to nurse herself back into an improved mental state before she could show her ghostly self again. She looked out through the pantry window to watch Simon make his way on Almond across the field.

Hmm, she thought. Now that's a rather interesting idea.

CHAPTER FIVE

Feeling better for having spent the day on her bed snoozing and reading, it was early evening when Selby got up for a cup of tea. Wandering into the study and turning on the lights, she nervously glanced at the chair in which the apparition had sat. There was no one there. She relaxed. Been driving myself too hard to finish the book, she reasoned – and too much cognac the other night.

After a light supper, she gathered fresh towels and ran a bath, chucking in lots of herbal bubble gel. Lying back, inhaling the lavender wafting up from the steaming water, she closed her eyes. Images from the night in her study popped up. Honestly, she said to herself, if you were going to hallucinate, why didn't you call up Mary Hemingway's ghost, so you could ask her questions for your book. She broke into fits of giggles. Sinking further down into the water, the conversation with the figment of her imagination ran through her mind. She liked my book. "Stop that," she said aloud. "Ego mixed with crazy. Ghost of Daphne du Maurier. *Che idiota*! Excessively overactive imagination. *Usi il cervello, cretino*."

"Not really," a voice said. "Was that Italian? I never learnt it."

Selby sat up and turned her head. Sitting on the loo was the same figure she had seen in the study. "No," she shrieked. She shut her eyes quickly, waited a few seconds and opened them again. Panic was rising within her. Her heart raced in her chest. "Must be calm," she whispered while looking again, trying to process the figure in front of her. "See someone. Sober. Hallucination."

She submerged her head and shoulders under water. When she came up, her face was covered in bubbles. Eyes squeezed closed, her hand felt around the edge of the bath for the face cloth. When it was put into her hand, she slid her entire body to the far end of the tub as far away as possible from the apparition. Pulling her knees up to her chest for protection, she wasn't sure what to do next.

"I am real," the woman said. "Not real as in the flesh, but as I said the other night, I can't explain what I am. I just know I'm here talking to you. I'm Daphne du Maurier. I lived in this house at one time. I happened in here. Then I read your book on that machine, liked it, and decided to stay – for a while at any rate. Okay with you?"

Selby realised she had been asked a question. Though petrified, it occurred to her that perhaps making conversation with the imaginary figure would reveal what deep-seated neuroses had conjured up the form in front of her. When it disappeared, she would decide which medical specialist was needed. Reluctantly, she opened one eye, then the other. She stared at the thing sitting opposite, wishing it would evaporate.

"Does a person get to choose if a ghost can stay," she said tentatively, hoping she would get no reply.

"Ghost. It's such a common, uninteresting word implying floating ectoplasm with no purposeful thought," Daphne explained. "I don't think I like being called a ghost. I'm a writer – like you. By the way, I shouldn't put the funeral scene in that chapter. Stick it in after Cuba. Build the tension."

Selby answered instinctively, defending the placement of the scene to which she had given a great deal of thought. "Considered that. Easier for him to have the ruckus in the bar after the funeral."

"I think it will reveal his future second wife's intentions sooner if you let the reader witness her stay in the house for the funeral. Allow her to dominate the household, boss the first wife around, make her feel inadequate."

"Mrs Danvers," Selby suddenly blurted out before stopping to think about what had just happened. She had had a conversation with whatever was sitting opposite her. "Oh my God, could you possibly be real? Or else, I'm a very sick girl with a terribly overactive imagination – spooky either way. Discussing my book from the bath with Daphne du Maurier. Who would ever believe such a thing?"

"You've got a point," Daphne said quickly. "This ought to stay *entre nous*, don't you think?"

"Who would I tell? Men in white coats and all that."

Selby chuckled, reaching for a towel and dressing gown before going into her bedroom.

Daphne called out from the bathroom, "You know that typing machine you write on? I can apparently press the keys down, but I don't know how it works. I'm used to a thing that tap, tap, taps itself in a nice rhythmic noise with a little bell at the end of a right-hand margin. Your machine is silent when you depress the keys. Can you teach me?"

Rounding in from the bedroom, Selby was so cross she could barely speak.

"You? At Menabilly? Was it you who left me locked in? I heard that blasted tapping through the wall – and that annoying little ping. Drove me mad all afternoon."

"I don't see I could've done anything useful, do you – under the circumstances?"

"Seemed to be enjoying my predicament, and you – it was you who touched my laptop, wasn't it? You just admitted it. Had me ranting and raving about losing my mind. Pushed me close to the edge. Erased whole sections of my book. Have you any idea how long it will take to go back and rewrite them?"

"I think, even in your present over-excited state, you can agree that I would," Daphne replied with a slightly conceited air.

"Why can't you go back to Menabilly where you came from? This is not the place for you. I need solitude, quiet. I like it that way. Bloody hell, am I really trying to reason with a figment of my imagination?"

"Thought we'd been over that," Daphne said dryly.

"And I can't go back there – to Menabilly, I mean. It's not a sympathetic atmosphere."

Selby sat down. It was all too much. The thing was standing in front of her clear as day. It had admitted to being a ghost though preferring not to be labelled as such. Did ghosts really exist? She wasn't afraid of whatever it was in front of her. If anything, she found it annoying. "It's late, and my mind's going around in circles. I can't think straight, but if you are real, and I find you here in the morning, there will be rules. One – absolute quiet when I'm writing. Two – never touch the laptop. Clear on that? Good. Going to bed. You sleep?"

"Alas, I do not, nor do I get tired unless I try to do something too ambitious." Daphne paused, uncertain whether to ask the next question. "I wonder, could I use the bedroom with the red and green flowered chintz? I've had a quick look around and taken a liking to that room."

Have you just, Selby thought, retreating to her bed. Unable to keep her eyes open a moment longer, she wiggled down into the middle of the mattress, pulling the duvet over her head for sanctuary. "Tomorrow. Ring doctor," she murmured before falling asleep.

When she woke the next morning, Selby lay in bed for a while looking around her pretty bedroom, admiring the design of the pelmets Joanna had suggested. The soft tones of the wallpaper were just the right backdrop for the curtains in the 'Garden of Eden' fabric which had caught her eye when she and Joanna had walked their feet off looking for samples to take to Cornwall. In the end, they had both agreed no one could compete with the original designs from the Chelsea Textile Company. She had used the fabrics for most of the rooms. The hand-embroidered curtains in her bedroom were designs of exotic birds, fruit, flowers and leaves, which the shop said and been taken from an English bed curtain of the early eighteenth century. She had toyed with the other fabric, but in the end, she had used it in the guest room down the hall.

She froze.

Down the hall – that thing – the conversation last night – had she dreamt it all? Going over the sequence of events, she felt sure it had happened, but what if the whole thing had been a delusion? She felt ashamed to have conversed with the thing, even discussing her book. Sitting up in bed, stacking pillows behind her back, she grabbed the iPad from the bedside table. Google: 'A delusion is a belief that is held with strong conviction despite superior evidence to the contrary...' "Do I strongly believe what I saw last night was real?" She hesitated to answer, realising that one way or another, she was doomed. Either she was delusional and needed urgent medical care, or her house had become the refuge for an annoying thing that talked too much and had too many opinions. It would disrupt the tranquillity she treasured and needed.

She re-read the definition – 'Superior evidence to the contrary'. "I am bloody well not going to google the word, ghost. Don't care what testimonials exist. I have never believed in all that stuff."

"Then where does that leave you, my girl," a voice asked. "Either you're psychotic or I exist."

"Who said that?"

"You know who said that. I introduced myself last night."

Selby winged pillows across the room in all directions. "Oh no you don't. Where are you?" When no answer came, she stomped down the hall to the spare bedroom, throwing open the door so hard it hit the wall behind with a bang. "If you're in here, get out. Do you hear me? Get out of my house." Chest heaving up and down, beetroot-red face, she stamped back to her room, slamming the door behind as hard as she could.

Wow. That's quite a temper, Daphne thought. I must remember not to get on a 'hard-chair' with her. In an invisible state, she watched the girl collect the pillows from the floor and get back onto her bed.

Selby lay there for a few minutes calming herself down before continuing to read Google:

'As a pathology, it is distinct from a belief based on false or incomplete information...delusions typically occur in the context of neurological or psychiatric disease...of particular diagnostic importance in psychiatric disorders including schizophrenia...and...manic episodes of psychotic depression.'

She threw the iPad across the room and was about to spew a string of expletives when she remembered that thing could hear her. What are you doing, she asked herself? You're playing into this delusion. Stop it. Ignore it. Maybe it will go away. She felt exhausted from the whole business. I am – not – going to let anything or anyone disturb the tranquillity of Rose Cottage, she screamed inside her head as she sprang up out of bed for a shower.

Closing the door of the bathroom, she looked around

to see if she was alone. Locking the door seemed futile. Just get on with things. Make pretend you neither see nor hear anything.

"Gosh, this is going to be harder than I thought." Daphne looked out the window at the pretty garden below while she considered things. "She's got to want me here or I shall have to leave. I couldn't put up with that kind of behaviour all day in any case. It's not in my nature to be around high-strung people. I've got to make myself useful to her, indispensable perhaps."

Selby stood under the hot shower until she felt in a calmer state. She got dressed and went down for breakfast. When she walked into the kitchen, she saw the table laid up for one, hot toast and coffee on a mat. "Stop this," she screamed, sweeping her hands across everything on the table, sending it all crashing to the floor. "Get out." She rushed out the back door, fleeing to the fields across the road.

"Now, what was wrong with that, do you suppose? I would've been chuffed to find my breakfast all laid out." Daphne walked around the house looking for jobs she could do that might please, but that wouldn't cause another explosion.

It was three o'clock when Selby returned to the kitchen. She was thirsty from the long walk she had taken to the sea. Her stomach growled while she swept up the china from the floor. Pâté on toast organised, she took a tray to the study now that she was in a calmer state to write. Hearing nothing more from the voice for the rest of the day, she settled into a good rhythm and a productive session at her laptop, rewriting what had been lost the day before. When she finally closed the lid, it was almost midnight. She went to bed.

From a deep sleep, she woke in the middle of the night. Something fluttered back and forth over her face. Ignoring it, she turned over, but a few minutes later, she opened her eyes again. Small high-pitched squeaks were coming from somewhere in the room. Switching on the light, she screamed. The room was full of bats winging their way through the air, flying swiftly overhead and around her. Selby sprang out of bed to grab her dressing gown which she flung in all directions to get to the door. Once out of the room, she sat down on the stairs for a while to catch her breath. Terrific. Now what? She was damned if she was going to the spare bedroom where that thing might be. Deciding it would have to be the sofa in the sitting room, she stood up to go downstairs when the door to her bedroom opened and Daphne appeared.

"It's fine now. I've managed to get them out," she said. "Not sure they liked the idea of me. I've stuffed some towels into the opening of the fireplace. It's never worked anyway – something to do with the ratio of chimney height to width of grate. I should have it closed up if I were you."

"There you go again, dispensing advice, prying, interfering, and bothering me."

"I was only trying to help. They're gone. You can go in there now."

Mumbling a swear word under her breath, Selby slid past as quickly as possible to get back into her bedroom.

That will do for now, thought Daphne. What a sweat it had been getting those bats down the chimney and into the room, but it had done the trick. The girl was now in her debt.

Selby lay awake for some time, thinking. There was no other conclusion. The thing was real despite the preposterous idea of a ghost haunting her house. It had already caused a ruckus, interfering with her routine, but it was more than a disturbance. She didn't want to share Rose Cottage with anyone. The desire for an uncomplicated life after splitting with Raphe had driven her out of London to find a peaceful place to live and work.

She laughed quietly to herself as she closed her eyes. "And what was the most glaring thing in the sales brochure, you imbecile; the thing that made you think Rose Cottage must be a good place to write? That Daphne du Maurier had once lived here."

Simon kept thinking about Selby Lyons and the coincidence of her being the girl who had been locked in the bathroom at Menabilly. His farmer had not mentioned the neighbour with the problem sheep was such a beauty and just a few fields away. A writer, he had said. He typed Selby Lyons into a Google search. The first item appeared was a book on the artist, Lee Krasner; the second one was on naturalist painter, Marianne North. The only book of fiction was *The Egg People of Brimstone*. The reviews were especially good for all three. He went into Amazon and ordered.

"Why not just go over there and ask her out, you idiot?" Daphne would accuse him of cowardice if she were here. No hiding things from that woman. She never left anything unsaid. He missed her interference though. She had been like a mother to him all these years, bringing him out of himself the year after his mother died; there for him during holidays from boarding school; there to listen to all his woes; there to deliver wisdom on this and that. He felt terribly alone now, almost as if there had been a death in the family. Wherever she had gone, he knew she would be back. On the other hand, he couldn't spend the rest of his life holed up with only a ghost for companionship. Wasn't she always saying he needed someone in his life? Ask the woman to lunch, he told himself – less of a date thing than dinner.

Deciding to ride over to Selby Lyons' house that afternoon, he groomed his mare, and cleaned tack and saddle. After a shower, he considered what to wear that wouldn't look like he had tried too hard. When he reached Rose Cottage, Latin music was coming from an opened window. He tied Almond to a fence rail. Feeling jittery as he walked to the door, he talked to himself in a quiet voice. "Just ask if she's free to come to lunch – that's all, you twit."

Selby opened the door, startled to feel a double beat of her heart when she saw Simon Rashleigh. He cut quite a dash in jodhpurs and riding boots. His thick brown hair was standing straight up in places from the riding hat in his hands.

"Hello. Sorry to stop by unannounced," he said. "I was out on a hack and thought I would just check on your sheep."

"Thanks, about the sheep. Afraid I seemed ungrateful

the other day. I'd just come back from Italy on a night flight into Heathrow. Writing today but taking a break. Been in a permanently bad mood lately."

"The local grapevine said you're a writer," he replied. "I'm one of sorts."

"Read two of your books."

Two. Did that mean she couldn't bear to read a third, he wondered? He was summoning courage when she spoke.

"Rude of me. Come in. Coffee? Doing some cooking."

"I can smell it from here. What is it?"

"*Agnolotti del Plin* – agnolotti pasta stuffed with roasted meats and spinach. Grew up in Italy. Coffee?"

Simon had not expected to be asked in, but the scent of whatever was cooking in the kitchen was irresistible.

"Strong? Weak? Milk? Sugar?" she asked when they walked into the kitchen.

"Black, thank you."

Selby looked up suddenly. "Know how to skin a rabbit by any chance? Needed one for this recipe. Asked a friend if he could get me one. Left it on the doorstep, fur, and all. Was just going down to the farmer to ask for help when you knocked."

"Look, I'm sorry for stopping in like this. If you're cooking for friends tonight, I'm sure you've a lot to do."

"Recipe takes two days to prepare and cook. Can you?"

Simon was considering the reference she had made to asking someone, a man, to get a rabbit for her. "Um, I haven't skinned a rabbit in a long time. The Game Keeper taught me when I was about ten. I could give it a go, I suppose, but I'll have to put my mare in your field. She's just tied to a fence post."

When he returned, Selby pointed to a hallway off the kitchen. "By the wellies inside the back door. You'll need this knife. Hope you don't mind my asking."

He hoped he wouldn't make a hash of it. Think, man, think. He heard the keeper's voice in his head: "Cut a ring round each leg, boy, just above the leg joint. Mind you, only cut enough to get past the hide. Don't cut deeply – it's a waste of good meat."

Holding the rabbit by the legs, he suddenly remembered the keeper had tied the rabbit to stakes as an anchor while it was skinned. He went back to the kitchen. "I need a bin to put the bits, and I'm afraid I'm going to need your help. Someone has to hold the legs while I pull the skin off."

"Oh, I don't think –"

He interrupted to explain in more detail, "I can't cut, hold, and pull on my own. Can you close your eyes or something?"

He showed her where to hold the rabbit. She looked the other way while he made the ring cuts above the leg joints, and on each leg, a single slice going up from the ring cut to the backside of the animal. Here goes, he thought, pulling away some of the hide, working from the ring cut at the foot joint down to the backside. The hide started to slide off. He cut through the bone of the tail. The keeper's voice echoed in his mind again: "Don't puncture the bladder, boy." Placing the knife on the table, he continued to pull the hide down the carcass with both hands.

Selby was watching by now, totally fascinated. "Like peeling a banana."

Perspiration rolled off his forehead while he worked his fingers into the sleeves of the hide of the arms. They weren't coming off as easily as the upper bit. After a few minutes, he got the hide from the upper torso down to the head, pulling until it rested at the base of the skull.

"Okay. Better look away now or possibly retreat," he said.

"I can stick it out."

Severing the head from the spine, the skin detached from the remaining meat. He broke the bones with the knife at the arm and leg joints. Selby turned her head, wincing at the crack and snap while he severed the skin from the bone with the knife.

"Phew, I wasn't sure I would manage it," Simon said with relief.

"Sorry about all this. I didn't realise how much work it involved when I asked. Thank you. Bet you didn't think you would be doing this today." She laughed.

No, thought Simon, but there's more than one way to skin a rabbit. She will have to say yes to lunch now. They went back to the kitchen.

"Coffee is cold. I'll make fresh. Have it with *cristolli*, ribbon cookies," she said, picking up a tray. "Made them this morning. I'll pop them in the oven – crisp them up."

"Wow. You've really been cooking up a storm today."

"Stuck on a section of a book I'm writing. Cooking clears the head and any foul mood hovering evaporates."

"I feel that way about cooking, though I didn't know anything about it until my trip to Madagascar. I changed the style of my books to include recipes of local cuisine which, after all, is influenced by a country's culture. The women in the village taught me. Smells coming from their kitchens were so pungent. Not sure I'd cooked more than a boiled egg before that trip, really. You wouldn't believe all the vibrant colours of the spices piled high in baskets in the marketplace." God, man – stop rabbiting on, he told himself.

"Learnt from my Italian nanny. Taught me everything. Had a lot of time together. Parents are artists, always in studios." She didn't say that Viviana had saved her from boredom and loneliness.

"What's next in the recipe?" Simon asked.

"I'm going to make the pasta. Then, I'll stick it in the fridge. After that, I've got several hours of roasting the meats – pork shoulder, chicken thighs – and now, thanks to you, rabbit. Clean the meats away from the bone, chop it, and let it sit in the pan juices. Start the spinach. Add herbs. Chill overnight. Tomorrow, stuff the agnolotti. Freeze what I don't eat. Make sage butter. Eat." She cringed – how much does one person eating alone need? Setting the ribbon cookies on the table, she poured hot coffee.

"These are great," he said. "Look, I mustn't get in the way, and it's almost time for Almond's evening feed anyway." He downed the rest of the coffee while badgering himself to get on with the reason he had come over in the first place.

"Give you some *cristolli* as a thank you. You'll need to crisp them up."

She stopped talking for a second before saying, "Got a

better idea. Come back tomorrow night. Sample what your hard labour produced? If you're free."

"Thank you," he said quickly. "I'd love to come back and taste – what's it called again?"

"*Agnolotti del Plin.*"

"What time?"

"Eight."

"Perfect, I'll bring a bottle of wine if you'd like. What would you suggest is nice to drink with it?"

"Something red with a zing."

"Okay then," he said, making his way out the door. "A red with some zing. See you tomorrow evening."

She cringed after he left. "Something red with a zing? What does that mean? *Idiota.* And dinner?" That was easier to explain – such a pity not to share Viviana's recipe after all that work. *"E solo cena, sciocca. Calmati!"*

Simon gathered up the reins, putting his left boot into the stirrup, lifting himself into the saddle. "Sorry, girl, things took longer than I expected. You won't believe what I just had to do, but it was hard to say no to such a beautiful face. Will tomorrow night come soon enough?" He kicked Almond into a gallop across the field.

CHAPTER SIX

Selby rose early. Stuffing agnolotti was a fiddly job, done one by one with care. The meats had rested in their juices in the fridge overnight. Pasta was chilled and ready. She cleaned the spinach, cooked it, letting it drain while mixing the ricotta with the cream and freshly grated nutmeg. The tomato sauce simmered on the stove for the morning. By five o'clock, everything was assembled and left to chill in the fridge until an hour before cooking.

"Pudding. Nothing for pudding," she said, panicking and grabbing Viviana's notebooks to look for ideas.

"It does seem an awful lot of trouble just for supper," Daphne said, appearing suddenly in the kitchen.

Selby jumped off her seat. "Not used to you popping up. Did I ask for your opinion? Where do you go anyway?"

"Here and there, I don't always remember. What are you doing?"

"Having neighbour to supper." She didn't want to

mention who was coming. "I've made a stuffed pasta dish with roast meats. It's quite rich so I need something light for dessert and – God, what about you?"

"Don't worry. No one will see me. I'll take myself off," she assured Selby. "I once had a heavenly thing in Capri. Now what was that? The chap whipped it up in a big bowl right in front of us on the terrace. Oh, what a lovely night that was with the moon on the water below. Wait. Was it Capri or St Paul de Vence? I couldn't say for sure."

It seemed that when Daphne got started looking back on her life, there was no stopping her. Selby thought it must be frustrating not to recall one's life: the good and the bad – everything that had made it yours. "It was probably *zabaglione*," she commented while continuing to search for ideas. "How come you say you have no memory of your life, and then you come up with little nuggets like a moonlit night in Capri?"

"I don't know the 'hows' or the 'whys' of my existence. I just know that I am. Memories from my life come back in spurts." Her expression switched from happy to unamused as she spoke.

"That's an idea," Selby suddenly said.

"What is?"

"*Zabaglione* is. Takes a lot of arm muscle though. I would have to do it before and chill it. Should be slightly warm and made just before serving, but it can be eaten cold. It's so delicious. What's the time?" She worked it out. Wash hair. Choose dress. Would she wear a dress? Might look like she had gone to too much trouble – a casual dress, why not? Which to do first? Get the work done, she decided, before gathering up the Marsala and cream to begin. It needed about four hours in the fridge to chill.

At seven thirty, she came downstairs to set the table in the kitchen, placing candlesticks and a small vase of flowers in the middle. She lit fires in both kitchen and sitting room and dotted scented candles on various surfaces. When the door knocker banged at eight on the dot, her stomach lurched.

"Just dinner, stop it. Don't even know him." She looked in the hall mirror – red lipstick, tanned face, clean hair, strappy, navy linen dress, and open-toed kitten heels. "Fine," she said.

When she opened the door, Simon Rashleigh was holding a large bunch of hedgerow flowers. He looked just as good as he had yesterday. Another heart-skip. "Beautiful flowers. Thank you. Come in."

He followed her into the kitchen, looking around the comfortable, large space he had not taken in on the day before. Long slabs of polished, black slate covered the counters. A large fireplace dominated a wall at one end of the room. Placed in front were two generous armchairs, divided by a coffee table stacked with books. In the middle of the kitchen, copper pots hung from rafters above an enormous, bleached, pine table. Terracotta pots, overflowing with herbs, crowded the deep windowsill above double stainless-steel sinks.

Selby eased the cork from the bottle of champagne and poured into two fluted glasses. "Thank you," she said, raising her glass in the air, "for the ladder rescue and for the returned sheep and the skinned rabbit. We've got some time before the *agnolotti* will be ready. Let's go to the sitting room." As they walked down the hall, she frantically tried to think of something to say. "Chilly tonight, isn't it? Hardly notice weather when I'm writing. Been taking a break for a few days." Her heart sank – the weather?

"I know what you mean," he answered back. "I haven't been as fired up as I usually am about the book I'm working on. So, a few weeks ago, I booked a flight to Ethiopia. Driving to Heathrow just before dawn tomorrow morning."

"Ethiopia? Tomorrow? Thought I saw a news report there was trouble there?"

"There is, but we can't cross off all the areas on the map where there's conflict? Should we stop visiting ancient sites we're lucky are still standing and ignore cultures who have inhabited these great cities for centuries? Tourism is an important source of income for them, and the cuisine is exotic. Take Ethiopia – spicy meat dishes with fenugreek, chillies, nigella, cardamom; all served on wonderful sourdough flatbread."

Selby could see the excitement in his face as he talked about the trip. Why did she suddenly feel flat? Ignoring it, she asked when he first knew he wanted to travel and write.

He didn't answer that it had been Daphne's advice. Having read Classics at university, he had no idea what to do afterwards. She had encouraged him to travel. "See the world," she had said. "Keep a diary. Perhaps you can write a book about your travels like my friend Clara Vyvyan. You've nothing to lose. Go." When he had returned home, Daphne had read his journals. Reworking them a bit, she had explained the mechanisms of writing, and how to enrich descriptions. "If I didn't think you could do it, Simon, I wouldn't bother, but you're a natural and almost there. Another few rewrites, you'll have it. Then, show it to a publisher."

"I guess it began as wanderlust," he said to Selby. "One thing led to another. A publisher liked the first travel journal, bought it, then commissioned two more – nothing complicated."

"Rather dismissive of a profession which takes perseverance, imagination, discipline."

He thought she sounded like Daphne now, and it made him laugh. "All true, but I wouldn't say they sell out the minute they hit the bookshops."

"Not a measure of a book that makes you believe you're living the moment – waking to a purple sunrise in the desert with a camel breathing on you, its drool falling over your face."

"Arabian Desert Journal – you've read it?"

"Massive sand storm; rotting fruit covered in sand flies when you ran out of provisions. Euphoria when you swam in the lake at the end of the journey." She didn't mention skimming his books last night on her Kindle.

"That's cheered me up. I'm never sure anyone really reads them. I've often wondered if people just buy them as presents to give away when a friend goes on a trip."

"They describe places I'll never go. Not brave when it comes to travel. Wouldn't go on my own." She instantly regretted painting a rather pathetic picture of herself. "Let's have food," she said, quickly changing the subject. "I just need a few minutes to sort things out. Can you put the screen in front of the fire, please?"

Simon looked in the mirror over the fireplace to straighten his hair with his fingers, stopping suddenly to sniff the air. Cigarette smoke. Perhaps that's why she has so many scented candles about. He noticed birds' nests on the mantle. The smallest was tightly woven with moss, hay, and lichen. He took it in his hands. "Only a sensitive soul would collect these," he murmured.

During dinner, they discussed his travelling adventures, and places he had yet to visit. The evening was at an end when Simon realised he had done most of the talking. Comes from living with a ghost, he thought. Standing at the door, he wondered if he could kiss her goodnight. "That was a wonderful dinner. My place next time when I'm back from Ethiopia in three weeks?"

"Thank you. Okay."

"Oh, and look, I don't mind cigarettes. I'm not bothered if people smoke in my house."

"What? Don't smoke. Used to – probably the fire smoking. Why?"

"It's just that I thought I smelled – um, that you'd lit the scented candles, um to get rid of the smell. I wasn't prying. I was just saying that –"

Interrupting him, she wished him a good journey tomorrow, and ushered him the rest of the way out, closing the door. When she went into the study, Daphne was sitting in front of the fireplace in the high wingback chair. Selby plopped down on the fender seat. "Guest smelled your cigarette. People don't smoke anymore, you know. No smoking when someone is here."

"Touchy chap, isn't he?" Daphne sniped.

"Rather nice, I thought. During dinner, I was wondering. If it was you on the other side of the wall when I was trapped in the bathroom, what were you doing at Menabilly? I know you used to live there and everything, but –"

Daphne instantly cut her off and began waving both arms around. "I do find it difficult having to explain things. It makes me feel low. A much more interesting topic of conversation is this man who was here tonight. He's handsome, don't you think, and he seems to have a good brain. He talks a little bit too much, but what he said was worth hearing, I thought. I'm sure he was getting ready to kiss you at the door." She lit a cigarette.

"How could you know that? Thought you said you would take yourself off some place? Doubt you would have come out with someone here, and I don't like the idea of peeping Toms by the way, so no more of that when I have friends over."

"Well, I did vamoose, but came back in the middle of dinner, and then retreated in here before getting bored, so I was hovering when he was leaving. It was only for a few seconds. There are times I can make myself invisible. You did close the door rather quickly after what he said about smelling cigarette smoke."

"Not used to this thing yet – dealing with ghosts who smoke or men trying to kiss me at the door."

Simon drove home slowly, relishing all the bits of the evening, and wishing he wasn't leaving on a three-week trip. He worried he had blotted his copybook with the cigarette thing. Why had she lied about smoking? Having had plenty of practise over the years with Daphne's cigarettes, it was so obviously cigarette smoke he had smelt.

He slammed on the brakes.

"Daphne?"

He tried to make sense of what was running through his mind – Selby, Menabilly, the locked bathroom. It fitted. Just the sort of stunt Daphne would pull. Turning the car around, he raced back down the road to Selby's house. It was dark at the front, but light was coming from a room at the side. Creeping, he stayed low enough to look through the window. Selby was laughing, and talking to someone, but he couldn't see who was sitting in the chair. He crouched closer to hear the conversation, but the heavens opened. He was about to return to the car when he noticed cigarette smoke rise from the armchair. Two arms sprang out either side and began to wave about in an excited fashion. Simon gasped. At the wrists, he could see a floral print blouse peeking out from the sleeves of a beige cardigan he had first seen as a seven-year-old boy.

"Daphne," he whispered.

The house was quiet in the morning. Selby felt clear-headed, ready to return to writing. Dinner with Simon Rashleigh had gone well; delighting her that Viviana's recipe had been cooked to perfection. The ease with which they talked had sent her to sleep with a sense of accomplishment and moving on with life. Was he really going to kiss her goodnight as Daphne suggested? Ridiculous, she thought, don't start taking advice about a possible romance from a woman who has been dead for three decades.

Now that she had accepted a ghost was haunting the place, Selby hoped they could coexist with the minimum of fuss. Perhaps ghosts really do exist as a normal occurrence in many houses, but people are too afraid to mention it for fear of ridicule. What would CC say if she told him? She had not mentioned the idea of Daphne when she had been in Tuscany. Viviana had grown up listening to stories of 'Babao', the Italian version of the bogeyman. There were tales of ghosts at the castle where she helped her mother clean. "Things disappeared sometimes," she had told Selby. "One minute the broom was in the corner, the next it was by the door."

It wouldn't do for Daphne to pull shenanigans like that; she needed peace to write. Opening her laptop, she read over recent paragraphs on Mary Hemingway:

"You're beautiful, like a May fly," Ernest said when first declaring his love in 1944. They were both war correspondents in London at the same time. Mary Welsh knew his reputation as a womaniser, yet felt helpless to resist the attraction that had grown between them. Though both Time *and* Life *magazines waited for her copy, revenue which she...*

Selby stared into space. It must've been tough for Mary to maintain a sense of herself in such a tempestuous marriage with such an overbearing character as Ernest

Hemingway. "Does this section work? Is it necessary?" she asked aloud.

Daphne answered from behind, "Your problem, my girl, is that you don't get outdoors enough."

"Oh, it's you," Selby said in mock surprise. "Not helpful when you just pop up. Jars me out of a train of thought."

"I'm just saying – I used to keep to regular routes, even when I was writing – especially when I was writing. Like clockwork, I took a long walk every afternoon to clear the cobwebs. It gave me time to mull over my characters, their thoughts and actions. When I returned, I felt renewed, often brimming over with fresh ideas and solutions. From my writing hut, I had views of the sea. It was positively inspirational, not like this north-facing dungeon at the back of the house. You should take one of the rooms upstairs with a view of the sea where the sun comes streaming through the window."

Selby laid on the sarcasm while continuing to type. "Hm. Yes, perhaps the green and red chintz bedroom. That's – if you've no objection."

Daphne went on. "Why not get yourself out and fill those lungs with oxygen? I used to swim twice a day in the sea this time of the year. Come on. Get up. Let's go for a swim. Well, you go for the swim, that is. You won't believe how much better you'll feel. Or we could walk to the moors and stop to buy a pasty. I'll show you a wonderful place to sit in an old earth-dwelling on the top of a tor."

Selby began to speak aloud the words she was trying to type over Daphne's never-ceasing chatter. "...*revenue which she badly needed, her only source of income...*"

"I met him," Daphne said.

"Look," Selby snapped. "This has to stop. Don't stand behind me, reading over my shoulder, making remarks. Go and do whatever it is you do when you're not bothering me."

"I'm just saying that I met Hemingway in London during the war. That's all. It might help your research. Wouldn't you like a first-hand account of the man?"

"Right. Get on with it and then get lost." Selby thought if she let the woman hold forth, she might feel sated enough to leave her in peace.

"London didn't seem such a big place, then. There weren't many nice restaurants where one could go to have a drink and something to eat, you see. So, one often found oneself mixing with all kinds of people. He was a handsome man. Not my type, but I could see the attraction women had for him. You knew he was there – that's the thing. One couldn't deny his presence. Wouldn't have done for me – too showy, too loud, too full of himself. Very 'See-Me'. Not surprised he had so many wives. Of course, divorce is so common today. Due to the war, I've always thought. Women got a taste of being independent. Then the men came home and wanted submissive little housewives. I'm not saying that a woman didn't need to do her bit in the home and with the children, but so many of us wanted our own careers. I don't imagine Hemingway was very sympathetic to his wives' ambitions. Apparently, he had a filthy temper, especially when he had drink taken. And I wouldn't stick a husband who insisted my writing take a back seat to his."

"Four of them did, though some lingered longer than

others," Selby replied dryly, "and I'm trying to write about the last one. Take yourself away now, so I can get some work done. Behind enough as it is – mostly having to do with you and the happenings of last week."

"Oh, I don't think you can blame me for getting locked in that bathroom."

"Possibly not, and since you brought that up, I've been wanting to ask about Menabilly. How did you exist there? Knowing you even the little I do, it seems out of character that you would be anywhere without making comments or interfering. What about Simon Rashleigh? Did you ever show yourself to him?"

Selby waited for an answer, looking behind her when none came. It had worked. Ask a penetrating question about Daphne's existence, and off she went. Now with a quiet room, she continued writing:

...and badly needed. She had found lodgings with two other women journalists, sharing expenses for rent and heat. It wasn't a big flat, but it had a shower, small kitchenette, and a pull-out sofa where Mary slept. Men were not expected as overnight guests. More than once, she had pushed Ernest away from the door to get herself inside if he walked her home.

As tender as Ernest could be one minute, a torrent of abuse could streak out the next, calling Mary "a smirking, useless female war correspondent" one night in front of the whole bar at a restaurant. He expected his women to be able to take 'it'. 'It' meant him, and everything to do with him. Sometime after his suicide when Mary thought about the scene she found after he had shot himself in their home, she recalled him saying years before, "You hired out to be tough, didn't you?" She had acknowledged early in the relationship that –

Knocking at the window interrupted Selby yet again. Turning in her chair, ready to banish Daphne from the house forever, she saw George Renfold peering in and waving.

"Grr. More interruptions," she said before getting up to open the window. "Working, George. Not convenient."

"That's okay. I'm here to let you know that I've fixed your broken fencing."

"What? You didn't have to do that. I was going to ask the farmer if he could help."

"I had some time on my hands today, and well, the loose wires were not going to hold the ewes in for much longer. Saves us both a lot of trouble."

"Thank you. Sorry. Writing. Can't ask you in. Another time, okay?"

Putting his hand on the window frame to lean in, he said, "The other thing I stopped by about, is that the family is getting together at home, day after tomorrow. It's supper, nothing fancy, but I'd love it if you could join us. Thought I'd come up here to ask after I fixed your fence line."

Selby was trapped. That's twice he's mentioned the fencing, she thought. "Of course, what time?"

"Pick you up at six."

"Just a dinner," she grumbled as she closed the window, though what she would talk about was a worry. "I'll make a dessert to take. With any luck they'll ask me how I made it."

When she finished writing for the day, she went to the

kitchen to look for a recipe. Daphne was watching the evening news. Ignoring the noise from the television, Selby began to assemble the ingredients, hoping to find everything needed for George's pudding. A few days in the fridge would intensify the flavours of the amaretto.

Daphne waved at Selby to come over. "Look. Isn't that the chap you had here for dinner? Isn't that him in the crowd on the box?"

Putting the whisk down on the counter, Selby peered closer at the screen. "Certainly, it looks like him." She turned up the volume.

"...in Addis Ababa was today occupied by large numbers of young people demanding the government's resignation. Passengers from a British airline have been held at the airport since their arrival due to large angry mobs gathered outside the airport terminal. An Ethiopian official explained that it's for their own protection. BA is waiting for a plane to return them to London."

Simon Rashleigh was standing in the middle of a crowd, waving his arms, trying to get the attention of an airline official.

"Yes, that's him. We talked about this kind of thing when he came to dinner," she remarked casually as she reached for the whisk again. "Told him I wouldn't jump at the chance to go to places having demonstrations and strikes. He said he wouldn't let it keep him from travelling. Lucky they're being sent home."

Daphne had noticed Selby's face while they listened to the news report. Concern had led to relief, and then she was sure a smile had followed. Don't we play our cards close to our chest, she thought.

Selby's arm began to tire from beating the six egg whites in the big copper bowl in her arms. It would take more muscle before they formed the stiff peaks needed for the pudding for George's family dinner. She concentrated on something else besides the burning sensation in her arm – his eyes, his smile, his laugh.

He's coming home, she said to herself.

CHAPTER SEVEN

he buzzing had been going on since daybreak. Pillows over her head only muffled the sound. Selby opened her eyes to glance at the clock. Groaning, she closed them again. It was only five in the morning.

"How can you sleep through that?" Daphne asked, suddenly visible at the bottom of the bed. "Get up. It's very lucky to have a swarm of honeybees visit your house. Did you know that? Come look." She vanished as quickly as she had appeared.

Reluctantly, Selby threw on jogging sweats and a T-shirt. Daphne's bursts of enthusiasm, if ignored, generated a relentless stream of consciousness. Must come from being dead a long time, she thought. The French doors in the sitting room were open. Daphne was on the terrace looking up.

"There – in the eaves of the slate roof."

"Do I want them there?" Selby yawned as she looked up.

"Let's see if they settle. They may just be a resting swarm. They're harmless and need a home – a bit like me."

"While they're making up their collective mind, I need caffeine in the vein." As she made coffee, Selby began to think about a letter she had received. It was an answer to one she had sent a few months before to a friend of Mary Hemingway's. Though she had not asked the question, the reply detailed Mary's complicity in her husband's liaisons while they lived in Cuba. Occasionally, when Papa and Mary were at their favourite haunt for dinner, if there was an attractive girl sitting at the bar, Mary invited her to have a drink with them, encouraging her to stay at their table to eat. Many bottles of wine later, the three would end up going home together whereupon Mary would sneak off, making herself scarce. The girls were always gone by morning.

"Slightly unexpected," Daphne said, swanning in. "They've gone around to the south side of the house. I've had a look upstairs. Until they swarm again, they're in your bedroom. I'm afraid it's out of action.

"Nothing unusual about that lately," Selby mumbled to herself before asking Daphne how they got into her room.

"You mean, apart from through the open window?"

"Stupid of me, didn't think you were talking about thousands of bees when you woke me at dawn. I'll need to sleep in there tonight. How do we get them out?"

"Swarms can number up to twenty thousand, but there aren't that many in your room. They're flying all over the place and having a good old snoop. When I went in, they seemed to cluster around me – very spiritual things, bees. I spotted the queen resting on the wall. When she leaves the original hive, she takes over half the worker bees with her, leaving the young queens to hatch. Only one queen to a hive – 'twas ever thus," Daphne explained.

Selby thought of Mary Hemingway. Was that the idea – did she have to allow Papa's philandering to stay Queen Bee? If the girls were on her patch for a one-night-stand, she could keep any budding relationship from developing into something that could threaten her position.

"Of course, if their pheromone markers are still on the entrance," Daphne continued, "they'll cluster together and head for a space under the facia board where they used to be when I lived here. It faces east so morning sun will keep it warm, and after the sun moves around, the hive won't cook in the afternoon – too hot and those worker bees do nothing but fan their wings to cool the hive down. It's quite a surprise to hear the noise from all those wings if you stand underneath."

Had it been a shock for Mary to realise she wasn't enough for Papa's appetite, Selby wondered? Did she take it personally or take a view that some men just have an overabundance of testosterone? If she had thrown a fit, would he have thrown her out? Sitting in the best seats at bullfights and restaurants, mixing with the famous and powerful – was that enough for a woman who had had a writing career of her own? She had lived independently in Europe while working as a war correspondent. Ernest's demands dominated the relationship, leaving Mary the object of his abuse, made worse by the substantial amounts of alcohol he consumed daily.

Daphne clapped her hands several times to get Selby's attention. "I just thought – maybe you'll have honey if they settle here again. We had the most delicious, gooey, deep brown honeycombs. When that part of the roof leaked, we had to send someone up a ladder. The bees had gone, but they left pounds of the stuff in the hive. We melted it on a low flame on the cooker and poured it through a filter. It cured my sinus trouble at the time. I remember that now. You could try ringing the British Beekeepers Association for advice if the bees are still here tomorrow. You're not listening to a word I say, are you?"

"If I listened to everything you said all day, I'd never get any work done. Going up to have a shower. When I come down, I expect to have the study to myself for the rest of the day – alone – that means without you barging in with Wikipedia titbits about the life and nature of bees," she said, leaving the kitchen.

"The study of bees is apiology, regardless what Mr Whicky-somebody says," Daphne grumbled.

By the end of the day, pleased with the new chapters she had written, Selby decided not to work after supper. How the next section would begin was crucial to the tension she hoped was building to the death of Ernest Hemingway. She needed time to think it over.

"A good session?" Daphne asked when Selby walked into the sitting room with a glass of wine.

"I think it was. There are days that are great for

coming up with fresh ideas. Other times seem perfect for editing, some for writing – I never know which it will be until I start typing. Then, there are days when you can do all three with the greatest of ease, you know what I mean?"

A wry smile crossed Daphne's face.

"For bloody sake, how can I ask such an absurd question?" Selby broke into peals of laughter. "It's ridiculous, but sometimes I forget I'm talking to Daphne du Maurier, the writer, instead of Daphne du Maurier, the ghost – sorry, know you don't like that word. Why don't you like that word? It is, after all, what you are." She took a sip of wine.

"It just sounds like something silly out of a children's book. I don't really believe in ghosts."

"That's rich, considering," Selby said as she plonked down on the sofa and put her feet up on the ottoman.

"What I mean is – I don't believe in the proverbial picture – you know, like what a child would wear to a fancy-dress party, the white sheet thing. All the being ever says is whoo, whoo. It suggests an entity with no brain, speech or will of any kind. Also, people use the word as an adverb to describe places of hopelessness, places that are somehow at the mercy of dark forces."

Selby grinned, and turned on her mobile, tapping Google. "Synonyms for ghost – here we are. Spectre...not nice. Sounds scary. Phantom –"

"Oh, heaven's no," Daphne shouted. "There was that Swedish film in 1921 called *The Phantom Carriage*. Scared the life out of me. I was only a girl, so probably I shouldn't have been taken to see it. Terrifying, I tell you, positively not phantom in a million years. What else does the phone have on the list?"

"Banshee – worse, I'd say. Shadow – no."

"Well, I am a shadow of my former self."

"Yes, but shadows are silent so that definitively rules it out. Mirage – don't know how that qualifies as a synonym; see you clear as day. Daydream, rather nice, I think, but not you, and not my idea of one."

"Not very nice," Daphne interjected.

"*Ignis fatuus* – something a Benedictine monk yells at an unruly schoolboy. Delusion – what I first thought you were. The others are not acceptable," Selby said while raising an eyebrow, "though I may use them when you piss me off."

"So, I guess it's to be spirit then. I'm fine with that. Think I had plenty in life. I still seem to have a modicum left in me, wouldn't you say?"

"No argument from me," Selby confirmed, getting up to make supper.

Later that night when she went upstairs to bed, it was quiet when she opened the door. The buzzing had gone. She turned on the light, and froze, wanting to scream, but not daring to do so. Stepping back, closing the door very quietly, she scurried down the hallway to Daphne's bedroom. "Bees," she whispered. "They're all over the walls and ceiling and bedcover, pillows, everything. My wardrobe is open. What if they're on my clothes? Looks creepy like that film of your book about the birds everywhere."

"I wasn't a fan of that. Hitchcock distorted my story," Daphne shot back.

"Anyway, I'm not going in there again. I'll have to get people here tomorrow to do something."

Daphne looked appalled. "Not to gas them, I hope. I won't stand for that. Call the BBA. They'll send someone to take them away or perhaps the swarm may not be there in the morning."

"Don't be silly. Of course, I'm not going to destroy them. Now, on to more immediate issues. Since you don't sleep, and since I haven't bought any beds yet for the other spare room..."

"Yes – splendid idea, you can bunk in here with me like a pyjama party."

"No – I had something else in mind, Daphne. Take yourself off some place so I can sleep in here."

"Leave my bedroom? But I lie on the bed – I have to do something during the night."

"I would rather it not be staring at me while I sleep."

"I wouldn't. I read and think about things – I remember scenes from my life. It's better at night. I don't know why, but in the day, there's very little I recall unless something pops up unexpectedly."

"You can do that downstairs in any number of rooms. Now, out," Selby insisted, before going down the hall to find sheets and a duvet.

A while later, when Selby was finally in bed, her thoughts turned to Raphe. He and Ernest Hemingway shared a remarkable talent for shooting arrows straight at the hearts of women with whom they were involved. She thought about Raphe's cruel words before he walked out the door: pathetic woman, emotional cripple, boring. She couldn't imagine Simon saying things like that. She had been in awe of Raphe like she had been of her father – a man who patted her head as he passed through a room. Don't think about all that now, she told herself. Concentrate on something nice – your cottage, the sea, hear the waves rush towards the shore, watch them move back and forth. Eventually, she drifted off to sleep.

Hoping to find something pretty to top the dessert for George's mother, Selby walked down the aisle of soft fruits at Tesco's. She picked up three punnets of raspberries. In the queue at the till, she saw him.

"Simon?" she said. "You're back. Saw you night before last on a news report at the airport in Addis Ababa."

"Long story. I'm okay, but tired and pretty fed up. Smelly too, so I wouldn't get too close. They put us on a plane last night, finally. We arrived at Heathrow this morning. It took ages to clear immigration. I'm just getting some food to take home. Haven't eaten in days. I'm starving."

"Better idea – my house – good ragu in the fridge – made it last night. Eat and then go home to crash."

Once at Rose Cottage, she offered Simon the use of the bathroom in the spare room. It wasn't long before he was back down.

"Thanks. I feel better, but I still wouldn't get too close. It's all rather embarrassing after going on the other night about freedom to travel and not letting things stand in the way et cetera."

She put a big bottle of apple juice on the table. He drank the entire thing before tucking into a large bowl of the meaty stew put in front of him. "There's more in the pot on the stove. Help yourself. I've got biscuits to make."

Selby took the dough from the fridge, shaped it into round nuggets, rolled each in crushed hazelnuts, and popped them into the oven before doing the washing-up. When she looked up, Simon was asleep in one of the big armchairs next to the fireplace. She went upstairs to change for supper with George's family.

At six o'clock, Simon jolted upright in the chair when the door knocker banged several times.

"George?" he asked when he opened the door.

"Simon?"

"Yes, it's me. Sorry, I must look a mess. Fell asleep in front of the fire."

George raised an eyebrow in response. "Did you?"

"Hello, George," Selby said, coming down the stairs. "Simon, I've got to go. Sorry. Hope you feel better soon." When she reappeared with the dessert, Simon had left.

"He looks awful," George said after she explained about the trip to Ethiopia. "He's always running off some place. Never sticks around for long."

They arrived in time for a quick drink before dinner. George introduced her to his siblings, his mother, Margaret, and father called Big George. Several times Selby caught Margaret staring her up and down. Then she saw the other son wink, giving the thumbs up to George. She felt like a prize heifer in a show ring. She sat down on a sofa near the fire. It had been laid, but not lit, making her wish she had worn something warmer.

They each found a place to sit or perch. Everyone stared at Selby. "Got chilly the last few evenings," she said.

"Too hot indoors," Margaret replied. "Feels like we ran a marathon when we all come in after a long day." She got up and left the room, returning a few seconds later with a smelly wax jacket to put around Selby's shoulders. "We're all hardy farm stock and forget other people have normal thermostats." Margaret laughed. "So, Son George says you write books. What kind of books? Sarah loves a good romance novel, don't you, girl? Big George and the boys, well they don't have time to read, isn't that right? The day starts early and finishes late. After supper, they watch telly, and then fall on their mattresses." She turned to her husband and tapped his knee to wake him. "We'd best go into dinner or you'll be embarrassing us all with your head-nodding routine."

Dinner was beef from their Red Devon herd, peas, broccoli, carrots, roast potatoes, and gravy. Everyone piled masses of food onto their plates as the serving dishes passed in front of them. "Come from a big family, do you?" Margaret asked Selby, between bites of food she was shovelling in at great speed.

"Only child," she replied.

Everyone stopped eating to look up at Selby with sympathy.

"We were six," Margaret continued. "Pass the gravy please, Sarah. Big George was one of five. We only had three. Still, that gave us plenty of hands to help around the place. How come you've only had three potatoes, Ben?

Yup, you need hands to help when you have a farm. When this place is yours, George, you'll need lots of extra hands. They start out little, but they grow up to be strong enough to contribute. Sarah's gone to secretarial school. She's already looking after the books, aren't you, girl? Ben's got the fields to do with Big George, and Son George and Ben share the sheep and cattle herd work. Proud of all of them." She gave them a big, warm grin.

When plates were cleared, Selby assembled her dessert, putting the platter down in front of Big George along with the hazelnut biscuits.

"Now that's a thing of beauty," he announced. "I can't eat raspberries though. They give me a rash."

"Never mind, Big George, I've got strawberries." She turned to Sarah. "Go and get the ones you picked this afternoon, and bring the pouring cream please."

Selby watched Margaret pick the raspberries off the top of the pudding and put them on a side plate. She then poured cream in quantity over the top, which everyone around the table proceeded to mash into the pudding as they served themselves.

"Delicious," Ben said. "I could eat this every day. What's it called?"

"Tiramisu. Italian. Grew up there so I have lots of Italian recipes."

"George, you didn't tell us Selby's parents were Italian," Margaret said.

"They're not," he replied, between mouthfuls. "They're artists. Well, I mean, they're British and moved to Italy to paint."

Sarah raised her eyebrows. "You mean they moved there forever?"

George looked embarrassed at his sister's unsophisticated view of the world. "For goodness' sake, Sarah. Some people do live other places besides Cornwall."

More silence and looks of sympathy followed for Selby.

"Now that's something I could not do. I couldn't leave Cornwall," Big George said. "I'd miss the farm. Wouldn't we, Margaret?"

"Yes, we would, Big George."

The women finished the dishes after dinner while the men sat in the sitting room discussing livestock prices. When it was time to go, Selby thanked Margaret who interrupted to comment herself.

"Your pudding was the special thing we ate tonight, dear. Thank you for bringing it. I hope to see you again here very soon. George, you make sure you bring this pretty girl back before harvest."

They didn't talk much on the way home. Selby had not been able to think of anything to say during dinner. Now, she worried about George's expectations – why he had asked her to dinner with his family. Arriving at Rose Cottage, Selby thanked George for the nice evening as they walked up the path to the front door. She dug around in her bag for the house keys, hoping to get inside as soon as possible. When George leaned in a bit closer, Selby edged a few inches away. Fumbling with the keys, she tried to get them into the lock while keeping an eye on George.

"I'm glad you met the family," he said, leaning against the door with his shoulder so that she couldn't open it without him falling through. "They're a nice bunch. My mother's a bit of a strong personality, but she's had to be to keep a farm that size ticking over. When can I see you again?"

Before Selby could answer, George pulled her towards him, kissing her on the lips. She wanted to bolt inside, but she didn't want to hurt his feelings. *Tell him how you feel. Be decent*, she screamed in her head. George leaned in for another kiss. Selby put her hand gently against his chest to move him away. "No, George, don't feel that way towards you. Best to say now before things get involved."

"I'm already involved," he insisted. "Can't we give it some time? There's lots about me you don't know."

"Need to be honest. Friends?"

"Friends," he moaned. "Got enough of those already. The Royal Cornwall Show though," he called back as he walked to the car. "You promised weeks ago."

She had not promised anything of the kind, but the guilt she felt for rejecting his advances kept her from saying so.

CHAPTER EIGHT

*W*ith only a few days before Selby was due
for lunch, Simon paced the floor, trying to
decide the menu. The feast she had prepared the night
before his trip to Ethiopia had been memorable. Pulling
the ceiling ladder down, he went up to the attic. Rows of
cardboard boxes holding his travel diaries were organised
by country. "An island off the south-eastern coast of
Africa," he muttered. "Cameroon. Ghana. Morocco. Cape
Verde. Aha, Madagascar."

Carrying the box down the ladder, he sat on the floor
and peeled the tape from the top. The scent of vanilla
wafted up even after five years. Photos of huge baobabs
slipped out of a folder on to his lap, followed by other
shots of white sands next to volcanic reefs jutting out into
turquoise waters. His book on Madagascar had been the
first to include native cuisine. He was hooked as soon as
he smelt the exotic scents coming from Malagasy
kitchens; they were complex, heady aromas. In basic

French, he asked about the sauces he greedily ate at meals with the family with whom he lodged for three months. The women laughed. Malagasy men were not found in kitchens. Humouring this tourist became an amusement. They let him record the recipes while they cooked.

Picking up a photo of Nomena, the community's matriarch, he remembered how she had not wanted to bother with him until one afternoon when he offered her a lift on his moped to a grandson's football match. He had stayed to watch the boy play, cheering when he scored a goal. The next morning, she had invited him into the cooking area. Together they had made *Romazava*, the one-pot dish every Malagasy family ate. Pieces of beef, pork, and chicken, cubed to the same size were added to onions, tomatoes, spinach, leafy vegetables, and crushed garlic – all to be eaten with a side dish of *Sakay* made from red chillies, garlic, oil and ginger. Everyone had watched as Simon tasted the *Sakay* that night. It had been fiery hot. Nomena had handed him the rice drink without saying anything. It had quelled the fire raging at the back of his throat.

On the day of his departure, the women had stood in a group each passing in front of him with small packages wrapped with string – *Baie Rose*, the Madagascar pink peppercorn; cloves, strong and oily, from the south-eastern part of the island; and vanilla pods. When Nomena had approached, she had held a package up for all to see. "*Sakay*," she called out. The crowd had enjoyed the joke.

Returning home to Cornwall, he had stored these treasured gifts in a cool, dark cupboard under the stairs. Now he would use some of them for the lunch he would cook for Selby. Poring over recipes in the journals, he eventually decided on smoked salmon with *Baie Rose* before lunch with a glass of champagne; a three-coloured beetroot recipe with crumbled goats cheese for the starter; *Romazava* for the main course; and chocolate for dessert.

On the day, he had only last-minute jobs to finish, yet he felt jittery. "It's just lunch, for God's sakes. You're returning hospitality." But he knew it was more than that.

He had planned the order of things the night before. During the main course, after a bit of wine, he would tell her about the 'Gods on Earth'. This was the name the Malagasy gave to the dead, whom they believed to be the most important and authoritative members of the family intimately involved in the daily lives of the living members, walking amongst them as ghosts. He would wait to see where the conversation went from there. If he was right – that Daphne had moved to Selby's house – he wasn't sure what he would say. The very idea Daphne would leave Menabilly for a stranger's house had never occurred to him. Was she gone forever? Of course, he wanted her back, and, of course, he missed having her there as she had always been. One way or the other, he needed the facts. On the other hand, he had plans for Selby Lyons. If he made her feel foolish with questions about poltergeists, he could jeopardise any chance of a romance.

When gravel crunched under the tyres of a car in the courtyard, Simon opened the door. "Selby, how nice to see you. Welcome to a different Menabilly than the one you met the last time you were here. Come in, please. I know I've seen you since, but I wasn't in a fit state at Tesco's to tell you what a wonderful dinner you cooked the night before I left for Ethiopia. Hope I measure up today. It took you two days to make that delicious feast if I remember correctly. You must've fallen into your bed exhausted afterwards. I felt guilty leaving you with all the washing up." He wished he could just shut up sometimes and not let every little thought fall out of his head.

"Knew you had an early flight. It didn't take long. Went right to sleep."

Did you, he thought, remembering the chatty scene between her and Daphne. "How about a glass of bubbly before lunch?"

She followed him through the wood-panelled Long Gallery into a large room with lofty ceilings and tall mullioned windows. A collection of African masks and tribal artwork hung on khaki-coloured walls. African sculptures dominated shelves either side of the fireplace.

"What a great room to show off these artefacts. Never got to see any of this the other day."

"Well, getting stuck in the upstairs loo kept you other-wise engaged. Why don't I give you the five-pence tour after lunch?" He handed her a glass of champagne.

"Thank you. Noticed scaffolding up on the side of the house when I drove up. So lucky Rose Cottage was in good nick when I bought it. Not sure I could deal with repairs to the roof and other structural stuff."

"There's a bit of a derelict wing that hasn't been touched since my mother died. The family moved here when I was a boy. Father didn't really do much to some of the upstairs rooms after the previous occupant."

"That was Daphne du Maurier, wasn't it?" she asked.

Simon stopped pouring the champagne into his glass. Was she baiting him? Of course not, you fool, he screamed inside his head. Calm down. Everyone knows she lived here.

"Yes, it was," he replied casually. "She let it from the family though I think she tried to buy it several times. Not sure she ever bought anything in Cornwall."

"Yes, I've heard she let quite a few properties. Apparently, she lived at Rose Cottage for a while as well," Selby said, sitting down in one of the chairs that gave a good view of the garden.

It hit him like a hammer. Daphne went to Selby's house because she knew it. There was the connection – made the day of the charity luncheon. "You're lucky that's not a well-known fact," he heard himself say. "People climb over fences here. They walk straight up to my front door asking if they can see where Daphne du Maurier lived. Can you imagine? It's a bloody nuisance."

"Need a wax mannequin of Mrs Danvers in an upstairs window," she said, grinning at the irony of discussing Daphne.

"The thought has occurred to me. Did you ever see the film?"

"Several times. Rainy afternoon, good idea."

"Do you believe in ghosts?" he casually asked.

"Not sure," she said quickly. "You?"

"I expect such things are possible. I once stayed in a castle in Scotland where I couldn't get myself through a door on the first floor. I just had the sense there was something untoward in the room. Ever had any experiences with things like that?"

Selby didn't reply for a moment. "I'm not sure. You know writers. Fertile imaginations – sometimes not knowing where reality ends, and fantasy begins."

"Yes, I suppose so." Allowing the thought to hang mid-air too long, he noticed Selby staring at him. He quickly reached for the platter on the side table. "I've hopefully recreated a Madagascar menu for our lunch. Starting with these – pink Madagascar pepper is really the star here, but you'll be relieved to hear it's mixed with creme fraîche and lemon on smoked salmon."

Selby put one in her mouth. "It's delicious."

"Glad you like it. The *Baie Rose* grows wild in the Malagasy rainforests. I hiked up to see how it's harvested and then camped in the jungle near a village. Hundreds of men, women and children collect the crop – no machines. It's a lot of work for such a small commodity. It's only slightly peppery. Can you taste the anise and sugar in the after-taste? Have another."

"Yes, I taste it. Was it your favourite place? Madagascar?"

"I thought it was one of the most beautiful places I'd ever visited. It breaks my heart that deforestation and habitat destruction have become so pervasive. The subsequent erosion and soil degradation will significantly impact on the local population; they rely on the land for survival. In addition, the world will lose a unique ecosystem – made up of coastal rainforests, spiny forests, palm savannas, mangrove forests, coral reefs – to name a few. But to get back to your question. No, Madagascar is not my favourite place. My favourite place is right here in Cornwall at Menabilly. I'm never happier than when I'm here."

Then why are you always leaving it, she thought to herself.

"Sorry, that was a bit flip. Don't know why I said that though it is true. I can't explain the hold the house has over me. I've just always loved everything about it. But of all the places I've travelled, Madagascar is high on the list. I spent weeks camping on my own, photographing for the book, using the capital, Antananarivo as a base. There's still a lot of their French colonial past in evidence, so the city is dotted with old palaces and government buildings from the nineteenth century. French influence in their poetry and music is also still prevalent."

"I would have expected their music to sound African."

"Some of it does, but in coastal areas, you can hear an Arab influence. Other places, inland, there are South American rhythms. Yet, somehow when you're listening to it, you're aware of something quite French. Music is important to them, not only in a social context, but also spiritually. It's crucial to their priests achieving the trance-like state to heal and foresee the future. They believe each spirit has a preferred musical instrument – wonderful really. Men play the conch shells at spiritual gatherings to summon the dead."

Suddenly aware of the opportunity that had presented itself, he shifted in his seat, turning towards Selby to watch her face closely.

"In fact, the Malagasy have an active relationship with the dead. They call them, 'Gods on Earth' – they believe they're intimately involved with the daily lives of the living members of the family. Can you imagine not being able to pick your nose because the ghost of Great-Aunt Louise might smack your hand? Who could relax with a ghost watching everything, every day?"

A nervous laugh gushed out from Selby.

The first course was already on the table when they went into a small dining room off the kitchen. "There's olive oil, parsley, goat's cheese and Malagasy wild black pepper over the beetroot," he explained.

"I didn't know beetroot came in different colours. The purple, yellow, and orange ones look like jewels." She glanced at the vibrant pottery covering the walls. "Beautiful plates. From your travels?"

"Yes, from different souks – a plate here and there, and before I knew it, I had a collection. It seemed a clever way to display them." Daphne's idea, he thought to himself. *"You've got boxes of the stuff cluttering up the hall. Why not stick them up on the wall some place,"* she had suggested.

When the first course was finished, Simon went to the kitchen, and returned with a tureen. "This is *Romazava*. The little devil in the side dish is *Sakay*, a fiery mash of Malagasy red chillies, garlic, ginger, and olive oil. Go carefully," he warned while pouring some red burgundy into her glass.

Fragrant exotic aromas wafted up from the steaming portion he placed in front of her.

"It's hearty – rich," Selby said after the first mouthful. "Full of depth." She took a tiny bit of the *Sakay* sauce on the corner of her fork and tasted it. The fire raced through her mouth and throat.

"Drink this." Simon handed her the rice drink. "It cools instantly. Then eat the meat. It will absorb the rest of the chilli. I was the butt of a well-enjoyed joke the night I first tried it in Madagascar. Probably not the first time they'd watched a tourist's face turn purple."

After a few minutes, the heat subsided. "Wow," she gasped. "That's quite a shock."

During the meal, she listened to his stories about recent trips to South America. They revealed another side of him. From reading his books, it was obvious that he was a good, descriptive writer, an observer who noticed subtle aspects of the cultures about which he wrote. However, it was his sense of humour and self-deprecating manner that were responsible for making her laugh. These were stories he had not written about though she thought they would easily amuse readers. It had been a long time since she had relaxed so easily in a man's company. All so different from Raphe's personality where everything had been met with such earnest. Take things slowly, she warned herself. You've been enjoying living on your own. Of course, she wasn't entirely alone, but does a ghost count, she wondered? Why all this talk of ghosts from Simon before lunch?

"This is dessert." Simon placed large tins on the table in front of her. "They hold various kinds of chocolate, all from the noblest of cocoa beans, the Criollo. It's fine and rare with a distinctly reddish colour – quite a complex taste of caramel, nuts, and vanilla, but each one is different, depending on the regions where the beans grew. First the wine though; it amplifies the flavour."

She laughed. "More wine? Think I may need a walk after lunch instead of a house tour."

Simon went into the kitchen, returning with a decanter. "California Zinfandel – intense and full-bodied, pairing well with our strong, dark chocolate." He poured into two glasses. "Now, the fun. Close your eyes."

"Really? Why?"

"Because the tin has painted pictures on the labels listing the characteristic of the chocolates. I want you to describe what you taste without knowing. It's more fun this way if you're willing to be a good sport."

Selby wasn't keen but agreed. "Okay, carry on."

"First, take a sip of water," Simon said, handing her a glass. "Now, the first chocolate – rub it against the palm of your hand to release the scent. Then, taste it."

Selby felt the small square in her hand before popping it into her mouth. "Dense. Dark. Not sugary. Not melting easily. Flowery, fruity, like a blackcurrant sweet I had as a child – and some spiciness."

"That was chocolate from Ecuador. Taste the wine now."

"Yes, the flavour is more intense with the wine. Delicious."

"Water now, before the next chocolate. Here you go."

"This is completely different. Creamy. Caramelly and peachy – it's so good. Now, the wine?"

Simon handed her the glass. "That was Ocumare 61 from Venezuela. Here's your water, and now the last one." Leaning down, pushing the tin away, he kissed her lips instead of handing her another chocolate. He had not planned it – it had just happened.

Selby felt dizzy and opened her eyes. All that wine has gone to my head – and his, she thought to herself, feeling her cheeks blush.

"Sorry. I didn't mean to embarrass you."

He had caught her completely off guard, sending the tone of the afternoon shooting in another direction. She liked Simon, but it took her a long time to get to know people. There had been too many times in her life when she had opened her heart and had it crushed. The room felt warm and claustrophobic. "Need a walk. Not used to so much wine in the afternoon," she managed to say.

Simon pulled away. "Yes. Right. I'll make some coffee to take with us. I won't be a minute. If you open that terrace door, there's a bench in the shade."

Selby's mind raced back and forth between making too much out of the kiss and analysing the turn of events. She decided it was best to ignore what had happened, to go for a walk, and think about it all later.

From the kitchen window, Simon noticed Selby had walked around to the front of the house. He watched her open the car and hoped she wasn't getting into it to leave. He rushed out. "Here we go. I've got two mugs of hot coffee, and if I remembered correctly, you have it black. Is that right? Where shall we walk? Over hill and dale or to some place where we can watch gulls dive for fish?"

When they reached the far end of a field that looked out over the sea, the sun came through the clouds. They sat down at the cliff's edge. "Peaceful," Selby said, feeling better for the sea air. It was agonising to sit there, trying to think of something to say. They had no history. She had an abhorrence of small talk. It had been such a relief during lunch to let him go on about his travels, needing only to laugh at his funny stories, adding a small comment here and there. It was at times like this – these pregnant pauses – that sent her diving for cover.

"Yes, it is peaceful. I used to come here a lot as a teenager. Sat for hours reading."

"What did you read?"

"Other people's travel books – funny now I look back on it. All those books flooding my subconscious as an adolescent. The whole time they were contributing to this insatiable desire for foreign cultures, the food, the art. Then, I ended up becoming a travel writer myself. I had no idea at the time that's what would happen, but I must've been living vicariously. Jan Morris was the best, especially her book on Trieste."

"Did you just stick a pin in a map to decide where to go first?"

"Not really, but it ended up being quite serendipitous. My books from earlier trips aren't – in my opinion – worth reading. It wasn't until I got interested in native cuisine that I felt I hit my stride. They also sell better, so I must have got something right. In fact, I've got boxes of my early stuff which I'm hawking at the Royal Cornwall Show tomorrow. I take a stand every couple of years on the first day. Would you like to go to the show with me? I only work the stand in the morning."

"Thank you, but I told George Renfold I would go with him."

Hiding his disappointment, Simon stood, and gave her

a hand up. "Ah, good. I'm glad you'll have the fun of seeing the show. It really is the most wonderful display in the county – man, woman, child, and beasts, all together for a good day out."

When they got to her car, she opened the door quickly, not wanting to give the impression that she was waiting for him to kiss her again. "It was a truly delicious lunch. Thank you, Simon."

"Very glad you enjoyed it."

As he watched her car disappear up the drive, he felt disappointed he had let things get carried away. "God, you're an idiot of the first order." He kicked at some turf that had seeded itself in the gravel. "And no self-control. You never drew a breath. No wonder she was so quiet. Stunning, beautiful woman though. Bloody fine lunch, too. Blast – and no further ahead about Daphne."

Selby plopped down on the sofa when she got home. She thought about Simon, and the kiss. It had been as delicious as the chocolate. She stretched out, letting the scene fade in and out, reliving the moment until she fell asleep. When she woke later that evening, her stomach was making demanding noises.

"You're too greedy – just had a big lunch. How can you be hungry again?" she scolded herself. She walked to the kitchen, and taking cooked sausages from the fridge, shoved them into the hot Aga. The thought of them with scrambled eggs and toast was irresistible. Alcohol-blotter, she reasoned while beating the eggs. She popped bread into the toaster. When the timer went off, she took the sausages out and left their dish warming on top of the opened oven door before quickly moving to finish the last bits of her feast.

"Yum, toast on plate, eggs on toast." She reached behind to stab the sausages with a fork, but they weren't there. She bent down to see if she had slung them over a bit carelessly. Checking under the table, she saw one of them roll out towards her foot. Something was eating her sausages. She screamed, running over to stand on a chair.

"Rats," she cried, and made a dash for the broom, swatting the space under the table with all her might before springing back on top of the chair. There was a sound of something scurrying across the stone floor. It took refuge under the cupboard by the fridge.

"Daphne," she yelled.

Daphne duly appeared. "What are you doing up there?" She suddenly reached down towards the floor with both arms. "Mouse? Mouse, is it really you? Of course, it is. There's the collar I buried you in." The sound of a barking dog filled the kitchen. She sat on the floor laughing, turning her face from side to side, oblivious to Selby's attack pose on top of the chair.

"What is this pantomime you're acting out for bloody sakes?" Selby asked.

"It's Mouse, my dog, my West Highland terrier."

"Your dog? You're a ghost haunting my house, and now you've got a ghost-dog? Are you serious?"

"Tut tut. We don't like that word, ghost, do we, darling Mouse?" Daphne cooed to something.

"This is mad."

"How lonely I've been all these years without dogs. I was never without one when I was alive. West Highland terriers, they're sturdy little chaps. I used to walk miles with mine daily. During the war, I had to hide in the woodland if we took a stroll – the Westies, being white, you see. Prid was closed to the public like many beaches, so no walks along the cliffs for picnics. I recall being quite miserable about that, now I come to think of it. We felt caged up, didn't we, Mouse? Oh, how I love the smell of you."

Selby had jumped down from the chair and sat on the counter to watch the incredulous scene playing out in front of her. "I can't see him, you know."

"Really? I can see him clear as day."

"Well, I'm happy for you both," Selby said in a flat voice, "but where does that leave me – sausages and all, I mean. Is this thing staying?"

"Where I go, he goes. That was always the way. Anyway, he's no trouble. He'll be with me."

"Where were you when he ate my sausages?"

"Oh, I doubt very much if Mouse is capable of eating anything. I can't."

"Then where are the sausages I had hopes of swallowing myself?"

Daphne bent down to look. "I see them under the table. He probably only shoved them around a bit. They look fine. I'm sure he won't do it again, will you, Mouse," she said, picking up the invisible shape.

Selby sat down at the table, listening to Daphne talk to the dog as she made her way up the stairs. "Great," she said, pushing the plate of cold eggs away. "A ghost-dog."

CHAPTER NINE

Whether it was tipping down rain or a sweltering day at the Royal Cornwall Show, everyone sought shelter at some point during the afternoon for aching feet and a cup of tea. It was the county's biggest annual event with horse shows, dog trials and all manner of farm-bred animals vying for prizes in exhibitions. The agricultural show stretched across fields covered by hundreds of concessions. Throngs of people moved along at a slow pace.

Selby had walked in the sun for hours, stopping each time George ran into someone he knew, waiting until the conversation finished. By three o'clock, she needed a break and protested. They agreed to meet in the CLA tent where he had reserved a table with some friends for tea. He was due in the far corner of the showground to help judge a selection of rare breeds. Once on her own, Selby took her shoes off and looked at the map in her hands to decide the shortest walk to a chair. If she cut through the poultry tent, she reckoned she could be under cover and on a chair in twenty minutes. While stopping to admire different breeds of hens and roosters, she heard her name being called. Simon was waving from across the next aisle. Her heart jumped in her chest, and seeing him walking over, she stepped back into her shoes and tidied her hair.

"Buying chickens?" he asked when finally standing in front of her.

"Just looking. Making my way to the CLA tent for tea and a chair."

"I'm going there myself to join some friends. Why don't we go together? I know the way from here. Didn't do too badly this morning at the stall, and I managed to catch-up with lots of people I haven't seen for a while."

When they reached the tent, a group huddled near the bar were loudly debating the recent government tariff on red diesel. She said goodbye to Simon as someone hailed him from a table across the floor. He started towards his group and then turned back to Selby. "Why don't you come with me until George arrives. I'm meeting old friends. They're all perfectly harmless."

Simon introduced Selby around before leaving to stand in the queue for tea. She was grateful for the chance to slip her shoes off under the table. The group were obviously old friends, judging by the winding up going back and forth. When Simon returned with a tray laden with cake, tea sandwiches and a pot of tea, he became the object of their teasing. Several of the women seemed to be flirting with him. A pretty blonde made a joke, reaching for his arm while she laughed.

Selby drank her tea and ate her cake while watching

the scene play out. A good county catch was probably how most women saw Simon Rashleigh. He seemed to be enjoying the attention – like some of those cockerels I've just seen, she thought.

George arrived a few minutes later, apologising for being late. He shook hands with Simon and said hello to some of the others before leading Selby to another table where his friends were gathered. It seemed to her that the afternoon was going to go on for hours more. George was perfectly nice. There was absolutely nothing wrong with him, but she found herself looking over at Simon more than a few times. Handsome, that was true enough – high forehead below thick brown hair, good cheekbones, a happy expression, full mouth, dimples either side of a mischievous smile.

This could just be lust, she reminded herself. Someone telling a story at his table had everyone's attention. When they all talked at once, she heard just his voice. It sent butterflies fluttering in her stomach. Oh, why did all this have to start up again? The feeling that you can't wait to see someone; the getting to know them; the early tentative conversations tailored to subjects of mutual interest or laid as traps to entice. Did she want to entice him? She looked at him again. This time, he turned his head, saw her, and smiled before resuming conversation with the woman next to him. She quickly looked away. What do I want with you, Simon Rashleigh? Why have you come into my life?

~

Simon raised up the boot to unpack empty boxes that had been full of books at the start of the day at the Royal Cornwall. Having gone to supper at someone's house on the way back to Menabilly, he was tired from the constant chatter. Unlocking the front door, he stopped immediately he got inside. "Daphne?" he called out, dropping the boxes, and running upstairs into her room.

"Are you here? I smell your cigarette smoke."

There was no sign of her, so he looked in his study. Papers from his book were strewn all over the floor.

"Stop playing games, Daphne. I'm seriously cross. This is you, isn't it?" he shouted.

Selby's feet ached from the previous day at the Cornish Show. A foot soak in Epsom salts was all she could think about. "Who can concentrate with swollen feet?" She walked down the hall to the study. Opening the door, she let out a shriek. "Not again." Burnt wood and char from the fireplace were scattered over the carpeting. She ran to her desk. The manuscript was there, thank God, but a closer look revealed all the research notebooks were missing. Running upstairs to find Daphne, she stopped on the landing, aghast at the scene in front of her. The content of dresser drawers had been dumped onto the floor. Shoes lay in piles in the bathroom.

"What's going on here? This can't be the work of birds or rats. Is this you, Daphne? Why have you done these things? Show yourself."

Had it been Daphne who had initially scattered pages

of her book? Rain began to lash against the open window. Dashing over to close it, she saw the Soay sheep grazing below in the garden. Every plant and shrub had been trampled and eaten. The sheep had not escaped on their own – of that she was certain. George had mended the fencing. This was a deliberate act. She burst into tears. "How do I cope with this? It must be Daphne doing these things. How do you reason with a ghost?"

Simon had woken, reluctant to get out of bed when he remembered the mess in the study the previous night. He was sure it had been Daphne though she had never done anything like this before. What had changed? Throwing on his dressing gown, he clapped down the stairs in his slippers. The only thing different in his life was Selby Lyons. Was Daphne jealous of Selby? It was a preposterous idea. He heard a car race up, brake suddenly, spraying gravel everywhere. The door opened and a crazed-looking Selby Lyons flew through it.

"Can't take it anymore," she yelled. "That thing is driving me mad. Gone crazy for some reason. Don't know what it is. Tearing up the place."

"What are you talking about? You're upset. I can see that."

Marching ahead to the sitting room, she was in too much of a state to sit. She began waving her arms around, speaking in staccato phrases, looking over her shoulder. "At wits end – don't know why I came here – don't know you well enough – my life lately – crazy things going on – crazy story. Unbelievable." She burst into tears.

Looking at Selby, he suddenly felt protective, and wanted to make it all right for her as quickly as possible. "Daphne's at your house, isn't she?" he asked.

She stopped crying. "What did you say?"

"I said the ghost of Daphne du Maurier is at your house. Isn't that right?"

"Yes, but how –?"

"Because she's been living here in my house, that's how. I was a seven-year-old boy when I first met her. It was the night after my mother's funeral. They had been friends for years. I know this all sounds absurd, and if you hadn't also met Daphne, I wouldn't be able to tell you any of this."

"Why? Am I such an ogre?"

"No. You're sweet and funny and smart and beautiful. I can't imagine for a second why you're bothering with me," he said.

"Who said I was bothering with you," Selby shot back.

Simon looked embarrassed.

"Sorry. Didn't mean that. Are you saying that you've lived with a ghost in this house since you were a boy?"

"Yes, but not just any ghost – the ghost of world renowned writer, Daphne du Maurier. Really, it was like having an eccentric aunt. She never offered silly answers like grown-ups are prone to giving pre-pubescent school-boys. I've missed her every day since she left. I got in a bate and said I wanted a change. She left Menabilly in a flash of temper and moved to Rose Cottage. I'm sure she heard you mention you had recently bought it. You know, when you were going down that ladder."

Selby suddenly felt stupid buying into all that stuff Daphne had said about admiring her writing when in fact Simon had kicked her out of the house she had been haunting all these years. That Selby had genuinely enjoyed her company made her feel more pathetic. Was she so lonely that she had jumped at the chance to have a friend, even a ghost?

"God almighty headache," she groaned. "My book, she's taken my research notebooks – a whole year's work – clothing, shoes thrown everywhere – Soays in garden – eaten best shrubs and flowers." She burst into tears again.

"I did say that the fence posts had rotted," Simon pointed out as gently as possible.

"No," she cried out. "George mended fencing. Someone opened the gate deliberately."

"Daphne has never done anything like this before, and it's slightly out of character if you ask me. Don't think I've escaped. My manuscript was scattered over the floor, and the pages missing include the reference lists for photographs and coloured plates for my book. I sifted through hundreds of photos to make those selections. I'm very cross about the whole thing." Simon walked out of the room.

Selby curled into a foetal position in one of the armchairs. The whole situation was too fantastic to believe. Without Simon's confirmation that Daphne really existed, she had begun to question her own sanity this morning after finding the chaos upstairs. Deep-seated psychosis can conjure up characters and events.

"You know, I thought it was rats or birds the first time my manuscript was strewn over the floor," Selby explained when Simon returned and put a steaming mug of coffee in her hands. "I never did find the missing pages. Now the research notebooks are missing, but I must have them back. Is this a game? Some silly treasure hunt?"

Yes. He considered the idea. If Daphne was going to hide something, where would it be?

"Come on," he said. Grabbing Selby's hand, he pulled her up the stairs to the linen cupboard, and opened a door on the back wall which led into a room. "This is Daphne du Maurier's bedroom, and where I first met her."

Selby looked around the sparsely furnished room. Shelves filled with books lined a long wall; the spines of their dust jackets were faded with age. An old-fashioned typewriter and stacks of typing paper sat on a table next to the window. Tattered, threadbare curtains barely clung to their fittings. She suddenly thought back to the day she had been trapped in the bathroom and had spotted the vent through which she had heard Daphne typing.

Simon searched all the drawers in a dresser and looked behind books on the shelves. Standing on top of a chair, he reached up to feel on top of a large wardrobe. "Aha. See? Here's something." He took down a batch of papers. "I thought I might find something hidden in this room. These are mine. Yours should be here some place."

Selby looked under the bed. "It's too dark under there to see properly. The stuffing in the mattress has collapsed. Looks like there's something in the middle, but I can't reach it."

He fetched a broom from the cupboard in the hall. "Try this."

She stuck the long handle under the bed. A yapping followed by her cursing made him bend down to look.

"Go on. Let go of that," she said firmly.

"I'm not holding it," Simon insisted.

"No, not you. Mouse."

"There's a mouse under the bed?"

"No, Daphne's dog," she answered in an exasperated voice. "Let go, you filthy mongrel."

"Daphne doesn't have a dog."

"She does, and they travel in pairs," Selby huffed.

"She's got two dogs?"

"No, for bloody sakes," she said, getting up from the floor. "Wherever the dog is, Daphne is generally close by. Aren't you, Daphne? Even in that invisible state you sometimes call up at will. The one when you want to eavesdrop or observe clandestinely."

They looked around the room, waiting for a reply. Simon got on his knees again. "I can't see a dog."

Selby raised her voice, feeling thoroughly fed up. "Nor can I."

"But I thought you just said Daphne's dog was under the bed."

"Yes, but I can't see him," Selby explained.

"I'm confused." He plopped down on a chair.

"The dog's invisible, Simon. You of all people ought to know that nothing is straightforward with Daphne. It just showed up the other day. Nicked my sausages right off the table."

"It can eat?"

"Don't ask," she snapped. "Try the broom from your side."

He lay down on the floor to stretch the handle into the mattress wadding, trying to move it aside to reach the bundle in the middle. He grunted from the effort before breaking out into fits of laughter. "He's licking my face. Stop that. Cut it out."

Selby had had enough. In a stern voice, she said, "Mouse. Naughty dog. Come here this instant."

"Don't yell at the poor thing."

"It's what Daphne says when he's left a mouse in the middle of the floor."

"Got them," he shouted. Pushing the bundle of papers out to the bottom of the bed, he used his robe to wipe them. Cobwebs and dead flies fell to the floor. "These can't be yours – the papers are yellowed, typed on something like that old machine on the table over there." He began to read them. "Listen to this."

"The sea mist, which cloaked the shoreline, shrouded all but the destruction at her feet, as Merryn Penrice gazed down upon the skeleton wreck that had once been a ship, and in the gloom of the moment, she thought of those she loved, whose mistress was also the wild sea. Then, lifting her skirt above the ankles, to step between ripped sailcloth threaded through broken barrels, she walked further to the wreck's long planks that rolled in the shallows like drunken sailors. A splintered mast, its mizzen-top anchored in mud, was bound by tresses of dark seaweed that beat the water's edge, leaving a frothy scum.

"And as sun bled through scarlet bands, streaking the horizon, she fell to her knees, praying that her lover would escape the same fate as the floating bodies returned by the tide. The

winter tempests, that forced foreign vessels to seek refuge on the north coast of Cornwall, delivered them to harbours with tall cliffs that sheltered from the storms, seducing them with the look of calm, but they were not safe havens, for under the dark water, jagged rocks like dragon's teeth lay waiting to shred the bellies of ships, leaving no survivors. Then, on some far away soil, women would weep, waiting for news of their men, ignorant that the sea had been the only witness to their end.

"Later, as she walked the narrow path that skirted the cliff face, she thought of Richard Penvose. They had held no secrets from each other that day in the far meadows, and a tranquil sense of well-being had taken hold, until the big bell rang out, and they had run to the village, arriving breathless and redfaced, to find an air of uncertainty in the church. The eyes of women darted to those already in widow's weeds, looking from one to another, too frightened to utter a greeting. For when the big bell tolled, a sense of urgency and foreboding touched all who heard the sound. They knew their men would be called upon to risk their lives, for the sea hoards treasure, delivering opportunity on a whim.

"Merryn accepted her lover would captain the first boat, and her body went rigid as scenes of tempestuous seas flew through her mind, until a flame of anger rose within her, filling all her senses. 'Not him,' she cursed under her breath, for they were fitted with a great love. She whispered to the sea, 'You've had father. 'Tis enough. Four days at most, and then deliver him back to me.'

"There was a sudden hush when the big doors closed, the shuffling of the old man the only noise, as he made his way slowly down the aisle, his shrunken frame like the twisted stick on which he leant. He turned to the villagers, and raised his

hand high, speaking in the loud voice, recognised by all assembled as the most experienced of them, and as the man who would decide.

"'Wreckage were spotted on the tide,' he told them. 'From cargo beached, she looks foreign. Ye know what that could mean, if true.'

"Time stood still for a moment, as some forgot the danger, and dreamt of what great thing they would buy with their share of the purse, when the booty was sold to the highest bidder in a town inland. The old man passed his eyes over those he had known all his life. Some men had the look of adventure, and some were marked with greed by the faint smile that twitched at the corners of their mouth, and yet fear spread over all, when he said the words they awaited. Then, mounting the steps to the altar, he stood like a captain on the bridge of a ship about to give an order.

"'Sailing tonight at high tide,' he commanded."

Simon stopped reading. "I know this story. Daphne used to tell it to me when I was a boy. It's not from one of her books though. I've read all of them."

Reaching for the rest of the manuscript, Selby took the next stack of papers, and read them to herself, passing pages to Simon for the remainder of the afternoon, until there were no more. "That can't be the end. Where's the rest of the book?" she asked.

They jumped off the bed, searching everywhere in the room. Simon went to the attic, throwing down any boxes that didn't look like Rashleigh things. There was nothing of Daphne's, no further pages about Merryn Penrice and her lover.

"I was hoping you might find my research notebooks

up there." Selby sighed and sat on the stairs. "An unfinished story by Daphne du Maurier under the bed all these years – if we hadn't been looking for my things, would it have stayed there forever?"

He sat down next to her. "How about that scene when the harbour was full of floating bodies. No one better to describe something like that than Daphne."

"Do you think Merryn ever saw Richard Penvose again?"

Daphne watched in a transparent state, nodding her head while thinking to herself, *Work on mine, not yours. What I wanted. What I need.*

In darkness, there was no warning before big waves crashed over her head. She gasped for air between swells. Salt water rushed down her throat. The swirling seas bubbled and churned. She held tightly to the broken mast keeping her afloat, but the whirlpool slowed, pushing her to the centre, sucking her into the vortex and pulling her under.

Selby woke in the middle of the night from the terrifying dream. She had been Merryn Penrice in the sea. Her nightdress was soaked with perspiration and her heart thumped in her chest. It had all seemed so real, she dared not close her eyes again for a bit. The house was cold when she walked downstairs. Light from a full moon cast a milky hue over the counters and plants on the windowsill. She reached for the kettle, filling it halfway before turning on the lights.

"Bloody hell," she screeched. Daphne was sitting in one of the chairs at the fireplace. "Scared the hell out of me. You've got guts showing up here. Thought you might have gone for good, judging by the wreckage you left behind."

Daphne remained silent.

Selby punched the switch on the kettle. "Simon and I looked for you today. Yes – 'Simon and I'. Don't look surprised. None of that's going to work anymore. We've compared notes. 'Good writers stick together', my ass."

"It wasn't flattery. I meant it, though you're quite suggestible," Daphne said in a pointed fashion meant to irritate. "I shouldn't be surprised if here on in you start seeing lots like me."

"The likelihood of that happening is slim," Selby shot back. "You're the only phantom I intend to pay any attention to forever more."

Daphne winced at the word phantom which she knew Selby had deliberately used to annoy.

"You've taken my research notes, and I'm not listening to anymore of that 'I don't know how things work' nonsense. Took a year to put that stuff together." Selby reached into the fridge for some milk. When she turned around to hammer the point again, Daphne had gone. "Exasperating woman."

Taking herself back to bed, she sat propped up on pillows with the lights out, sipping the hot drink and thinking about her dream. "Poor Merryn, she could've done with a moonlit night such as this."

CHAPTER TEN

*S*imon was heading downstairs after a restless
night when he heard the familiar tapping sound
coming from Daphne's room. He swung round and ran
down the hall to her bedroom. She was sitting at her table
typing.

"You've caused quite a stir, you know. Selby was here,
but then I guess we can agree that you were probably also
here, can't we?"

"Can't we what?" Daphne asked in a flat tone.

"Can we agree that you're often around, but not always
visible, so that you can listen and observe," he said impatiently. "That was news to me. I must say, it makes me feel
quite uncomfortable when I think of past girlfriends I've
had here over the years. I just thought you took yourself
off to this room if I had guests, so I wouldn't feel self-
conscious."

"Don't flatter yourself. I'm not a peeping Tom.
Honestly, who would want to snoop on your boring old

love life anyway?"

"It mightn't have been so boring if you hadn't been here all the time."

"I think we've discussed the fact that I am certainly not the reason you have no paramour."

"Let's not go over that old chestnut again." Realising he would have to take a stronger line to progress things, he changed his tone. "Stop changing the subject. Where are Selby's research notebooks? I insist you tell me now. This has all got out of hand. We're both fed up. You've never done anything like this before. What's got into you? Is it Selby? Are you jealous of her?"

Daphne stopped typing to reach into her sleeve for a handkerchief.

Simon hadn't heard her cry since the first night they had met. "Come on, old girl," he said, feeling guilty for the telling-off he had given. "I thought you'd be happy I found someone I like. Of course, I've no idea what she thinks of me. Don't you like Selby? Can't imagine you going to live in someone's house if you didn't like them."

Letting out a big sigh, he sat down next to her. It was nice arguing with Daphne again. "You know, I was worried you might have gone forever. It made me sad I'd never told you what you've meant to me all these years. There were so many times I couldn't wait to get home from boarding school to see you. Remember when we used to play hide and seek on the first night of half-terms after Pa had gone to bed? How about the time I had measles when you painted red dots on Father while he slept? Oh, what holy hell he gave me when he discovered the spots were red ink. We laughed in my room listening to the whole discussion between him and the doc."

Simon stopped laughing. "This is different now, Daphne. I want Selby in my life if that's in the cards. We can't both live in houses between which you go, dumping contents of dresser drawers, letting sheep out, and hiding our work."

Remaining silent, she just stared at the page in her typewriter.

"Tell me where you've hidden her notebooks, and we'll forget about all this. We found some pages from one of your books, by the way. We sat reading them for over an hour. Ah yes, but then you probably know that. I remember you telling me that story when I was a boy. Did you know some of it was under the bed or had you forgotten about it?"

Daphne started to type away at a fast pace, tearing the paper from the machine after a few lines, and handing it to him.

"There's nothing here. It's blank," he said.

"Exactly."

"Exactly what?"

"When I type, that's what happens."

"I don't understand. Are you saying that you type, but nothing appears on the page?" He paced up and down the room, looking at Daphne, the typewriter, the page in his hand. "All these years when I've heard you typing? It's been like this?"

Daphne got up, walked over to the sofa, lit a cigarette, and sat down. "That's the gist of it. I think of a story. The plot develops in my head. I sit down to type, but nothing shows on the paper. The book ideas just go around and around in my head until I think it will burst."

"But I hear you typing. If nothing appears on the page, why do you type?"

"Because it helps me to get the ideas out of my head. It gives me the sense of writing, you see."

"How many books have you...ha ha...ghost written?"

"Lots – ten – twenty – well, some of them are no good. I don't know because I can't proofread them, can I? Thought I'd found a solution at Selby's house on her writing machine, but I didn't have any better luck."

"Laptop," Simon corrected. "You never touched my computer here."

"Oh, that monster's too big. Petrified me. I used to try after you went to bed."

"Well, that's probably because it had gone into sleep mode."

"It sleeps?"

"No, never mind. What you've described just now. Is it the way things work in your world? Wretched and unfair, I must say."

Simon heard the front door slam. Selby yelled his name: "Simon? I need to see you."

Stepping into the hallway, he called out. "I'm upstairs."

"She's here, isn't she?" Selby asked when she got to the top of the stairs.

He pointed to the linen cupboard. "In there."

Running through, she saw Daphne standing to the side of the wardrobe. "I want to know what happens. I want to know about Merryn Penrice. I nearly drowned in my dreams last night. I was in the sea. I was Merryn. She

131

was clinging to a broken piece of the masthead. The sea was tossing her from wave to wave. It was horrible. After you disappeared – again – I couldn't get back to sleep. So, I started inventing different plots, but I can't resolve anything because it's not my story. I want to know what happens. What is –?"

Simon interrupted. "I think there are more important matters just now."

Daphne put her hand up to stop him saying anything else. "I would be delighted," she said. "Sit comfortably, and I will tell you about Merryn and her captain."

Selby and Simon obeyed, sitting up on the lop-sided bed, turning towards her like two children whose mother had promised a bedtime tale. Walking to the big window to look out at the blue of the sea in the distance, Daphne began:

"Only the whistle of curlews pierced the dead air in the village that night. Sea mist, drifting thru alleyways, curled around stone dwellings, and wisps of the damp air stole in through cracks in doors and broken panes of windows, mixing with smoking fires. Those sleeping in lofts felt the heat rise from the smouldering peat, but they shivered when they smelt the salty mist, for it was a reminder of the dense fog that kept boats blind, unable to return for yet another day.

"On the eighth night, fearing the worst news, women in the village no longer slept. Merryn paced the cliff path, before turning to face the grey and full sea before her, and for a moment, she marked the time and place of her decision to set sail to search for her lover. She had come upon it suddenly, while in a dream. It was a bold plan, but she was the daughter of Jack

Penrice, legendary ship's navigator. He had given her the Cornish name for 'born of the sea', and though a girl, he had taught her all that he knew, and how to read a night sky, and how to point into the wind to best advantage over a cresting wave. She feared a raging sea, but she knew how to manage its tantrums.

"When the village was quiet, and a sufficient wind in the harbour, Merryn stole down to the quay with sail bags to row to her father's boat. She stood for a while, busy tying knots she would need in a squall, until finally, with the anchor up, the boat shifted, floating out on the tide. Her heart pounded in her chest while she hoisted the sail, which flapped before billowing out, and yet, even as the boat slipped away, she looked up over her shoulder to her cottage at cliff's edge, wondering if she would return.

"Smelling deeper water approach, she knew there was no turning back. Her hair flew behind her with the first gust, and when a spray rose up, splashing the deck, the taste of salt on her tongue was exhilarating. She drank deep of the sea air, and something primitive and wild filled her senses, and the thrill of being back at sea shot through her body. With no idea of time, she might have sailed forever, forgetting her mission, but when the ride of a wave lifted her high, the cold air brought her back to the present. The wind cut through to the bone, and she blew upon her hands, longing to stretch them down into the water, to pull his body free from a watery prison. And then, as the white capped seas broke, she knew she would find Richard Penvose, or die trying.

Daphne had been walking back and forth over the floor. She glanced over at Simon and Selby. They were both asleep. Selby's head was on Simon's shoulder.

"Looks like Merryn's fate must wait to unfurl," she whispered.

A few hours later, Selby woke in Simon's arms. "Fell asleep," she said, noticing the blanket covering them.

"Hm, yes I saw that too."

"Daphne?"

"Who else? Bit of matchmaking, I suspect."

"Do we need matchmaking?"

"I think it's fair to say that Daphne hasn't been too impressed with my abilities in that department in the past. She may also be trying to mend fences, but she still hasn't offered to return your notebooks."

"Dreamt about her story again," Selby confessed. "Pity she never got to finish it."

"It must just be how things work in her world. When she tries to write, no words appear on paper. She tried using your laptop. It produced no better results than her tapping away on her old Underwood Standard over there."

"What has she been doing all these years? Typing them out for the sake of it?"

"Apparently, after discovering the blank pages, the poor thing got very low, but couldn't stop ideas from coming. She needed the noise of the typewriter to get the stories out of her head. I heard sniffles when she explained it all to me earlier – not like Daphne to cry over anything."

Selby sat up. "Simon, why can't we write down her story? Daphne could dictate it."

"And then what? We take it to a publisher and say, 'This is a book by the ghost of Daphne du Maurier?'"

"Agreed, but in principle, if it's been such torture for her all these years, why can't we just get the thing written for her?"

"I don't write fiction," he said.

"How do you know you can't?"

"I wouldn't be as good at it as you are. I loved that book about the egg people in the village up north. Pure delight."

"Only bit of fiction I've ever written. Didn't know you'd read my books."

"I didn't want to appear sycophantic."

"Telling someone you like a book they've written can hardly be called that. You do have strange ideas."

"Yes, and your idea that we write a book Daphne dictates is not? Anyway, how do you know she'd agree?"

"She would!" Daphne interjected, taking form in front of them.

"Can't you let us know when you're in a room listening to every word," Simon said in an exasperated voice.

"Never mind all that. Let's talk about the book, can we? We could do it. Together. I very much like the idea. When could we start? Oh, I've so many story ideas for books. You can't imagine how –"

"Hang on, hang on," he interrupted, "let's not get carried away. Let's just discuss the one we found under the bed. We were both so exhausted, we fell asleep. Sorry – that's not a comment on the tale, I hasten to add. For starters, the book couldn't have your name on it."

"Yes, I heard what you said. I don't care. I just want to tell my story and see it in print."

Selby offered cooperation contingent on various conditions. "I'm in the middle of my own book – if – I can ever get my research back," she said emphatically. "Plus, I definitely need to be writing my book at my cottage."

"I've had an advance from my publisher," Simon added. "My agent rang up yesterday, wanting to know if I was on track for the September deadline."

"Well that's all right. I can go between the two houses. I don't mind – rather a challenge," Daphne replied enthusiastically.

Selby and Simon exchanged glances. "Challenge indeed," Simon mumbled under his breath.

They had settled on a routine. Daphne would dictate to Selby from eight to ten in the morning, and to Simon from three to five in the afternoon. At the weekends, they would meet up to edit each other's sections, and check that text and continuity were in good order. It seemed a straightforward plan.

Having convinced Simon that they could handle writing both their own work plus Daphne's, Selby began at six every morning until Daphne showed up to give dictation. At first, she felt exhilarated by the pace, but after three weeks, everyone except Daphne was exhausted. Selby was finding it hard to keep her mind on Mary Hemingway, especially with Merryn's uncertain fate. Was Daphne going to kill her off? Staring into space one afternoon, debating how the story might develop, she got up from her desk. She needed a break – from everything – from worrying about Merryn – from Mary and Ernest – from writing.

Taking Viviana's recipes out of a folder in the kitchen, she sat down to read, tasting the ingredients in her mind to decide what to cook. Eggs, flour, olive oil, baking powder, butter, chocolate, hazelnuts, sugar, orange zest – all the ingredients were in the cupboard for a hazelnut torte. To the rhythm of a samba, she began. When the torte was in the oven, she checked the time. If she was going to take supper to Menabilly this evening as a surprise, it couldn't be anything too complicated. She was more relaxed around Simon these days. There were things to discuss with Daphne's book though they got icy stares if they dared suggest changes of any kind. The power of what was written remained solely in Daphne's hands.

No time to make the pasta herself, she settled on a recipe using dried fettuccine. A piece of swordfish from the freezer went into the microwave to defrost. When the timer sounded, she cut the fish into small cubes before throwing it into a pan with some olive oil over a medium heat. Then, she added chopped onions, pepperoncino flakes, followed by a tin of plum tomatoes and some anchovy. The mixture simmered away while she cut some mint from the garden. Adding it to the sauce, she lowered the heat before turning it off to let the flavours meld together. The fettuccine, which took minutes to cook, would be done at Menabilly. She was finished. After a shower, she slipped into white jeans, a T-shirt, and trainers.

It was six thirty when she arrived at Simon's house. Plenty of time for him to have cooled off after his usual feisty session with Daphne, she reckoned. The pair had known each other so long that they butted heads if either thought they could win a point if there was something to debate. When she walked into the house, it was quiet. She looked around for Simon until finally finding him in the sitting room, lying on a sofa. "That bad today, huh?"

"Selby? This is a welcome surprise." He jumped up to give her a kiss on both cheeks.

"That's not the half of it," Daphne interrupted, flying into the room. "You should see what's in her car. A whole supper, it looks to me."

"Spoiled the surprise, you old hag. Come on, you –" she pointed to Simon – "need help carrying the stuff in."

"Have you really brought supper here?" he asked as he followed her out to the car. "God, if ever there was a time I needed food, but felt too done-in to cook myself, this is the night." He looked around to see if Daphne was behind him. "She was in a foul temper today. You wouldn't think that could happen to a ghost, would you? But she was spitting when I said I didn't think the relationship between Richard Penvose and his first mate worked in chapter fifteen. Then, she kept repeating herself, and got cross when I told her."

"You've never known her in writer's mode. I can be a vile creature at various junctures when I'm in the middle of a book, but I know exactly what you're talking about. Not looking forward to the next editing session. I feel a storm brewing, and it's not the one that swept Merryn off her boat."

Simon peered into the boot. "Can't wait to eat whatever it is you've made."

"It's nothing too elaborate. Just needed a break this afternoon. It's been a fairly relentless routine we've agreed to." She handed him the big bowl of sauce for the pasta and then reached in for the torte and the box of fettuccine.

"What do you need? Let me help," he said when they got into the kitchen.

"A big pot for the fettuccine, another to reheat the sauce, plates, and a table – can we eat right here at this one? Fettuccine is temperamental. It has to go from the pot to the sauce to our mouths."

"Absolutely. Shall I put the kettle on for the pasta?"

"What have you made?" Daphne asked, swanning into the room.

"*Fettuccine Al Pesce Spada* and for afters, *Torta di Nocciole*."

"Now in English, Miss, if you please."

"Swordfish fettuccine and hazelnut torte for dessert."

"Wow," Simon said. "When did you have time for all that? Though you probably whipped it all up in a flash."

"Not quite a nanosecond, but I didn't work on my own book this afternoon. If I'm not in the mood, I don't force it. Sitting at a laptop staring into space is, I believe, counterproductive."

Daphne shrugged her shoulders. "Never really had the problem. I always kept to routes – strict routines, plenty of fresh air, a swim in the sea, a walk over moors with my dog. The breaks solved any writing dilemmas."

"Where is that dog, anyway?" Simon asked.

"He's been disappearing a lot lately. I've no idea when he'll come back until I see him in front of me."

"What kind of wine, Selby? I'll go to see what's in the cellar."

"White would be my choice, but I think tonight we'll probably be glad to drink anything." She turned to Daphne while stirring the sauce. "Tell me something. Are you going to kill Merryn off?"

"Don't be absurd. How many of my books have you read, anyway?"

"You can't be implying they're all full of happy endings, surely."

"Of course not. Anyway, I'm not saying. You'll just have to wait and see."

"You haven't decided, have you? I sense you haven't made up your mind. Would've thought the great du Maurier had clear, definite ideas about the book right to the last page."

"It doesn't always work like that as you well know. Dictation is a new thing for me. When one speaks the word, one gets a different sense of things, you see. My mind just takes over. Sometimes I'm not sure what I'm going to say until I've said it."

"Another thing, what's the title of the book? You haven't told us."

"Really? I thought I had. *Pistol Meadow*."

"Of course, that makes sense."

Simon came back from the cellar with two bottles in his hands. "That's a bit ambitious," Daphne remarked, "especially as you both need a clear head tomorrow when we meet up again."

"We're not drinking both tonight for God's sake. One is to stick in the fridge for whenever."

Selby interrupted before a row broke out. "Okay, supper in three minutes, but I could use a bit more mint. Any growing in some pots somewhere? Hope you don't mind, I helped myself to things in your fridge for a salad."

You could have anything you wanted in my house, he thought. "Of course, it's fine. I'll fetch that mint."

A dog barking in the garden caught Daphne's attention. "He's back, the scoundrel. Just in time for an evening walk along the cliffs. I'll leave you to enjoy your feast."

When Simon returned, he stuck some flowers in a vase and put them on the table. "Here's the mint. Did you hear that thing barking up a storm at me? I've been attacked in my own garden. Of course, the worse thing is you can't see the little blighter. It's rather nice for Daphne though. If she must live this existence, at least now she's got a companion that's like her, don't you think?"

"I gave up trying to put myself in her shoes weeks ago. It's an uncomfortable exercise imagining a ghostly existence. Hard enough in this reality."

Dimming the ceiling lights, Simon lit the candles on the table while Selby brought the hot pan to the table. Tossing the pasta with tongs to coat it with the rich sauce, she spooned the swordfish from the bottom before dishing out generous portions into two large bowls. Neither of them spoke while they ate. It was satisfying to watch him enjoying the fettuccine. Having spent enough time around Viviana, she looked with suspicion on anyone who didn't eat good, home-cooked food with gusto.

When he had scraped all the bits from his dish, Simon let out a long sigh. "Oh, that's better. Thank you. Delicious. I'm feeling human again." He poured more wine for them both. "So, tell me – the woman you mentioned who taught you to cook. She was your nanny, I think you said?"

"Yes, but more than that. My parents were always very busy." She hesitated for a few seconds before going on. "They ignored me after we moved to Italy. Suddenly, I was invisible to them. They became caught up in the world of the art colony, their work – no time for a seven-year-old. They were popular in their circle. My mother is a beautiful woman."

"Ah, that explains things," he said.

"Flatterer. Anyway, Father's work began selling. Mother's took a little longer. Couldn't get their attention. I began speaking in short sentences. Had some pretty rocky, unstable years."

"You strike me as the emotionally balanced type."

"Ha – really? You count taking dictation from a ghost as proof of a stable mind? I stayed with Viviana when I went back to Tuscany recently though I did run into my father in a manner of speaking. I don't really communicate with my parents except at Christmas. Viviana and I were inseparable until I went away to school at St Mary's Calne in Wiltshire. Then university, afterwards London – lived with a man some years older, nasty break-up, moved to Cornwall. An abridged story of my life." She suddenly felt naked for having revealed intimate details.

Sensing her embarrassment, he filled in the silence. "In that case, I think Viviana deserves a toast. To the great woman who taught Selby Lyons how to cook like an angel," he said, smiling and raising his glass.

He really was quite charming. "To Viviana," she echoed. "I'll get the *torta* ready. Daphne told me the title of the book tonight, by the way. *Pistol Meadow*."

"Yes, why not? It fits, doesn't it? I like it. Very good. You know what else would be very good, especially with the hazelnut pudding? There's a delicious half-bottle of demi-sec champagne in the fridge."

Selby laughed as she cut two generous pieces of the hazelnut torte. "Not sure that's a clever idea. Tomorrow, ahem, remember? The schoolmistress will be smacking our hands with a ruler if she doesn't think we're up to standard."

"Let's be naughty children, then. We've been slaving over her bloody book for three weeks, plus writing our own stuff. Frankly though, and I'm embarrassed to admit this – lately, I'm finding my book so dry compared to hers. However, now on to more critical matters." He eased the cork out of the bottle. Sitting back down, he inched his chair closer to hers, inhaling the scent she was wearing. "Don't worry," he said in a soft voice, "I learnt my lesson the last time. I won't blunder in again."

"Everyone is entitled to a few mistakes." Selby leaned in to kiss his lips. He put his hand on her back, hoping to prolong the embrace for as long as possible.

In an invisible state, Daphne suddenly called out from across the kitchen. "I'd put clotted cream on that if I were you – much nicer that way."

CHAPTER ELEVEN

oticing Daphne out of the corner of her eye, Selby read the new pages she had written that morning. "Stop the pacing. Can't concentrate with you fidgeting behind me."

"I'll go and see how Simon's getting on."

"Don't do that. You know he's writing his own stuff until this afternoon. This won't work if you can't let us be."

"I've waited so long, don't you see. All these years, typing on that machine gave me the sense of writing. Listening to your tapping away makes me feel idle."

Selby turned around and looked sympathetically at Daphne. "It must've been a shock when you noticed the page was blank."

"It was a very low point. I couldn't go back to the type-writer for some time. Then, it was a matter of immense boredom. It was what I had known in life. When I found myself in spirit form, I expected to be able to do the same.

"What happened exactly? Did you die and then just wake up at Menabilly as a ghost?"

"Though the memories are hazy, some scenes stand in my mind like tableaux. I see me bedridden in my room at Kilmarth – such a pretty house overlooking Par Bay. I'm poorly but continuing to write. I float above my body and look down at it. My typewriter is on a tray on my lap with the finished pages spread over the bed. I'm frightened. I know it's a matter of time. I drive my spirit back into my body and open my eyes. Then, there's nothing. Must've died, I guess, but I've no recollection of the moment. But strangely, once in spirit form, Merryn's story wasn't vague. It was still there, gnawing at me. I could think of nothing else. Perhaps because it was the one thing I could remember in such detail, I have such an ardent desire to complete it. Does that make sense? In any case, I floated in a haphazard existence until Constance Rashleigh happened along. She could see and hear me. When she explained that I was at a house called Menabilly, I had a sense it was where I was supposed to be. I now know it had been a beloved place to me during my lifetime. Gradually, some of my memories returned though why some and not others, I've no idea.

"What was Simon's mother like?"

"Oh, Constance was a lovely, fey kind of creature. We had great fun because she saw the amusing, ironic side of things. She had no problem with my existence and agreed the secret room at the back of the linen cupboard was a good place for me. Boxes of some of my stuff were still in the attic. They were brought down along with my typewriter and other things.

"With an urgent need to write, I sat at my desk and began. When I discovered the blank pages, I let out a blood-curdling scream. Constance came running to my room. I remember her hair practically standing on end, and the skirt of her dress flying up. I think I was going mad, revolving around and around in circles faster and faster. A whirlwind of typewriter paper filled the room. Perhaps that's what my kind do when they get angry? Never having met others like myself, I've no idea.

"When I stopped acting like a dervish, I explained. She tried to comfort me, but there really wasn't anything anyone could say that would make me feel better. After that, I just drifted along as if in a dream for a time until I became aware of being in my room at Menabilly again. I have no memory of where I had been nor for how long. It must've been a considerable time though because when I returned, Simon was seven, and Constance had just died. I settled down into what became my existence, and there was the boy, you see. He needed me. What was I supposed to do but accept things as they were and carry on?"

Selby was silent for a few seconds before speaking again. "But how did the pages you had already written about Merryn get from Kilmarth to Menabilly?"

"You mean – that they were there under the bed? I can't say how, like so many things about me."

Selby looked up at the clock. "Damn, it's midday, and you've been rattling on, cutting into my time for my own book." She turned back to scold Daphne further, but she had vanished.

~

Daphne had not enjoyed looking back. Talking about the end of her life had caused her to feel out of sorts, so she had left Selby in mid-flow to see how Simon's writing was getting on. Laughter was coming from the garden when she appeared at Menabilly. Looking through the window, she saw a blonde woman with her arm draped around Simon's shoulder. They were sitting at a table.

"What's this?" Daphne whispered, moving in closer to eavesdrop.

"Oh, Simon, you are funny. I really have missed you."

"Felicia, I don't believe you ever gave me a thought."

"But I did, I do."

"Really?" he said, a bit too quickly

"Yes, really. Why do you think I've driven all the way down from London to surprise you?"

He smirked. "Because you've just finished some work and need a break. That's generally the only time we managed to see each other as I recall."

"True, I've just finished a big canvas, a commission from Barclays for a boardroom. When the paint was dry, I got paid. I thought to myself – who better to celebrate with than the lovely Simon? What shall we do this afternoon? How about a swim in the sea? We could take advantage of the sun. It's much warmer down here than it was in London when I left this morning. Why not have a picnic on the rocks where we used to sleep in the afternoons? You know, that summer I was here all of August."

"Yup, a good summer." He got up from the table. "Not sure I've got the makings for a picnic. I'll have a look in the kitchen. Otherwise, we can stop on the way to Lantic Bay to pick up some things. Look, also, Felicia, I should tell you that I've got a book going now and a few other things in my life, so I'm not free –"

Felicia put her hand up. "Darling, I'm not here to bust up any local romance. Just thought I'd stay a few days and then move down the coast to Penzance to a chap I've had my eye on for a while. Is that okay with you? No strings, no plans, just a good, cosy catch-up, okay?" She leaned over to give him a peck on the cheek.

"No, definitely not okay," Daphne thought.

Hot sunshine had been a good reason to carry lunch out to the terrace. Selby sat eating the salad of boiled egg, tomatoes, and ham while thinking about everything that had happened recently. An unfinished manuscript by Daphne du Maurier, hidden under a bed for thirty years, was astonishing enough. That she was now involved in getting the rest of it written, and taking dictation from a ghost, was unbelievable. She felt alive just being part of it. "Imagine if you suddenly dropped dead," she said to herself. "You wouldn't pine for the book you're writing now. Merryn's story is exhilarating; being with Simon and Daphne is exciting. But no more work today." She took her dishes into the kitchen. "I'm going for a swim. Take advantage of the hot weather before the afternoon melts away." After slipping into a bathing costume and grabbing a beach towel, she raced for the car and put the key into the ignition.

"And where do you think you're going?"

Shocked to hear a voice from the back seat, Selby yelped, "Bloody hell, Daphne."

"It's not fair. You promised to finish editing those three chapters. That way, we can begin the new one tomorrow morning."

Starting up the engine, she began reversing out. "It's too hot to work. I'm going for a swim, and I'm not asking your permission."

What beach are you going to?"

"Lantic Bay."

Daphne panicked. "Not a good choice, it's always crowded in summer – dogs, screaming children. Polridmouth Cove – Prid as locals say – now that's a nice sandy shore, much easier to get to than Lantic where you park thirty minutes down the beach or navigate that steep walk down.

"Not my experience – Prid was covered with bodies the last time I was there," Selby argued.

They were not the reasons she wanted Selby at Prid. Simon and Felicia were already at Lantic Bay picnicking, and God knows what else. Think of something, she said to herself. It will not progress the book to have Selby and Simon estranged for any reason. Why did that blasted girl have to show up now?

Lying down on the blanket next to Simon after their swim, Felicia sighed. "It's just as I remember. Days like this make me wonder why I live in London."

"That's where the energy is or that's what you told me when I said I was moving back to Cornwall."

"Yes, I know I said that, but looking at the light here today makes me wonder what it would be like not to live in a city. After all, the Newlyn School was here and the St Ives movement."

"Felicia," Simon said, lifting his head to look at her, "you and I both know you have the attention span of a gnat. You'd be bored silly living in the country. I know you. You work solidly for days on end. You like leaving your studio, trolling about, meeting up with friends at odd hours at odd places. Things close up early in Cornwall. It wouldn't work for you."

"I might be in the mood to change the way I live – all that running around, late nights, hangovers in the morning. I need a healthier lifestyle. I could accomplish much more with fewer distractions – be more prolific. Why not? It worked for you."

Simon turned over on the towel. "Yes, but I grew up here. I've got a home and the responsibilities that go with running the estate. I don't need the kind of things you need."

He had not taken the bait. A subtler approach would be needed if Felicia was to get her man back. Patience, she told herself. Let things take their natural course. She would have a whole month if she said the friends in Penzance had decided to holiday in France.

In an invisible state, Daphne had listened to their conversation. It was obvious to her there was a plan brewing. You're not pulling any wool over my eyes, miss, she thought. It's all too clear to me what you're up to. This is not good. I shall have to intervene before Selby walks down and finds this cosy scene, but can I manage it?

"You see?" Selby called out. "Just as I said – no one is here. I've got the beach to myself. Everyone is up the other end. Did you hear that, Daphne?"

Remaining invisible, Daphne said nothing, concentrating on the burst of energy necessary to move a solid object.

Selby locked the car. The sun was bright, and the concrete of the little parking bay was hot under her bare feet. She was thrilled to have told Daphne off. "Not a cloud in sight," she said. Looking at the view in front of her, she stepped over the thick chain hanging between two metal posts at the top of the path going down to the beach. Her second foot caught the edge of the chain. She fell forward and tumbled down the steep incline until slamming into a large hillock halfway down.

Breathless from the shock of the fall, she lay still for a few minutes, trying to make sense of what had just happened. When she finally looked back up the steep descent, she shouted to herself in a cross voice, "Always in a hurry – if you had parked at the other end like you usually do, this wouldn't have happened."

Her towel, handbag, and a bottle of water lay sprawled in various parts on the sandy hill. Standing up to retrieve them, pain shot through her foot. She collapsed. A second attempt made her cry out. Putting weight on her ankle was excruciating.

Daphne looked on, feeling guilty from heaving the chain up far enough to catch the edge of Selby's foot, but it was for everyone's own good. Now she must figure out how to get Simon away from the clutches of that other woman.

Simon knew he was in for a scowl and a telling-off from Daphne for missing dictation, but he would stick in a session before dinner to sort things. "Felicia," he said, standing to collect the remains of their picnic, "I have a project with a kind of deadline. It's been a lovely after-noon, but I've got to get home to do a few hours before supper. There's a half-hour walk up the beach to the car."

"Of course, I completely understand. Work must come first," she said in her most understanding tone. "What was that silly song we used to sing with your cousins? You know, the one we always sang at the end of an afternoon at the beach when we packed up – about the woman doing the washing."

He began to sing.

'Twas on a Monday morning
That I beheld my darling.
She looked so neat and charming
In every high degree.
She looked so neat and nimble-o
A washing of her linen-o

Felicia joined in and they sang the chorus at the top of their lungs.

Dashing away with the smoothing iron,
Dashing away with the smoothing iron,
Dashing away with the smoothing iron,
She stole my heart away.

They laughed and were about to start the second verse when Simon hushed her. "Did you hear that?"

Felicia listened. "It's coming from up there," she said, pointing to the sandy cliff above. "Someone is calling out – they sound in distress, don't you think?"

They grabbed their things and began the steep ascent in the direction of the voice. Halfway up, they saw a woman above them waving her arms. Simon stopped. It looked like Selby. They hurried the rest of the way until arriving at the spot where Selby was sitting. "What are you doing here?" he asked.

Selby quickly took in the blonde in the skimpy bikini standing next to him. "Is this your private beach, or can anyone swim here?"

"I mean what happened? Are you hurt? Did you fall?"

"Yes, Simon, I did fall, obviously. I began crawling back up to my car when I heard singing. I called out hoping someone would hear." She noticed the straw basket and blanket. "If I'd only known you were down below with your picnic." Her voice was full of sarcasm.

He shifted uncomfortably. "Ah, we were singing a Cornish song. Good thing we heard you between choruses."

"Wasn't it?"

Struck by the interplay between the two, Felicia hooked her hand through Simon's arm. "Hello, I'm Felicia Barrett."

Marking her territory, Selby thought.

"Oh, sorry. Felicia, this is Selby Lyons, a friend who lives nearby. Look, let's get you home, shall we? Can you stand?"

"If I could stand, I would have done so by now, don't you think?"

Simon winced, looking at Felicia with embarrassment while putting his hand out to help Selby up. She tried to walk but cried out in pain.

"It looks like a sprain to me," Felicia announced.

"You a doctor?" Selby asked.

"No, of course not – just saying, your ankle looks a tiny bit bigger on the right side."

Selby looked down. What a cow. As far as she could tell, her right ankle was now swollen to twice the size of the other.

"Lean on me," Simon said. "Can you hop on the other foot?"

Selby put her arm around his shoulder while smirking in Felicia's direction.

"Simon, she can't possibly hop like that all the way up this steep incline. We could make a chair between us – spread the load." Felicia smiled back at Selby.

"Yes, I can," Selby snapped back. Telling herself she would do it even if it killed her, she hung on to Simon, adding a bit more weight than necessary. He was drenched in perspiration when they got to the top of the hill.

"Is that the chain you tripped over," Felicia asked in an innocent voice. "The one with the steep descent warning?"

Ignoring the bitchy comment and anxious to get home, Selby got into her car, but when she tried the accelerator, the pain made her cry out.

Seeing an opportunity to get rid of the woman, Felicia suggested she drive one car and Simon the other.

He felt uneasy about getting in the car with Selby who had obviously made certain assumptions based on the skimpy bits of fabric barely clinging to Felicia's body – a body fit for a *Sport's Illustrated* swimsuit cover, he thought. There was nothing for him to feel guilty about. Besides, why should Selby mind? Unless she was jealous? Was that presuming too much? It was early in their relationship. Did they have one? She didn't talk much about her feelings. When they had seen each other lately, Daphne's book dominated the conversation. Either way, Felicia had just shown up at his door. An old friend that's all. He shrugged.

"The plan is a sensible one, Selby. We can drive your car to where mine is parked, but how will you manage once home? I can't see you going up and down the stairs in the shape you're in. You're coming back to Menabilly. I insist – at least for tonight. We're going to get frozen peas on that ankle. If necessary, I'll call the doctor in the morning."

With a sour smile, Felicia agreed. "Of course, it's a much better idea that you come home with us."

· · ·

The spare room was bright and cheerful, and Selby reluctantly agreed to stay on the bed. Placing a pillow under her foot, Simon layered several packets of frozen peas wrapped in tea towels on top and under her ankle. Felicia brought dusty, old editions of *National Geographic* magazines with one of her smiles. A cup of tea came next with a promise of some supper later.

Selby could hear them chatting and laughing downstairs while she lay staring at the walls, her ankle throbbing, pain radiating up her leg. She assumed Felicia was doing whatever sexy blondes do when merely crooking their little finger. They obviously had a history. Had it been a long relationship, an important one? Maybe she was a frequent guest. She knew so little about Simon. Anyway, she had no legitimate reason to feel jealous. Was she jealous? Why would he bother with her when he had whatever perfection Felicia's body was offering? "Stop brewing over all this. Rather be on my own bed," she complained while slapping the blankets in frustration.

"Well, that's not going to happen until that ankle of yours goes down," Daphne said in her most sympathetic voice. "Dear girl, I was so sorry to see them bring you here in that condition. Is it very painful?"

"Where are you? I can't see you."

"In the room but not able to show myself for some reason. I seem to be all out of juice. Perhaps it's the heat. I came back here when you got to the beach," she lied. "How did all this happen?"

"Tripped over a chain at the top of the footpath. If I hadn't been in such a hurry to get down, it wouldn't have happened, and why was I in such a hurry to make the most of the sunny afternoon? Because lately, you've been monopolising any free time I have."

Daphne barked back. "I told you not to go to that beach – always a tricky descent." She could see the girl was upset, and in some pain, so she softened her tone. "It's a pity you're not fit to get to Dr Rashleigh's Bath, a rock pool at Prid. This time of year, it's like a warm bath. Salt water is very healing. Maybe when –"

Selby interrupted, "As I was saying, then I heard singing and started shouting for help. Simon appeared with that practically naked girl."

"Ah, yes, the leggy blonde."

"Dirty blonde is what I believe they call that shade," Selby quipped.

"I wouldn't worry about her. She's an old friend who lives in London. An artist and not a bad one – that's one of hers on the wall opposite. I remember now. A few years ago, she used to come down a lot."

Selby looked across at a large canvas she had noticed earlier. It dominated a space on the wall between two dressers. A seascape, a modern work, but full of realism and movement. The wild sea flew across the canvas with great passion. It was impressive. "Not my sort of thing. Looks just like the sea I was caught in when I was Merryn in my dream. And I'm not worried by the way. Don't know why you said that. Why should it matter to me if Simon has girls here?"

"Perhaps it doesn't," Daphne said casually. "Oh, I do like that music they're playing downstairs. Can you hear it? It's been so long since I've heard music in this house. I can't resist going down."

Great, now even Daphne had deserted her. Selby rotated the bags of peas on her ankle. "Bored," she said, noticing the stack of magazines Felicia had brought. "*National Geographic*, my foot. I'm leaving here first bloody thing in the morning, swollen ankle or not."

Daphne watched the scene playing out in the kitchen. Felicia was busy demonstrating culinary skills and using a whisk with great flourish on a bowl of eggs. "Simon love, where do you keep the Dijon? I want to make a nice salad dressing for Selby. I thought we could all have cheese omelettes and a salad. What do you think?"

"Didn't think you cooked," he answered.

"I don't, but I can make some basics, generally things that are good after late nights." She busied herself finishing everything to take to the woman upstairs whom she considered might be a rival for Simon's attentions. After preparing a tray, she carried it up. This should keep her quiet for the night, she thought. Then, I'll set a romantic table in the garden with lots of candles and open another bottle of champagne.

Felicia came into Selby's room with a tray in her hands and put it down on the bed.

"Now – cheese omelette and salad, and I thought you could use some bubbly, so I brought the rest of our bottle," she said in a smug manner. "Oh, and this." She took a book from under her arm. "Have you read any of

Simon's books? They're terribly good. This one's on Morocco. It was such a fun trip – came back brown as a berry all over my body. I'll fetch the plates tomorrow. We might be late, and I wouldn't want to wake you. I did tell Simon to turn down the music in case you were sleeping, but he just loves to dance, doesn't he?"

She closed the door behind her.

"Came back brown as a berry," Selby said, imitating Felicia's voice. She tucked into the salad and cheese omelette. It was delicious and the champagne, very welcome. She downed the rest of the bottle and fell asleep.

Later in the evening, Simon helped to bring everything in from the garden to load into the dishwasher. An unusually warm summer's evening had provided a lovely end to a completely free day away from all work on his book and Daphne's. He had relaxed and enjoyed himself. Felicia had cooked the cheese omelette to perfection.

When he went upstairs to check on Selby, he opened the door, and crept over to the bed. Selby's eyes were closed. He was about to leave when Daphne spoke straight into his ear.

"What about my book?" she asked softly.

"God, you scared me. Where are you?" he whispered back. "I can't see you."

"I know. What about my book?"

"Daphne, you really are a selfish witch. Poor Selby lying there, probably still in pain, and all you can think of is you, you, you."

"All you can think of is Felicia, Felicia, Felicia," she mimicked.

"Don't be silly. You know very well she's an old friend. Well okay, an old girlfriend."

"Pretty though."

"Yes, she is, but you can't make a good relationship out of pretty. Besides," he said, looking over at the bed, "I'm rather counting on other things developing. Do you think she's in pain?"

"Selby's biggest problem tomorrow when she wakes up will be boredom. She's not good at sitting in one place. You've got to get her back to her own house."

"You just want her near her laptop, so she can work on your book. You are awful."

"Shush, you'll wake her, and that's not true. If I were Selby, I should like to be in my own house while I recover, and so would you. You know that."

"But how would she get up and down the stairs? I doubt she'll be able to stand for a few days. That ankle looked bad to me. I suggested a doctor, but she bit my head off."

"She can go up and down the stairs on her bottom like any sensible person would. Why don't you ask your Mrs Mop to go over to Rose Cottage during the day? I'm sure Selby will be recovered by Friday."

"Don't call the lady who is good enough to come here to look after the house 'Mrs Mop'. Mrs Taylor is a lovely woman from the village who has known me all my life. She knew Mother. In any case, that's an idea. I'll ring to see how she feels about it."

The moment Simon went out the door, Selby opened

her eyes. She could now see Daphne in front of her. They both stuck their thumbs up in the air. "Yes, but it comes at a price, my girl. I want you both back on my book by the weekend."

CHAPTER TWELVE

*M*rs Taylor was neither young nor tall, but her short, stocky frame and forthright manner gave the impression she was well able for anything. She rarely left the village where she lived, feeling confident that if something wasn't in the local shops, she didn't need it. Twice a week when she went to Menabilly 'to do for Mr Simon', she wore the same cleaning smock over the same dress. On Saturdays at home, she washed and ironed them with the rest of the family laundry. It was only herself, a cat, a black lab, and her husband. Mr Taylor pottered about since retiring from the China Clay works. He kept the veg garden, cleaned out the chicken coops, and scattered the day's scraps before a daily doze in front of the wood burner.

Once every six weeks, Mrs Taylor broke with routine to meet up with a group of friends she had known since childhood. Now in their early seventies, they booked appointments at the local hairdresser on the same day, looking forward to the comfort of speaking a kind of shorthand based on local knowledge. The gossip they exchanged over cups of tea lay like a ball of yarn until every bit of news unravelled. It was tiring but satisfying. The one thing about which she did not gossip was Menabilly. From her first few weeks working there, she had decided there were some things best kept to herself.

When she collected Mr Simon's friend, it was obvious to Mrs Taylor there was no love lost between the two women. She supported the dark-haired girl on crutches into the passenger seat. The blonde stood at the door, like mistress of Menabilly, waving goodbye. At Rose Cottage, she helped Selby up the stairs so she could shower and change. Then, she settled her on the sofa in the sitting room until taking in a tray at midday.

"Brought a sandwich and some soup, dear."

Selby sat up, surprised she had slept so long, but feeling she could sleep as long again. "Thank you. It's so nice of you to come here. What will Simon do without you this week?"

"He's fine managing on his own. He shared in the housework as a boy before I came into their lives," Mrs Taylor replied.

"Did you know his mother?"

"Backalong, I did – a nice woman," she said while fluffing up pillows behind Selby's back. "I'm away home shortly. I done some dusting and hoovering, but mentioning I have a free day in the week." She waited for Selby to say something. When she didn't, she carried on. "Mr Simon said you're a writer like him. Hope you don't mind me saying, better fit would be me here once a week. There's a fair amount needing doing."

"That bad? Only recently had a go at things, but it's not a routine. Get stuck into whatever I'm working on and forget about everything. Thank you, yes, if you can spare a day."

"That's all right then. I'll just do up the dishes and make a cup of tea before getting along. I'll leave the door abroad if you want to call out for something in the meantime," she said before returning to the kitchen.

Daphne was sitting in one of the chairs either side of the fireplace while watching the housekeeper work. When the tea was made, Mrs Taylor plonked herself down in the other.

"What are you staring at?" she asked.

Daphne flew up. "You see me?"

"Aye? Course I see you. My nan had the gift. Passed it to me. I'm not saying I go around seeing ghosts everywhere, but seen you right enough from the first day I started work for Mrs Rashleigh."

"Why didn't you say anything?"

"Because it weren't my place. She needed you. Your company brought her out of herself."

"But you're always asking Simon if he smokes?"

"That was just to keep him on his toes." She chuckled. "A bit of fun to poke at you both. Yes, I can't say I haven't enjoyed my little pranks. Cheered me all the way home when I'd pulled a good one."

"Well, that's a fine thing."

"Don't get all high and mighty with me, and while we're on the subject, you're up to something, and I'm not sure I like it. And mind, I've noticed you've made yourself scarce at Mena lately. You been hiding out here? Had one of them barneys, did you?"

"I don't know what you mean," Daphne said in a petulant voice.

"Yes, you do. I see right through you." Mrs Taylor was pleased with the little joke she had made. "What's the connection between you and them two? Leave them alone. He needs someone nice like her."

"You can't be talking about the blonde thing?"

"You are cakey, but then it might be due to your state."

"It is not, and no one has ever accused me of being thick – dead or alive."

"What's it like, anyway? Been wanting to ask you that for years."

"What's what like?"

"You know – being dead and all. Not afraid of death myself, but oh whee, I would get bored just watching the living. Course I've heard you typing in that room of yours behind the linen cupboard, so I suspect you keep occupied."

"You know about that?"

"I crept in while you were both in the garden one day. Dusty place – thought about giving it a good do, but decided it was nothing to do with me."

Mrs Taylor took a long slurp of tea. Obviously to quench a parched throat, Daphne thought. The woman hadn't drawn a breath since confessing to observing her these last thirty years.

"Oh, I was chacking. That's better, now. Seen your books on telly. *The King's General*. About Mena, wasn't it?

Saw *Jamaica Inn* with them smugglers. Mr Taylor and me, we go up there on the moors sometimes for a tasty meal. Cosy place, nice people serving. Saw that other one also – you know, the one about that evil housekeeper."

"Strike any chords," Daphne shot back.

"They were good yarns anyway, is all I'm saying. What are you going to do with all that stuff you've typed? Must've written hundreds of books up there by now."

Daphne repeated what she had told Simon and Selby about the end of her life and having to leave her story about Merryn unfinished when she discovered that no words appeared on the page; how typing, nevertheless, got the stories out of her head. The communication she had had with Simon's mother, and the close friendship that had developed with her son had given purpose to her existence all these years.

"I've struck a bargain with them to finish my book, you see. I go between the two houses, dictating. They do the typing. We're nearly halfway through. They can't wait to hear what will happen, and I'm having a grand old time getting it all out of my head and on paper. It's made me feel lighter in spirit than I've felt in a long time."

Mrs Taylor took a tissue out of her sleeve and blew her nose. "A sad tale – caused a good squall, but what now? That other girl is here. How are they going to work on that book of yours with her around though I know people don't see you unless you want them to. Noticed that when we had that rotten window – saw you watching the bloke who brought the new one. You were standing right next to him."

"An observant creature, aren't you?"

"Course you're tied to these houses from living in both when alive," Mrs Taylor explained as she washed up her cup. "My cousin, Rachel – she knows about these things. Spirits have a connection to houses where they lived before passing. How are you going to tell Mr Simon what you want him to write? That incomer will hear him talking in his study, and from all the bickering you two done over the years, they won't be quiet times."

"What a snoop you've been," Daphne said with affection in her voice. She liked having Mrs Taylor to talk to. The housekeeper had not put a foot wrong all these years at Menabilly since Simon's mother had died. Hearty meals had been cooked for father and son, and the house kept in order. When Simon had come home from boarding school, she had made sure he went back with everything clean and tidy. She had cut his hair and had cleaned up scrapes on his knees when he was a boy. "You're right. The likelihood of Simon and me whispering is unrealistic. Speaking of the blonde, I'm not so sure her motives are as innocent as she's made Simon believe."

"That's something we agree on. The party gave me one of those fake smiles of hers this morning at Mena – a real upcountry smirk. You should see all the clothing she stuffed into her case, more than needed for a few days stay – asked me for an iron and board when she came into the kitchen. I took it up to leave in her bedroom, and, oh my, I wasn't prying or nothing, but – some of that black lacy under-stuff sent the colour through my cheeks."

"You see? She has intentions, plans for Simon. You wouldn't pack sexy underwear if you were just going to visit a friend, and that's not all. Do you know when you collected Selby from Menabilly this morning – that woman – she stood at the door, waving like she owned the place."

"Made the same note to myself."

"Anyway, after the car had pulled away, and Simon had gone inside, I heard her say, 'That's you gone, Selby Lyons, and good riddance.'"

"No? Did she really?"

"She did. Proof she's the vixen I thought she was. So, I blew as hard as I could on her neck – sent a shiver right through her." Daphne looked pleased with herself before saying with conviction, "She must be stopped."

Mrs Taylor cackled. "Ah now, that shouldn't be a problem for the likes of you and me. We can run rings round these pups."

They broke into peals of laughter. "This is much nicer being able to chat with you," Daphne said. "Now, the first thing we need to do is to get her room changed to Blue Lady."

"What's that?"

"It's the bedroom at the end of the corridor at Menabilly. The room where Felicia has dug herself in is too close to Simon's for any mischief on our part. He could come in and see me there if she screamed or something."

A shiver rippled down Mrs Taylor's back. "Never liked it in there."

"Of course, you didn't. I never saw her myself, but lots have over the years."

"Saw who?"

"A woman in blue has been seen from that window. You know – someone like me. Since before my time, really, but I did have the occasional guest who claimed to see her. I was never sure if it was the gins they'd drunk, or if they really had seen something."

"It's worse in that bathroom," Mrs Taylor confessed.

"Yes, I heard that too – the feeling that someone is watching you. How do we get Felicia out of the bedroom she's in and moved to Blue Lady?

As if on cue, Mrs Taylor said, "Easy. Got a cat, Percy – he brings dead mice into the house regular like. Sometimes, we don't find the things 'til the smell is ripe enough to make our nostrils twitch. I'll gather up the more putrid ones from the compost pile and shove 'em under her bed. It won't take long before the stench fills the room. Then, you hover. Do some of them things that irritate, like you do with me. Oh, don't bother with that mutt of a face – it's wasted on me. Plenty of times over the years I had to fluff up cushions 'cause your ladyship had plonked herself down."

"I could've made a lot more mischief," Daphne said in a defensive tone. "There were countless occasions I was sorely tempted to turn the heat up on the stove to let something burn, or hide your car keys, but I didn't, so count yourself lucky. Now, what do you suggest we do first?" She moved in closer to hatch a plot to rid Menabilly and Simon of Felicia Barrett.

When Mrs Taylor got home, she placed her bag on the catch pit in the porch, and grabbed the day-old newspaper to hold the scraps from the tea she would begin to make.

"All right, then?" she asked, seeing her husband snoozing in his chair.

"Aye?" He opened his eyes and straightened up. "Time to walk Albert." Mr Taylor grabbed his flat cap and jacket, which was generally a ritual that got the Labrador springing up, but the dozing dog didn't fancy a walk in the rain. "Come on, old boy. No use pretending to sleep 'cause I ain't cleaning up no mess later. Up you get."

Albert growled. "Getting teasy in his old age, isn't he," she said. "Go on, boy, so you don't hold Pop up when tea's ready." Albert didn't budge but continued to growl.

Percy, the large orange cat joined in, hissing and coughing. "More hair balls, I suspect. I'll spoon some oil down his throat tonight." The cat suddenly pounced from the window to Mrs Taylor's feet. Albert began barking. "What's having them tonight?" she shouted. "You been feeding digestive biscuits again? Told you. Animals can't take all that sugar. How many did you give 'em during crib?"

He could barely hear what his wife was saying between Percy's hissing and Albert's barking. Grabbing the dog by the collar, he flung him out the door, and followed behind.

Percy arched high, hissing and spitting. "What is it, me 'ansome? A mouse? Get on with it, then. Stop making such a fuss." Percy was not interested in whatever his mistress was saying. He didn't like strange dogs in his house. Determined to chase it out, he pounced repeatedly, ending up hooked to Mrs Taylor's tights by a claw. "Right. That does it," she screeched, grabbing the big cat to carry outdoors. "That's for you tonight – my new tights in ribbons."

The rest of the evening was quiet, but when Mrs Taylor got into bed, she felt guilty about Percy. She had decided to fetch him when she felt something jump up on the bed. It settled on her legs. Turning on the light, she saw a definite impression in the middle of the duvet. When she reached her hand out towards the spot, something licked it. She left it there for a few minutes before taking it away.

"Wasson? The light," her husband complained. "Can't sleep with it."

"Dreckly," she told him, and then continued to ponder the mystery of what was on her bed. *Don't know what you are or where you came from, but here you cannot stay, not without a lot of bobber lips from them other two.* Tomorrow she would ring Cousin Rachel who knew about such things.

Felicia had gone out for the afternoon, so Simon had taken the opportunity to hole up in his study with Daphne to work on *Pistol Meadow*. Reading from over his shoulder as the type appeared on the screen, she made comments if something wasn't perfect.

"No, no, no. It wasn't the lovely shore. I didn't say that. Lonely. It should be 'lonely' shore."

Simon barked back, "Can we agree that we'll just get the dictation down. For bloody sakes, woman, after supper I'll go back and edit the chapters we've done."

She continued, *"Sheltering from the downpour beneath the eaves of the church, the men drew close to hear news of the first boat returned."* Daphne paused and tapped Simon on the back. "Have you got that, boy?"

"Yes," Simon said, using all his willpower not to explode again.

Daphne went on, *"'What news of Penvose? Speak man. Our kin were with him.'*

"'No story to give,' the elder answered."

Simon interrupted. "Why did Merryn sail out to look for Richard? Wasn't she used to him being gone for long stretches in all weather?"

"She was indeed, but this voyage was different. This time her heart sensed danger. In dreams, she saw him drifting on a floating barrel. A sea-witch pulled him from her embrace. A woman like her –"

"Yoo-hoo! Simon."

"That blasted woman is back," Daphne cursed. "What now? We've made progress this afternoon. Can't you get rid of her?"

Felicia knocked. Simon got up to open the door.

"Simon love, I've just been with Uncle Mike and Sarah at Werrington. They haven't seen you since I was last down that summer when we went to the cricket match there. You know – when Uncle Mike insisted you play for their side. Remember? He wants us to come over for drinks and a dinner party they're giving tonight. Would that be okay with you? They want to see you again. Apparently, you're positively hermit-like down here. Is that true? We must change all that. Seven thirty, okay? Tie and jacket for you." She gave him a peck on the cheek before rushing out the door.

"Well, I couldn't really say anything, could I?" he asked, looking around for Daphne.

As she became visible again, Daphne shot daggers in his direction, and lashed out. "How about the word, 'No'? I've heard you say it plenty of times to me. A dinner party instead of the editing you promised to do after supper – traitor." She disappeared to her room behind the linen cupboard. This was a serious development. The woman was positively digging herself in for winter.

Upstairs, Felicia felt on a high. She hadn't told her uncle she was coming to Cornwall. Stopping in unannounced at teatime, she casually dropped hints that Simon would love to see them again. They invited her back for drinks and dinner. Uncle Mike and her father were always trying to pair her up with a respectable soul like Simon Rashleigh. It would be good for him to get out more, she reasoned. They needed to go out, together, mix in with a nice crowd. If she ended up living in Cornwall, they would want a fun group.

Looking through her clothing, she chose a turquoise silk dress that sat off the shoulders. She spread it over the ironing board and switched on the iron to heat up while she had a quick shower.

Daphne floated into Felicia's room and noticed the dress laid out on the ironing board. Focusing on the concentration she needed to move any material object, she opened the water compartment, and pushed the iron on its side. The water leaking out would ruin the fabric, she reckoned, and count as the first of many mischiefs she planned to execute. Mrs Taylor would be proud of her. She looked through the other dresses hanging in the wardrobe. It was not a wardrobe for a Cornish summer though she liked the green one, but the navy shift with the slit up to anybody's knickers worried her. Three pairs of expensive looking shoes sat in a row on the floor. Spotting the four-inch heels, she wondered how anyone walked in them.

Not having a sense of smell, it was some time before Daphne noticed smoke rising from the iron. "What's this?" she suddenly called out. Knowing she would never manage to upright the thing, she flew to Simon. "Upstairs. Fire. Smoke."

He jumped up from his desk and ran up the stairs by twos into the smoke-filled room. Small flames rose from the fabric under the iron. He pulled the plug before throwing water from a jug onto the dress. Then he opened the windows to let the smoke out.

"Felicia. What the hell?" Really, he wanted to shout through the door to tell her off, but when he heard the shower going, he trounced down the stairs and sat on the bottom step to wait.

"My dress. What happened?" she cried, a few minutes later.

Simon ran back up the stairs. "Your dress? That's rich. You could've burned down my house. How could you turn the iron on and leave the room? Any fool knows better than to do that."

"Did you just call me a fool?"

"Mrs Taylor uses that iron weekly. It's never burst into

flames before," he said, leaving the room and slamming the door.

Daphne had retreated to her room in a panic after fetching Simon. She had not noticed that the girl had switched the iron to the 'on' position. Whilst the incident had created the desired tension between Felicia and Simon, the consequences could have been dire. That she might have set fire to her beloved Menabilly was a shocking thought. Feeling weak from the effort, she sat down to consider things. "I need a different strategy, but what?" There were limits to her abilities. "Now, let's see," she said. "What would Mrs Danvers do?"

CHAPTER THIRTEEN

*W*hen Felicia and Simon returned to Menabilly from the dinner party at Werrington, an evening around other people had dissipated the frostiness between them. They shared a cognac in the kitchen and swapped details of conversations with dinner partners until she went up to bed. He washed their glasses while thinking about the evening. It had been fun. Why didn't he mix more with people? Lots of invitations winged their way to him on a regular basis. Easier with a partner, he assumed. Just so difficult finding one. He missed seeing Selby. With her, he could talk about food, travel, his books – and Daphne. That was the best thing – being able to share Daphne with someone else. Someone who wasn't the slightest bit afraid of her. Someone who stood their ground against the ghost who had so abundantly blessed his life. He had realised only lately that he had taken Daphne for granted all these years, assuming she would always be a part of his life. He felt guilty about it. What must it have been like for her, not being able to put words on paper? Writing was in her blood. Grandfather George du Maurier had authored two bestsellers. Uncle Guy du Maurier had written the celebrated patriotic play, *An Englishman's Home*. Imagine, he thought, eighty-six years ago Daphne had published her first book. The failure to recognise she may have had problems in her ghostly existence made him feel ungrateful and selfish. Finishing her book was the least he could do to show his love and appreciation, but it would not be easy while Felicia was visiting.

"Sorry, dear," Mrs Taylor said to Selby. "Should've rung the bell, I know. I let myself in through the kitchen door. Just stopping long enough to check on things. I've brought an apple cake I made, and I'm leaving an oggy in the warmer for midday. How's the ankle?"

"Thank you, that's so kind. The ankle is much improved. Walked around the garden earlier. Need to strengthen it, but think I was lucky it's just a sprain. Not moving again this morning though. Don't want to push it. Plenty of work to keep busy."

"You stay right there. I'll make us both a cuppa with a nice slice of cake before I head off again."

Mrs Taylor went into the kitchen and saw Daphne. "Can't say I'm surprised to find you hiding here, and not at Mena. Laying bets that iron business was your mess. Am I right? Mr Simon was on the phone to me, acting nought but a child, asking if the iron was broke, and how fires burn down old houses all the time because someone does something stupid. I had to agree with him there. You're lucky that –"

"Mouse."

"Yes, I've got the mouse for the girl at Mena in my bag," Mrs Taylor said, lowering her voice.

Daphne leaned down towards the floor. "You're back, Mouse. Where have you been, naughty dog? I've been looking all over for you."

"Well, I never. Is that a dog down there? I can't see it myself. I never seen a dog with you all these years – I mean a ghost-dog. Wonder why I can't see it?"

"I can see my Mouse just as clear as anything. Now, get down, there's a good boy," she said before turning her attention back to Mrs Taylor. Mouse had other ideas and began barking.

Selby grabbed the crutch by her side, hobbling as quickly as possible. It wouldn't do for Mrs Taylor to hear a dog and start asking questions. Her ears pricked up as she moved down the hallway. "Shush, Mouse," she heard Daphne say. When she arrived at the kitchen doorway, both women were bent low, whispering.

"What's going on? You can see her?" gasped Selby. Both Daphne and Mrs Taylor stopped talking to Mouse to look up. "Since when?" She shook her head in disbelief.

"Since always – it's in the family," Mrs Taylor said with hesitation as she straightened up. Grabbing a fresh cloth to wipe across spotless counters, she kept her hands moving to avoid looking at Selby. "Nan had the gift. Passed it to me."

"It's not in my family," Selby said. "I'm sure of that. How come I see her?"

"Probably to do with living here. It's where she lived sometime during her life."

Daphne nodded. "Eighteen months to be exact."

"So, if Daphne went back to any of the places she lived during her lifetime, people there would see her?"

"There she goes, analysing everything. There are things no one knows the answers to. Can't you accept that?" Daphne pleaded.

"Think I've been a pretty good sport accepting I've got to share my own house with a ghost. Honestly, no gratitude. Most people would have called in an exorcist long ago – and there are still times I fantasise about it," Selby insisted. "This development does take the pressure off though. I've wondered more than a few times if you ever heard us talking. Lord knows, there are days when the woman doesn't draw a breath."

"Can't blame her," Mrs Taylor said in Daphne's defence. "All these years, she only ever had Mr Simon."

"Yes, and if you had only told me years ago that you could see me, I would not have had such a lonely time of it while he was away at school or in London."

"Weren't my place," Mrs Taylor snapped back. "Told you that."

"Didn't have a problem with playing your little tricks though, did you?"

Selby watched the exchange between the two women and started to laugh. "Finally, Daphne, you seem to have met your match. Does Simon know?"

"We thought it a better fit not to mention it for a while.

My little jokes – ones I've had good laughs from all these years – well, he may be 'mazed when he hears," the house-keeper said, looking slightly ashamed.

"She used to tell Simon she could smell cigarette smoke, didn't you, Mrs Taylor?" Daphne said in a mocking tone.

"Harmless little things that helped to pass the time."

"That's not all. What about the –?"

Here we go again, Selby thought. "Going to leave you two to reminisce. Welcome to the Daphne's Ghost Fan Club," she said.

Mrs Taylor started up again when she was sure Selby was out of earshot, "Now, back to what we was hatching."

"We were talking about Felicia," Daphne said. "I admit things didn't work out with the iron. It was brainless of me not to notice it had been switched on. It's not easy moving things in my state either. I don't have much dexterity, and it took a lot of 'juice' to knock over the iron. The odd thing is that when I'm fully charged again, it comes back with a whoosh, streaming into me, and well, you wouldn't want to be holding a Ming vase. We need a new strategy. That woman is worming herself into Simon's life. I heard him agree she could stay on next week. If I'm to start shenanigans tonight, I need Felicia in Blue Lady though I'm not really sure what I'm meant to do once she gets there."

"Make her feel uncomfortable. Just give her the idea there are happenings at Mena, but if you're too plain about it all, she'll go running to Mr Simon. No," she said, shaking her head, "don't go overboard like you did with the iron."

"You're a wealth of ideas, but you're not the one who has to do the thing."

"Wait, I got an idea. Let Mouse loose in her room. He jumped on my bed last night. Thought I was imagining things until he licked my hand. I'm used to such things, but that girl is not. She won't know what's what. Should send her grey with fright."

"I'm not sure. I could try. I'm hesitating because though he was an obedient dog in life, he now seems to have a mind of his own – disappearing off sometimes like he did the other day."

"Stay away from Mena until tonight. I'm due there shortly. I'll see what can be done to help things along. I've got Percy's 'offering' for under the girl's bed." She poured tea and cut some cake to take to Selby. "It's proper rank, this mouse. It should get her moved to Blue Lady. It's in my handbag, triple-wrapped so that no one will notice the smell until it's open to the air. Anyways, it'll work better than setting a bleddy dress on fire." She hastened out of the room before Daphne could utter an acid reply.

"This'll right you," Mrs Taylor said as she set the tray down in front of Selby.

"You are an old goat, keeping that secret all these years."

Mrs Taylor winked at her. "I've been called worse."

It was a cosy scene. Felicia and Simon sat at the table in the kitchen, trading sections of the newspaper. Mrs Taylor announced her presence. "Shall I do upstairs first, Mr Simon?"

"No, look, I'm going to my study. Felicia won't mind if you start in here, will you?"

"No, not at all. Just ignore me."

Mrs Taylor wished she could do just that, but she was on a mission. With Simon out of the room, she had a chance. "Did you sleep well, Miss?" the housekeeper asked.

"I think I did though I got quite a fright what with nearly burning the house down before we went out for dinner. I still don't see how it happened. Are you sure that iron is in good working order?"

"It is. Does for me just fine. Maybe it wasn't square on the stand."

"I would never have left it in a precarious position, but what other explanation could there be?" Felicia turned the pages of the fashion section.

"Ah well, I couldn't say. It's an old house. Backalong, generations of Rashleighs have lived and died here, but I'm not to talk of it."

"Talk of what?"

"Nope – not worth losing the job over."

"I won't say anything. What are you talking about? Ha – are you saying there're ghosts in this house?"

"No. Now I never said such a thing. I never even said the word, 'ghost'. You won't put words in my mouth, Miss. I need this job. I've got a husband with no job, a mortgage, a dog, a cat to feed and food to put into our mouths and –"

Felicia interrupted. "Mrs Taylor, please, you actually have still told me nothing."

"Now, beggin' your pardon, I've got to get on with my work." She reached for the handbag she would need upstairs.

What an odd duck, Felicia thought, and she certainly had been insinuating there were ghosts in the house – all nonsense. If she did end up with Simon, she would live here and would have none of that silly business. He had been a bit distant though since her arrival. Did Selby have him in her sights? No matter, with time she would bring the old Simon back round again. He had been mad about her that first year they had lived together. Then, that trip to Morocco had got in the way – snakes, spiders, smelly goats in trees, filthy nomads.

He had sat for hours talking to them while she was stuck with the women, trying not to look at the disgusting stuff they were brewing in the pot over the fire. Simon insisted they accept their invitation to dinner. She had used every bit of willpower not to toss the whole thing up on his shoes in the car on hairpin turns back to the hotel afterwards. Feigning migraines and stomach trouble, she had stayed poolside for the rest of the week while he had trekked to Berber villages. If she could handle all that, she could manage village gossip about ghosts, she told herself. Still, she believed some old houses were creepy, but it was best not to dwell on such things. "Get out of here today for a while. Show him you can amuse yourself when he's writing," she mumbled to herself, and went back to reading the papers.

Sometime later, Mrs Taylor came rushing into the kitchen, huffing and puffing. "Oh, just awful, a dead mouse in your room, a terrible smell, a stinky, rank smell

– found it when I went in to tidy things. I've had to change you to a different room. Moved your things so you didn't have to go back in there. Windows are opened now to air the room."

"Really? It didn't smell when I got up this morning."

"That's the thing, see. Once the body starts to decompose, maggots work fast, the skin splits and the insides spill out – with the vile smell. Had to put some of your perfume up to my nose just to move your things. Hope you don't mind I took the liberty?" Mrs Taylor paused to refill her lungs. "And here's the guilty party. Right under your bed, it was." She pushed the tissue holding the decomposing mouse forward and under Felicia's nose. The stench was overpowering, sending Felicia out the back door, gagging and retching.

"That'll do nicely," Mrs Taylor decided as she folded the tissue over the ripe corpse, and wrapped it within plastic bags for the outside bins. "Not a hardy type, thank God."

Daphne worried that Mouse had not been to Menabilly since coming back into existence. Would he go wild when he got to his old stomping ground? It was too tiresome to think about, but being able to control him was crucial to the success of her mission. Unpredictability was not a wise thing in the circumstances. Mrs Taylor had driven over from Menabilly at midday to confirm that Percy's mouse had done the trick. Felicia was now in Blue Lady.

"Are you ready for tonight?" the housekeeper asked before getting back into the car.

Daphne replied that *she* was, but she wasn't sure about Mouse. She was still worried about being able to control him.

"Take him down to that beach below Mena," suggested Mrs Taylor. "It's a good, open space. You can yell for him without nosy folk. An overcast day like today won't attract bodies. No one likes that place anyway. I'm off now. There's a lot more work at Mr Simon's with a houseguest staying."

Daphne whistled for the dog who walked to heel to the sitting room before making a running jump for the sofa and Selby.

Expelling the air forced from her stomach, Selby cried out, "This dog isn't the weight of a Chihuahua. Can't you train it to bark before it hits my gut? And can you get it off me? Now."

Daphne leaned down; her hands wrapped top and bottom of an invisible shape. "I'm sure it wouldn't matter what I told Mouse to do. I've no experience of this reckless darling. That's why I'm taking him to the beach below Menabilly to go through some commands – remind him who's boss. Perhaps dogs don't have to obey their masters in my world. One makes these assumptions about how things work, but there are no guarantees I'm right about any of it."

"Yes, we know – 'I do not know the why or the how of my existence' et cetera et cetera," Selby said. "Good session we had this morning, wasn't it? I've missed Merryn. How are Simon's bits coming along?"

Daphne didn't want to mention they had only managed one dictation since Felicia's arrival. "We're making headway," she lied. "But he's in a nervous state and feeling under the gun from his editor who rings up constantly. Imagine asking him what page he's on. It would've driven me mad. That was one thing about which I used to put my foot down. Publishers knew that to pressure me into a timetable to either begin or finish a book was high treason. Writers should not write to deadlines. If you're a journalist, that's different. The truly creative spirit must come when it's ready. Once we got that straight, there was never a cross word between me and any publishing team.

"Ahem, and you don't think being Daphne du Maurier had anything to do with the smooth sailing of things," Selby teased.

"I wasn't always famous, you know – got a seventy-five-pound advance for my first book. Did I ever tell you that? Anyway, I laid down those rules from the start of my writing career. Simon's September deadline is making him quite ratty now. He seems in a state about the middle of the book. He's working as much as possible, considering houseguests are not conducive to concentration."

"No, blondes generally aren't," Selby quipped.

"I resent that. Why do people always have it in for blondes, anyway? I've known many women with dark hair who were irresistibly beautiful to men. Snagged just as many as my blonde friends – more maybe because brunettes are permitted to have a brain. Anyway, Felicia is just a distraction. She had her chance in London, and whilst Simon is a generous chap, it's not like him to go back to something that didn't hold him in the past."

"Now who's being generous? How do you know she didn't break up with him? Left him pining?"

"Because I was there when he arrived back from London. The boot and car were loaded with boxes and cases, so I knew he had made up his mind – no hound-dog face. Next morning, he said the house looked tired and worn. We had a wonderful time getting it looking smart. I never cared too much about that sort of thing when I lived there – too busy writing. I assumed Simon was sprucing up the house so that he could entertain more, but he didn't. He really is happiest either writing or travelling. I'm not suggesting he should start having wild parties, but –"

"Why shouldn't he have wild parties and friends to stay? Writers tend to live too isolated an existence – at least that's what my godfather is always saying."

Yes, thought Daphne, but that girl is after more than friendship.

Felicia had filled her backpack with sandwiches she had found in the fridge. The long walk over fields, circling around bulls, and clambering over numerous stiles, made her wonder if she should have gone to Prid as planned, but she had noticed the beach on a map in her bathroom that morning. On a whim, she turned left instead of right, hoping to find the place. When the sea finally appeared, she was eager to get down the cliff path. Grey water stretched as far as she could see. She breathed in the salty, fresh air. It felt good to be outdoors even on an overcast, windy day. She wished Simon could have come as well.

Since seeing him again, she felt sure they could be happy together. What a fool she had been to let him go, and for taking him for granted when they had lived together. This time would be different. An art studio could be built in the garden on the west side of the house near his study. They could keep her flat in London for exhibitions or parties. Could she stand the slow pace in Cornwall? She might not notice if she kept busy painting. If she got cabin fever, she could hop on a train to Paddington. She looked out at the sky. The light was special here. What could she accomplish without the distractions of pubs, parties, and her bohemian crowd?

Small rocks gave way beneath her feet. She steadied herself, travelling back and forth on switchbacks to reach the bottom. In a cave out of the wind, and the picnic on a blanket, she ate her lunch while watching sandpipers poke the sand for sea grubs. Then, she packed up everything to have a run up the beach towards a rocky cliff face at the shore's far point.

At Menabilly, Mouse ran wildly from one end of the garden to the other, sniffing under bushes and shrubs until he lay at her feet panting. Daphne purposely ignored the dog, so he wouldn't start barking within earshot of Felicia's bedroom. When we get to the beach, she decided, I'll run through commands to use in the girl's room tonight.

"That's a good boy," she said, once they had left the garden. "Now, come. Good. Sit." Mouse followed instructions, happy to have a game with his mistress. Pointing to tree stumps, she asked him to jump up. The dog obeyed perfectly. "You've done well, my boy, deserving of a good paddle in the sea." They were standing at the water's edge when she noticed the spring tide had begun to flow through gullies at speed. "Another forty minutes, there will be no beach left to walk down, Mouse. Course, that won't really bother us." She laughed. "But you did leave a wet patch on Selby's sofa the other day when you came in from the rain, naughty boy. Up towards the point now, and I'll throw some sticks." Mouse bounced along behind her, running, and splashing in the water. She threw stick after stick, giving instructions to stay, fetch, retrieve, sit. "Now to work on that bark." She picked up the stick, holding it in her hand. He began barking.

"No, that won't do for tonight. Shush." He stopped, and looked up at her, cocking his head from side to side, listening, waiting for the next command.

"Good boy. There you go. Better now, not so noisy. Shall we try it again?" The dog shot off like a rocket, disappearing up the beach.

"A nuisance, that's what you are," Daphne said in a disgusted voice as she floated along the beach until she found him. Mouse was jumping back and forth, barking frantically at a struggling Felicia who was knee-deep in a mud hole and sinking further into the quivering sand. Daphne panicked at the advancing tide. She looked further up the beach. They were at the strandline, the highest point on land that tidal water would reach. "No. Don't move. You'll sink deeper." Felicia clawed at the sand, trying to hoist her body up, and pulling at her thighs with her hands. "Don't move," Daphne shouted again with all the energy she could muster. "You'll make it worse."

Felicia looked ghostly. Dried mud was caked on her arms and body. "Pull me out," she screamed.

Daphne knew she would never manage that kind of strength. Seawater rose above Felicia's knees. She would have to get Simon as quickly as possible, or the worst would happen.

"I'm going for help. I'm not strong enough to get you out. Listen to me. Stop thrashing about. Just sit back to spread the load. Every time you try to pull your legs free, you're creating a vacuum under your feet and around your legs, making things worse."

"Please don't leave me. I'm afraid," Felicia wailed.

"Must get help," Daphne said before willing herself to Simon's study.

Once in front of him, she yelled, "Hurry. No time. You'll need Almond for the quickest way there. Felicia's in a mud hole on the home beach – up to her knees – tide approaching. Go. Quickly. She's at the far end, near the notched rock face."

He sprang up, ran out of the house to the stable yard, grabbed a coil of strong rope and stuffed his mobile into a plastic bag. With no time to fix a saddle, Simon whistled for Almond and slipped the bridle over her head. His hands shook as he tried to buckle it in place. Throwing the coiled rope over his own head and under one arm, he hopped on her back, and set off at speed across pastures. If he got Felicia out, but the tide advanced too quickly, they would need to swim through the sea on Almond to safety.

Once on the shoreline, Simon looked to the rock face at the other end. It was too far to spot Felicia, but he could see rising water covering Almond's hooves. He wasn't keen on a fast run on a beach. Horses could get soft-tissue injuries pushing off from the yielding surface, but he had no choice. As a boy, he had visited this spot frequently with Daphne. If he kept inland, there would be less chance of Almond stepping in a hole.

"Let's have your fastest gallop, girl."

CHAPTER FOURTEEN

Felicia's face was drained of colour when he found her. He called her name, but she seemed to be in a daze. "I'm here with rope. Slip it under your arms," he shouted, quickly dismounting. "Almond will pull. Don't struggle. Let the horse do the work." Sending Almond back a few feet, he tied the end of the rope over her neck and underbelly. It wasn't ideal, but it would have to do.

"Felicia, I need you to listen. Can you hear me?"

Nodding her head, she looked up.

"Okay. The tide's coming in. It's a spring tide, much faster. We don't have long. Can you catch this rope?"

Landing near her right hand, just out of reach, she leaned forward. "Don't move," he yelled. "You're sinking deeper."

Felicia howled.

"I'll throw again," he said. This time, the rope landed on top of her. "Quick, over your head, under your arms –

hold on for dear life. Almond girl, back. That's right, girl."
He pushed against the mare's chest, urging her back while
keeping an eye on Felicia's body. Now that she was lying in
a twisted position on her side with only her face arched
above the surf, he couldn't tell if he had shifted her
enough. "Keep going, girl, back, back."

After several minutes, she shouted. "I'm out."

Simon waded forward, stepping with care before
putting his full body weight on the sand under the water.
"You could still be near a hole. Let me get you closer."

He pulled her through the water which was now up
past his knees. They had to get away as soon as possible.
"Can you stand?"

"Yes," she answered, but when she tried, her legs
gave way.

"Almond, come here, girl. Down, girl. Down. Get
down in the water." He pulled on the bridle to reinforce
the command. The horse knelt, her nostrils flaring at the
seawater lapping her chest. Simon helped Felicia onto
Almond's back and then pulled her to a standing position
before jumping on. With one hand around Felicia's
middle, he pulled the rein on the right. "Steady. Keep
moving, girl," he said. He could feel the mare's body
quiver under his legs

He didn't like being atop a horse in deep seawater
because they don't turn when treading water but travel in
a straight line. Then, if they lose their sense of direction
and get distressed, they swim away from land. As much as
he wished they could remain in more shallow depths, he
had to get them out past the rocks which clustered near
the shoreline.

Once in deeper water, he steadied Almond, keeping his voice calm though his heart pounded in his chest. "That's right, girl. You're doing fine." From time to time, the horse found sand bars to rest a few seconds before Simon urged her on. They had to reach the boat ramp before the tide was fully in. Almond would need it to get out of the sea. Another few miles, and he would believe there was a chance. Turning her head from left to right, her back twitching, Almond shifted down into deeper water again. She stretched her neck out, moving in rhythm with her legs until raising her head higher to pick up speed to mount a sizeable sandbar. It lifted her out of the water enough for Simon to change direction. He pulled the left rein, pointing her inland. It was their only hope. The rest of the shoreline was rocky cliffs. If they missed the ramp, Felicia and he would have to jump off to float with the current until they could find a place to get out of the sea. Would she have the strength if the worst happened? Several times, he had felt her body slump like a rag doll. What he didn't want to think about was Almond if they had to abandon her. Without him, she could panic and head out to sea.

From her laboured breathing, Simon could sense Almond's fatigue. He allowed her a rest again for a few minutes. "We're almost there, girl, but you're going to have to get off this sand bar, back into the water one last time for the big swim." Squeezing her sides with his calves, he spoke words of encouragement. "You can do it, girl. I know you can." The horse moved forward just as a rising swell appeared. It carried them up and then down. Almond's head went under water for a second. When she came back up, her eyes were wide with fear.

Further along the shoreline, he spotted the place. The ramp was still partially uncovered. "I see it, girl. Almost there," he kept murmuring as they swam through the last few hundred yards until the mare stood in the shallows, breathing hard.

"The best mare," he whispered, barely able to speak while he slid off and led them to the concrete boat ramp. Then, he reached up for Felicia with the words she had been waiting to hear. "We're on land. It's over. You're okay."

Feeling ashamed of how close she had come to drowning all of them, she couldn't look at him. "So sorry," she said in a croaky voice. "The water, the tide. Came in so quickly. I thought I was going to..." She burst into tears. He wrapped his arms around her, rocking her gently, patting her back while he checked his mobile for water damage. When he reached the farm hand, he asked for the horse trailer. Then, he rang Mrs Taylor to explain what had happened, and to ask for blankets for their arrival home. Felicia had begun to shiver uncontrollably.

"I can only imagine," he said to Felicia. "But you're out of the hole. We're all safe now. Let's get you home and into a hot bath. It's over."

Almond walked further up the ramp and on to the dirt track. She lowered her head over a large pothole filled with rainwater from last night's downpour. Blowing her nostrils over it, checking to make sure it wasn't salty, she drank it down to the mud.

"My sentiments exactly, girl," Simon said softly. "And

when we get home, I'm going to drink an entire jug of it – and then something stronger."

An air rescue helicopter appeared overhead, hovering before calling down through a loud speaker. "Are you okay?"

Simon signalled up that they were fine and assumed some concerned soul had alerted them. Now on hard ground, he and Almond would recover, but he wasn't sure about Felicia. She was white as a ghost.

Whatever the consequences of Mr Simon discovering that she knew about Daphne, Mrs Taylor realised she would just have to take them. The housekeeper had telephoned the sea rescue people immediately after Daphne had appeared in the laundry room to explain about Felicia and the mud. The two women had sat quietly waiting for the outcome. When Simon rang asking for blankets, the relief was enormous, but it didn't take Daphne long to see the ramifications now that all was well.

"This messes everything up, you do realise? Naturally, I'm happy the girl got out of the hole – a terrible end for anyone – and that Simon and Almond are fine, but we'll need to cancel our plans to drive her away from him and Menabilly until she recovers. She'll probably have to extend her stay, and the writing of my book will get further delayed."

Mrs Taylor turned her back on Daphne as she lifted the sheets from the dryer.

"Saints alive, woman, they've only just come out of the

water. I know how you feel, but there's nought to be done. We're lucky everyone is saved, not at the bottom of the sea, bless their souls. Let's see how things turn – she may want to get away from here as soon as possible. I wouldn't stay by the sea if it had nearly swallowed me up. I'm going upstairs to run a steamy bath for the girl, tuck some hot water bottles into the bed. She should have tea with brandy and probably an extra duvet. Wouldn't hurt for you to ask Miss Selby to come over, neither. The girl may need someone her own age tonight. She's had a terrible shock. And ask her to bring a warm nightdress or pyjamas. I know she has both. This girl sleeps in skimpy things. Won't do her no good putting those on. Also, best you tell Miss Selby to say she phoned them rescue people in case Mr Simon asks. Keeps me out of hot water, see."

"Oh yes, I forgot about that little detail. I shouldn't like to be in the room if he ever does discover you've been playing jokes on him all these years."

"There may be more important things to think about, mind. It's not a mad thought the girl will want to thank the person who raised the alarm today, and that, my lover, could set the cat amongst the pigeons."

Selby turned over the various outcomes that were too horrific to imagine. The important thing is that everyone is all right, she kept repeating to herself. Yet, the uneasy, queasy feeling in her stomach felt like she had just received the worst news. Daphne's power of description had, of course, painted vivid pictures: Felicia, pale,

197

ghostly, mud-caked; Simon riding at break-neck speed; Almond swimming in deep water to bring them to safety.

Feeling the sense of relief change to anger, she turned to Daphne. "It seems from what you say about that stretch of beach, it could've gone either way. Damn reckless of her – it might have resulted in both their deaths, not to speak of poor Almond's. She should have told Simon where she was going."

"Well, of course, she should have," Daphne agreed. "In my day, it was proper etiquette to say where one was off to if one was a guest in someone's house if for nothing else but local knowledge for the outing. Clara Vyvyan...do you know who I mean? No? Well, she lived in a house called Trelowarren, a beautiful house on the Helford River."

Daphne stopped speaking.

"Where do I get this information? One minute, I can't remember anything from my life, the next, something pops in, clear as gin, but will I know it tomorrow, I always wonder? Anyway, about Clara – she and I used to travel abroad to remote areas to walk and climb mountains. The very first thing we did was to gather local knowledge so as not to look a fool. It would've mortified Clara to have ended up in a mud hole, needing rescuing. Any local around here could tell you that bit of beach is often empty of people and for good reason. I did frequent it, but I knew what to look for. Coastlines change though. One should never assume because one knew a place ten years ago that it's stayed the same. The land is always shifting. The sea etches into the rock face. Wind and weather tear away banks and cliffs. Local knowledge is always important."

"Yes, well, thank you for that little geography lesson,"

Selby said, looking back down at the pages in her lap. "How is Simon?"

"You haven't seen Mouse, have you? I think he got a fright at the beach, and he hasn't answered my whistles all afternoon."

"No, I haven't seen that mongrel, but if I find that he's been sleeping on my pillow again, you're both going out the door."

Daphne thought it was better not to make excuses for the dog, but she was worried. He had not been around since finding Felicia. "To answer your question, I don't know how Simon is because I left to come here before he returned."

"And why did you feel the urgency to race over to tell me the latest?"

"That's a bit hard-hearted, and I refuse to believe that you are unmoved by Simon's brush with death today. All rubbish, I say. There was another reason I came over here though. Oh yes. Mouse. No, something else. Now, what was it? Ah, yes, Mrs Taylor suggests you go over to lend support and to bring a nightdress. Apparently, Felicia doesn't have –" Daphne stopped, putting her hand up to her mouth.

"Go on. Doesn't have what?"

"Um, doesn't have anything warm to wear to bed," she said quickly.

Getting up, throwing her notebook down on to the table, Selby replied with a sharp edge to her voice, "Why would she? She obviously thought the Cornish Riviera would be warm enough – one way or another."

"Yes, well, it's the 'another' you should be worried

about," Daphne blurted out. "You're in a rather off mood today if you don't mind my saying."

"No, I'm not. How many times do I have to tell you? Who Simon does or does not do the 'anothers' with, is none of my business. Now go somewhere else, please. I'll be over when I can."

"Can I tell Mrs Taylor you're bringing something for the girl to sleep in?"

"Yes, yes, yes. Now, vanish."

When she got upstairs to the bathroom, Selby leaned against the wall, overwhelmed by the emotions racing through her. She had done everything to hide her feelings from Daphne.

"Simon, dead," she whispered, shaking from the mere thought of it. How would she be feeling right now if he had died? She undressed and stepped into the shower to let hot water pelt down on her shoulders. Her thoughts came flying in one after the other. None of us ever knows what's about to happen. If he had died today, I would have been heartbroken not to have told him how I feel. He had said nothing about his feelings – a kiss at lunch, nothing more than the usual stuff men say at the beginning of romances. They hadn't known each other long, but the time spent writing Daphne's book had brought them closer. They laughed at the same things and thoroughly enjoyed making fun of Daphne. But about his past life with Felicia, she knew nothing. Presumably, she was still at Menabilly because Simon wanted her there. Reaching for the towel, Selby stepped out onto the bath mat. None of that would matter if he had died today, she reminded herself.

After dressing, she searched for a warm nightdress to take to Felicia. She found a little flannel number with large lambs on it that her mother had sent a few years ago, thinking she was still a child who wore nighties. It couldn't be more perfect, she decided. Throwing it in a bag, she left for Menabilly.

Having helped a shivering Felicia into Mrs Taylor's capable hands, Simon tended to Almond. Bolting out of the trailer, she ran to the gate and back several times. Eventually, she stood in the middle of her stall, flank muscles twitching, eyes half-closed, body slightly swaying. "The vet won't be long, girl. I just want him to look you over. Then you can have a rest in layers of fresh straw if that's what you want." Though now on solid ground, none of them would quickly forget the day's events. His own body moved from side to side as if still in the sea.

He walked the mare back and forth when the vet arrived. "A fit horse in middle age like Almond should recover in a few days," he told Simon. "Give her a hot bran mash with some carrots. Add some turmeric to warm her muscles."

Simon felt relieved that there had been no damage, but he stayed with Almond to make a fuss over her when the vet had left. He hosed the seawater off her body, afterwards towel drying her in the sun. The mare seemed to appreciate the massage. Several times, he thought she might lie down at his feet. He felt guilt about risking her life, but Daphne had been right to suggest riding to the beach. If he had not, the outcome may have been very different.

When Simon returned from a hot shower, Almond had eaten the mash, and the hay net was empty. She was out of her stall, leaning her neck over the gate as he approached. He grabbed a pitchfork to turn the deep layer of straw in her box. "Have a well-deserved rest, girl," he whispered.

As he arrived back from the stables, Selby's car was pulling up to the front door. He wanted to rush over to tell her he had thought only of her when facing the worst today. It had seemed an eternity before he was certain Almond would turn herself inland instead of drifting out to sea. While in the shower, the enormity of it all had hit him. His body had shuddered when he thought of Felicia's ashen face, the terrified look in her eyes as they arrived at the spot where she was trapped. Fuelled by adrenalin, he had managed to pull her out, not thinking about the next challenge until he noticed how high the tide had risen. Though he had reassured Felicia and Almond, he had not been certain of the outcome.

He walked to Selby's car, opened the door, and offered his hand to pull her up. "How's the ankle?" he asked.

"How's the ankle? You nearly drowned today, and you want to know how a little sprained ankle is doing? It's fine now, thanks. More importantly – how are you? Daphne told me the details. How's Felicia? Almond?"

"I haven't seen Felicia. Mrs Taylor said she's still sleeping soundly. She was in a bad state, so I rang the doc.

He gave her something strong to calm her down. It may have knocked her out. I would take you to see Almond, but I've just settled her. I feel awful I had to push her to the hilt, but if I hadn't..."

Selby could see he was having difficulty finishing the sentence. "Can't imagine what was going through her mind at certain points. Look, I've brought a nightdress for Felicia. Mrs Taylor suggested she needed something warm. Would you like me to look in on her?"

"I think we should let her rest. She's been through hell today. Have you got time to stay for a bit? A drink perhaps – or stay for supper. I could use the company. Mrs Taylor is leaving something."

"Yes, I can stay for both. The evening has turned sunny and warm. Gin and tonic in the garden sound good?"

"Been thinking about one for hours. Can you get some limes and ice from the fridge, and maybe crisps if you can find any? Then, you can tell me how your book is coming along. I'll get the drinks ready in the sitting room. Meet you there?"

"Fine. Won't be long." Selby wondered if he was really feeling as together as he appeared. He had only just managed a smile. You don't nearly end up at death's door one minute and make jokes the next. She gathered up the various bits in the kitchen and took the tray down the hall to the sitting room, stopping at the door. Simon's hands were up against the wall, his head hung low.

"You okay?"

"I'm not sure," he answered, "possibly delayed shock. I've been out with Almond all afternoon. This is the first time I've stopped apart from an eternity in a hot shower." He took the ice, adding a few cubes to their glasses, squeezing lime into each. When he tried to pour the gin, his hand was shaking so badly, it went all over the tray.

Selby gently took the bottle and mixed the drinks. "This should fix you up," she said, offering the glass. "Would you prefer to stay inside?"

"No, I'm fine – let's go out. There are some chairs and a table under the big Cedar of Lebanon in the sunken garden."

The mud pulled her body deeper, sucking her torso down further. Unable to move, Felicia cried out, jumping in her bed, opening her eyes, looking wildly around the room until she realised she was at Menabilly. Safe. Whatever the doctor had given her had left her mouth feeling like the Sahara. Dragging herself out of bed for some water, she plonked back down in a chair near the sink, overcome with lethargy. She tried to make sense of it all – one minute she was jogging up the beach, the next she was past her ankles in the mud hole. Her first impulse – to lift one foot, then the other – had sucked both trainers off, sinking her deeper past her calves. Clawing at the sand either side, trying to lift herself, had made matters worse. Until the woman explained that moving created a vacuum, she had been too panicked to rationalise the best course of action. Uncontrollable shaking began again as she thought back on the scene. If no one had come along the beach, she would be dead now – drowned – a horrible death – a lifeless corpse, submerged in water – body anchored in the mud – hair floating in slow motion, eyes open in disbelief.

"No, I'm alive." She repeated it over and over again.

When she calmed down, the other memory surfaced. He had ridden his horse to save her. Though she had been only vaguely aware of his approach, eventually he had convinced her to focus. He must care for me if he risked his life, she thought. Holding her tight atop Almond, swimming through the sea, it had made her feel safe to have his arms around her. Now, it sent a thrill through her body. She wanted to see him, to kiss his face, to thank him for saving her life. She felt better for getting out of bed, but was she able to get dressed and go downstairs to look for Simon? When she stood, her legs buckled. Leaning against the bathroom door for support, she looked out the window, noticing the blue line of the sea in the distance. It panicked her, and she shifted her eyes quickly away to the green of the garden below. She saw them sitting at a table. "What's Selby doing here?" she whispered. Stepping back from view, she watched their body language for several minutes before lying down on the bed again. "When you're stronger. When the fighting spirit has returned."

CHAPTER FIFTEEN

"Wonders never cease," Mrs Taylor murmured while she fixed up a tray. "I keep saying to myself what a different house would be here tonight if the worst had happened. I took some apples to Almond. Nothin' wrong with her appetite though she didn't move too quickly to the gate, but she'll come right in a few days. It's the filly upstairs I'm worried about. We've not heard a squeak from her. That stuff the doc gave her must've knocked her out. It should have worn off by now. Taking some broth up to her. She won't want proper food after everything, but this will keep the wolf from the door for the night. We'll see how she is in the morning. I've told Mr Simon I'll come in until she's got her legs again."

"Do you ever wonder why some things happen when they do?" Daphne asked.

"Nope. I just get on with my life, my work, mind my own business, and the rest takes care of itself."

Daphne didn't believe that for a moment. "No, I mean – here we were, wishing Felicia would leave, and this awful thing happens. Now, she might up and away. Never wanting to see the place again."

"Don't be daft, and I wouldn't count my chickens," the housekeeper warned. "Mind, there's no telling what'll happen when she's better. She may feel a strong bond with Mr Simon. You know, all them stories from the war? How some strangers stayed close for life when one of them pulled the other from death's door? Some married after such things."

"Over my dead body."

Mrs Taylor stated the obvious. "That will not be an obstacle. I've left a fish pie for them other two in the warming-oven. I'll be off home after I take this upstairs."

Shouldn't want anything that swims in the sea if I'd nearly drown in it, Daphne said to herself as she left to find Simon and Selby.

They sat for some time until Selby broke the silence. "You must be exhausted. Just say when you hit a wall and need to collapse." He seemed to be in a dream somewhere. Letting him drift until he wanted conversation, she could only imagine what must be going through his mind after the day's events.

"This Cedar of Lebanon is Daphne's favourite tree, you know. She's always saying it's the best place from which to admire the house. I could count on finding her here if I was on a 'hard-chair' with her when I was a boy.

Sorry, I was away with the faeries. Yes, I must be exhausted, not unreasonably, of course, but to tell the truth, I still have so much adrenalin pumping through me. If we weren't in the middle of Daphne's book, I'd hop on a plane."

Selby asked how long he stayed away when he travelled, but she was thinking – how often do you run away from life.

"Travel for three months, write for six. It has always suited me, and I always came back with a fresh perspective on things."

What things, she wondered. "And the other three months of the year?"

"Oh, those," he said. "Life, I guess. Something always pops up."

"Must be hard to keep relationships going," she said, and then wished she hadn't.

"It is. No relationship develops without nurturing; even I know that. Perhaps I just haven't had any I wanted to develop enough to stick around. Had my share though. Felicia and I –"

Daphne announced her presence, staying only long enough to let them know that a tray had gone up to Felicia, and that Mrs Taylor had left a fish pie in the oven for them. "Though a bacon and egg sandwich might be more to one's liking tonight," she added before disappearing. She wanted to sneak into the girl's room to see if she was sitting up; gauge the chances of a quick recovery.

Felicia was sleeping peacefully when Daphne looked in on her. Bodes well, she thought. Any number of grizzly scenes could have kept her tossing and turning. Looking out of the window at the good, south-facing views of the garden with the sea beyond, she wondered why some people didn't take to such a lovely room, leaving all that rubbish about a Blue Lady aside.

"You – today," she heard Felicia whisper. "At the beach."

She turned to look at the girl who had lifted her head up from the pillow and was pointing a finger in her direction. Panicking, she wished for Mrs Taylor's help and vanished, finding herself in the middle of a small room. A black lab began barking.

"Shush," she whispered to the dog as she looked around, wondering where she was.

A man called out from another room. "Quiet. Any more noise and you go out for the night."

The dog heeded his master's command but continued staring at Daphne. A low, guttural growl grew back into a loud bark. Mrs Taylor came out to investigate. Seeing Daphne, she pulled the door closed, putting her finger to her lips. "What are you doing here?" she asked in a hushed voice. Grabbing her coat off the hook, she went out to the yard.

Daphne followed. "I just thought of your face and ended up here. Never been able to do that before – into someone else's house, I mean, except for Menabilly and Rose Cottage. Anyway, I'm here because I got into a panic. Felicia saw me. I was in her room checking on how she was doing, and she saw me. She spoke to me and said I was the one at the beach. I was in an invisible state in her room, so how could she have seen me?"

The housekeeper walked back and forth thinking. "I've no answer for that. In the morning, I'll ask Cousin Rachel before I go to Mena. She's the keeper of knowledge like this since Nan died. Get away from here now. We keep farmers' hours, and five comes soon enough. Any more ruckus and himself will come out to snoop. Nothing to do about it tonight," she insisted before going back inside. But Mrs Taylor was worried. How *would* they get rid of the woman if she could see Daphne?

The scent of something heavenly filled the kitchen. Taking Mrs Taylor's fish pie out of the oven to a mat on the table, Selby served up two plates. While she savoured every mouthful, she made a mental note to ask the house-keeper for the recipe.

Simon pushed the food around on his plate without tasting any of it until Selby finally said something. "Why don't I make Daphne's bacon and egg idea?" she asked.

He got up to go to the fridge. "I can make it myself."

"Just for tonight, I'm going to be bossy, okay? It'll be ready in a few minutes."

"Thanks. I think I'll have a quick look at Almond in that case while you're doing that. Be back in a –"

Screams interrupted his sentence. They ran out to the hall. Felicia was standing at the top of the stairs, crying hysterically, jumping up and down in one spot. Simon rushed up to her. She flung her arms around him, babbling incoherently, pointing to her room, shaking uncontrollably. Speaking in a gentle, soothing tone, he walked her down the hall. Selby retreated.

After ten minutes, he came back to the kitchen. "I'm sorry. She's in a bad way and going on about something on her legs in the bed – probably reliving today's horrors. I must stay with her and try to calm her down. She needs me," he said before disappearing back upstairs.

"Fine. You stay with her – it's obviously what you need, too," Selby said quietly as she left Menabilly.

Daphne had gone along all these years with a certain knowledge of her existence, not the whys and wherefores, but the basic facts: she had willed Simon and his mother to see her, otherwise she was invisible to the living. Mrs Taylor had 'the gift', as she called it, so that didn't count. Then her departure to Rose Cottage where she had chosen to show herself to Selby. How Felicia managed to see her tonight was a mystery.

Were those the rules in her world? Once you show yourself to someone, you remain visible to them? No, that can't be right, she reasoned. Slipping into invisibility was something she did regularly around both Simon and Selby. It was too confusing. Over the years, she had wondered how it all worked. Analysing it got her into a more muddled state, and though deciding it was better to accept what was, questions remained, nevertheless.

Why, for example, didn't she see others who had 'gone over'? She hated the phrase. Gone over where? 'To the other side' was another pearl. Silly. People bought into all kinds of stories about what happens after death though perhaps an essence of oneself remained in places that held joyous memories. She wished she could ask someone about these things. Simon's mother had gone to that medium. All she came back with was that she would be here for as long as she needed to be. If the medium meant she had a mission, she considered it had to do with writing *Pistol Meadow*. Whatever happened now, she knew that Simon and Selby would find a way to finish it.

She had grown fond of Selby – very like me in lots of ways, she thought – an independent soul, strong character, good brain. She puts iron gates up as defences though, forged from all that business with the parents that I heard her explaining to Simon. When will she drop all that nonsense and realise he's so perfect for her? And dear Simon – I've nurtured his soul, lavished love, dealt a rollicking when necessary. I'd like to think I've had a hand in what he's become – a loving spirit, capable of giving and receiving love. If only that damn woman hadn't shown up.

Walking into the sitting room, Selby threw her handbag down on the table, startling Daphne out of the deep conversation she had been having with herself, causing her to fly to a corner.

"Makes a nice change," Selby said. "Haven't managed to make you jump since I've known you."

"I was deep in thought, considering how I came to be here and why."

"Afraid you've got less existential questions to

consider, Dame Daphne, and much more pressing problems to solve."

"Don't call me that."

"Oh yes, read some place you hated the 'Dame' bit.
Think you said it sounded a bit like a pantomime. Did you
give an interview saying that you would've rather had
Menabilly conferred on you? Very funny. There must've
been something nice about the honour though."

"There was. One," she answered before reciting a
doggerel.

"Who wrote that?" Selby asked.

"A chap called Sir John Wolfenden."

From Daphne's quiet reply, Selby sensed it had been
an emotional recitation. Deciding to take a softer
approach, she explained that Mouse was probably in Felicia's bedroom.

"What?"

"Yup, I've just come from Menabilly. We were in the
kitchen when suddenly Felicia screamed at full volume
from the top of the stairs, shouting about something
sitting on her legs. Having had the pleasure of your mutt
doing the same to me, I'm making an educated guess.
Simon rushed up to look after her. Quite a touching little
scene."

Daphne sensed Selby was leaving something out, but
decided to ignore it for information on her dog. "I've been
calling that Westie all evening. I don't understand where
he goes. He's off sometimes for days. This is not good
news though. It makes things damned difficult. How am I
to get him out of her bedroom?"

"Simple. Get yourself over there now and grab the thing by the scruff of the neck."

"Yes, that would've been a good plan were it not for the fact that I checked on Felicia earlier this evening while she was sleeping. She opened her eyes and saw me."

"Ah, that explains the state she was in tonight. Thought people couldn't see you except when you wanted them to?"

"I've been going over such things in my mind all night. I'm no closer to any answers. I was on the beach with Mouse this morning when he disappeared. When I found him, he was barking at Felicia in the mud hole. I transported as quickly as possible to Simon, and that's it – nothing out of the ordinary. What a fright I got tonight when she spoke to me."

"A certain justice in that, but you've got to grab hold of the mongrel. No telling what deranged state it will send Felicia into."

"Wait a minute," Daphne said. "Felicia in a state? That's exactly what we do need."

"What do you mean?"

"You're not going to like it, and I'm not sure I should confide."

"Confide what?"

"Mrs Taylor and I had a plan to scare Felicia into leaving Menabilly. Yesterday, when she was there cleaning, she implied there were ghosts in the house. I was to go into her room tonight to get Mouse to jump on top of the bed. When Felicia turned on the light, she would see neither the dog nor me, but she would still feel him on her legs. That was supposed to give her a real fright, so she would pack up, and leave you and Simon, and..."

"So that we could finish your book? Honestly, you are a rotten ghoul."

"No, no – so you and Simon could fall in love."

Selby walked over to the drinks table to pour a swallow of cognac into a snifter glass. "Just the one," she said, smiling at Daphne. "I know better since the night I met you when I had an overly generous amount – let you out of the bottle, so to speak." She sat down on the sofa thinking about the whole situation, feeling touched that a plot had been hatched to clear the way for her and Simon. "Dearest Daphne," she said with affection, "if Simon and I are meant to be together, it will happen. It's nothing to do with you."

"But it is, you see. I want him settled with someone he can love. That girl is selfish. She won't make him happy. Plus, you're a bit backward in expressing yourself. All that tosh earlier this evening, hiding your true feelings when I told you that Simon could have drowned. I know you better than you think – you're a bit like me. I was never very good about expressing my own feelings though I gave characters in my books plenty to say on that score."

It was late, and Selby didn't think her chances of winning the argument very good. "Let's talk about it tomorrow."

"Mrs Taylor is speaking to her cousin, Rachel, in the morning. She knows about the spirit world. She's going to ask how Felicia could see me when I did not will it myself."

"Always wondered why you chose to show yourself to me," Selby said.

"I think it's something to do with the book," Daphne replied with hesitation. "I'm not altogether sure, but I was thinking about it before you arrived back just now."

Selby groaned. "Ah, yes, of course – the book." She went up to bed.

CHAPTER SIXTEEN

"There might be a tear in the ether," Cousin Rachel explained to Mrs Taylor, "or them things about saving a person's life. Better fit would be what Nan always said – that if a spirit interfered with the living and a life was saved, there could remain a thread, connecting them evermore. And another thing – the spirit may not be able to close the opening. Could be it remains visible to everyone until it's time for it to shove off, you know? Understand this though – spirits either remain or come back for a reason. Yours will have a definite purpose for being here. Otherwise, it would've gone long ago."

It was all too confusing. She asked if Nan had ever spoken of anyone from parts around who could help with such things.

"All her cronies have long been dead. Nothin' much else to say, but what I said – it may be visible to everyone now, maybe forever, and possibly to the life it saved."

Mrs Taylor wished her cousin had not constantly

referred to dear Daphne as 'It', but, nevertheless, this was not good news. Would Daphne remain visible, unable to get Mouse out of Felicia's room? No one else could see the dog to grab him. She would have to get Felicia out of the house long enough for Daphne to go into Blue Lady.

By the time she arrived at Menabilly, she had hatched a plot. Simon was sitting at the table with his head in his hands. He glanced up when she came into the kitchen. "Pardon me for saying, but you look awful, Mr Simon."

"I slept in a chair in Felicia's room all night. She had delayed shock from everything yesterday, and by the way, Mrs Taylor, you've known me since I was a boy. I would rather you called me Simon, please."

"Very nice, I'm sure, but I'm a creature of habit, Mr Simon, and too old for change. How is she upstairs?"

"She was asleep when I came down just now."

"I'll take her some ballast. See how things are."

"We had an awful time last night. She was hysterical. It took ages to calm her down, and to get her to sleep. Then, she kept waking, checking to see if I was still in the room."

The housekeeper saw the opportunity to rattle forth with her plan. "She needs a dose of fresh air. Perhaps out of the house for a bit – you know, have a change of scene – take her out of herself. What about Fowey for a few hours? Maybe find her a little something to cheer her up?"

"I suppose I could if you really think it would help. I'm worried about her. She had such a crazed look last night, I considered getting the doctor again."

"Let me have a snoop."

Felicia was sitting in a chair by the window when Mrs

Taylor walked in with tea and toast. "Better in morning light, my girl? I saw Mr Simon downstairs."

"He slept in this chair all night," Felicia said, feeling embarrassed the housekeeper had obviously heard all the details.

"He was worried about you. Such a kind man, Mr Simon is. He's having his coffee. Then he's going to Fowey. Why don't you go too, and –"

"Oh, I don't think I..."

"He was saying he wants to find something nice for you – to cheer you up and all."

"Really? Did he say that?"

"Yes. Very concerned, he was. Thinks the doc should come back. Men! They're no good at coping with things like this, are they? Oh, it's okay when we're standing on our two feet, looking pretty, doing their bidding, but the moment our nerves kick up, they – well, you know what I mean, don't you, my lover?" She let the words percolate for a few minutes while she tidied the bed.

Felicia didn't reply. She was considering how her hysterics might have made her look – how she had screamed like a banshee from the top of her lungs.

"So, I've got to be getting back downstairs to my work," Mrs Taylor said at the door when she finished the bed. "I'll pop in while Mr Simon's gone this morning."

"I think I would like to go with him," Felicia said quickly, "just for a little while."

"Good girl. Just the tonic. Do some shopping. Have some lunch in that nice pub by the water."

Felicia gave a little cry.

"No, I mean that nice pub at the bottom by the church.

I'll just pop down to say you're going. In an hour? Enough time?"

"Yes."

"She'd like to go," Mrs Taylor said dryly to Simon.

"Really? I didn't think she would agree to leave the house."

"Well, women have a way of surprising. Why not find a nice present for her in one of them shops? I'd be clucking if Mr Taylor bought me something, not that he ever would."

"I'm not very good at waiting around in shops," he said, "but I've had a list of things I need from the DIY since last week. Do you think she could manage on her own while I go there?"

"A snoop along the high street might work. Make her feel you want to give her something nice."

"I don't want her to think –"

"No, course not, but the opening of a wallet distracts most females, if you don't mind me saying. Get her thinking about something besides yesterday. She may come right. All that business last night roaring up – delayed reaction they call it."

Simon sighed. "If you think it will help. I'm checking on Almond before I go up to shower."

When Simon left for the stable, Mrs Taylor rang Selby. "Tell Daphne to wait an hour. Then get herself here with speed. Mr Simon's taking Felicia to Fowey. There's no telling for how long. That dog must go from Mena."

. . .

"How's my girl this morning?" Simon asked Almond when he arrived at the stables. He slipped a head-collar on her. "Let's see how you're doing."

Taking her into the yard, he walked her up and down, searching for any signs of lameness. "A bit hesitant, aren't you, but I don't see any problems. Are you ready to be turned out onto some nice fresh grass? I think it would be good to get you into a larger space."

He moved Almond along the track to a paddock where he slipped his hand under the rail to open the gate. Leading the horse forward, he unclipped the lead rope. She bolted to the other side, kicking out behind, trotting back and forth along the far fence line. "Full of it, aren't you? Good sign all is well," he called out to the horse who whinnied back several times. While he walked back to the house, he couldn't help feeling cheered up by Almond's sound gait and reaction to fresh grass. Perhaps Fowey would be a tonic for him as well as for Felicia.

"If you're asking me, it's a daft plan," Mrs Taylor said. "If you had control over that dog, it might be an idea, but you don't. If – and here's the ball of wax – if, the girl couldn't see you, it would be fine, but she can. Rachel told me this morning there might've been a tear in the ether; maybe everyone can see you now."

"Well, we must find out if people can in fact see me," Daphne said. "How does one go about that? One can't just walk down Main Street in Fowey."

"Why not? Any locals who knew you are either in one

of them homes hanging on by a thread, or under the sod. You are a hundred and twelve."

"Very funny, but I had lots of friends younger than I. Anyway, I couldn't go to Fowey even if I wanted to. I've tried plenty of times to wish myself to Paris or London or even to friends' houses in Cornwall. I've only ever managed Menabilly, Rose Cottage and your house in the last few days. It does seem, of course, that I can attach myself to Selby or Simon and go where they go, so I suppose I could traipse behind one of them to see what happens."

"There, you see. A solution. Easy."

"But I'm not doing it," Daphne shot back.

Selby had been listening to the two of them going back and forth over the same ground while considering the dilemma herself. "I think I have the solution," she finally said. "George Renfold lives with his family a few fields over from here. I could ring him – make an excuse to stop by. Daphne could come in afterwards, and we can see what happens. If people see her, she can say she's lost and needs directions. If no one says anything, we can assume that she's invisible again. The whole thing can be sorted in fifteen minutes."

Having reached a consensus, she took out her mobile. "Hello. George? It's Selby." Daphne and Mrs Taylor listened to Selby explain that she wanted to bring a bottle of whiskey as a thank you for his having mended her fences.

"All set then," she said, turning off the phone. "We'll go over before their supper."

"You remember there's no parking in Fowey," Simon said to Felicia, "so, I'm going to drop you along Main Street up ahead. I'll drive through the one-way system to leave the car at the top. It's probably not a great idea for you to walk too far today. I've only got a small list for the DIY." Sensing anxiety, he glanced over at her. "I won't be long. I'll easily find you in one of the shops down this street. Just have a look to see if you can find something – think you deserve a little retail therapy – my treat."

"That's very sweet of you, but it's not necessary," she said, opening the door of the car.

He stuck his head out the window. "Hey, look in that place called Salt; it's got quite nice stuff."

As she walked through the door, a canvas handbag with a navy body and red strap caught her eye. Very nice, she thought, but what I really want from him isn't in a shop. He doesn't know how I feel, but I can't just blurt it out. Perhaps something subtle like a small book of poems would work. I could leave one marked; slip it under his pillow tonight.

She left the shop and wandered further down the street, stopping at an open shop-front. "Isn't there a book-shop some place around here?"

A man looked up. "Down the bottom, near to St Fimbarrus's. It's the big parish church. You want Book-ends, my lover."

Muscles in her legs ached with every step down the steep main street. When she arrived in the square at the bottom, she stopped to rest, leaning against a shop-front window. A large, sepia-coloured photograph on an easel caught her eye. Putting her hands up to her eyes to shade the glare reflecting off the glass, she quickly backed away, and then inched back to have another look. "That's her," she whispered.

Hearing the bell ring when the door opened, the lady behind the till looked up. "Good afternoon."

Felicia pointed to the window. "That photograph on the easel there...may I see it please?"

"It's a lovely photo, isn't it? We sell copies of it here in the shop. We have it in black and white, if you'd prefer, instead of the sepia tone. Shall I show them both to you? Most of her books are against the wall. If you're interested in original covers and older editions, over there," she said, pointing to a shelf. "We specialise in her books – well, and, of course, also other writers connected to Cornwall like Winston Graham, Leo Walmsley, Denys Val Baker, A. L. Rowse, and Sir Arthur Quiller-Couch. There are new, second-hand, and antiquarian copies. Was it just hers you were interested in?"

Though she had begun to guess the answer, Felicia asked in a tentative voice, "Who – um, who is it in the photo?"

"Oh, sorry, I thought you knew. I always assume everyone recognises that face. It's the writer, Daphne du Maurier."

Felicia stumbled out of the shop, trying to make sense of what was going through her mind. It's an absurd thought, she told herself. Looking around for some place to sit quietly for a few minutes, she noticed the church, and went inside. "Was it her in my room last night and at the beach? Spitting image," she kept repeating, "but that's not possible. She's dead, unless I've seen a –"

The deafening bells in the church tower suddenly chimed the midday hour. They startled her out of the confused state into which she had descended. What she was contemplating not only made her feel foolish, but the possibilities were terrifying. She needed Simon. Rushing out of the church and up Main Street, she popped into every shop, getting herself in a state when she couldn't find him. Running back down the hill, she spotted him leaning against the window of Bookends. She sprinted over, nearly knocking him down.

"There you are," he said. "I was just about to look inside for you. I've been into all the shops up and down the street. Sorry if I missed you. I ended up taking the stuff from the DIY back to the car. Did you find something?"

Felicia pointed to the window, her hand shaking. "Her," she said. "On the beach. In my room last night."

Simon's knees buckled when he looked at the photograph. "Who?" he asked in as nonchalant a voice as he could muster.

"Her," she said in a hushed voice, looking around to be sure no one was close enough to hear what she was about to say. "The ghost of Daphne du Maurier."

Think, man, think, he commanded himself. Laughing a bit too loudly, he said. "You're frightening me, Felicia."

"I know. It's a scary thought," she agreed. "Have you seen her as well?"

"What? I meant I'm worried about what you've just said. Perhaps it was too soon to expect you to bounce back from the shock. Look, the doctor who came to the house yesterday – his office is just around the corner. Come on, let's go there. He might be able to take a walk-in. Just depends on how busy he is."

"No. No doctor. I just want to think about things myself for a minute. The woman on the beach looked just like the photograph in this window. I know what I saw. She lived at Menabilly, didn't she?"

"Yes, she did, but um, long before our side of the family went to live there. A more plausible explanation," he said in his calmest voice, "is that you saw a woman on the beach who looks like this photo. The old boy who drove to Menabilly to raise the alarm said he met a tourist who was all out of breath from running to find help. He's got a small lean-to there – you know, the boat ramp where we came out of the sea?

Felicia shook her head.

"I'm not surprised you didn't notice it. He knew Menabilly was minutes up the hill, so he raced in his Land Rover to find someone."

She thought about things for a few seconds before protesting, "But what about last night in my room? I saw her again."

This was certainly news to him. Had Daphne been in Felicia's room? "Do you think what the doctor gave you produced a hallucination? I'm no expert on these things. Let's go ask him."

Averting her eyes from the photograph, she leaned against the bookshop's window. "I don't know. I'm confused."

"The other thing that's just popped into my head is

that you had a very narrow escape yesterday. Let's face what a serious thing it really was. If it hadn't been for that tourist, you wouldn't be standing here. Let's not dwell on that for too long though. Perhaps last night, feeling dopey from the medication, you kept reliving the moment. Perhaps you want to thank the woman so you're conjuring up her image?"

"And what about feeling something on my legs in bed last night, a weight?"

"Is it also surprising that you would still feel the weight of that mud crushing against your legs?"

Thinking back on the mud, she shivered, but he had a point. His was a more rational explanation. The other idea was too fantastic to believe. She began to feel foolish. What must he think of her? Forcing a smile, she grabbed his hand, doing her best to push away what she had so firmly believed a few minutes before. "You are sensible. I thought maybe I was losing my mind. It must, as you say, be delayed shock. I hope you don't think I'm ready for the loony bin."

"Of course not. None of this is that surprising when you think what you went through yesterday," he said with huge relief in his voice. "We ought to be celebrating yesterday's outcome, not dwelling on the details of it all. Let's go in there. They've got quite good food. We'll have some lunch."

Felicia let Simon lead her in. They sat at a table in the back.

"Two chardonnays," he said when the waitress appeared, "and two Ploughman's Lunches, no onion."

"You remember?"

"Of course, I remember. No onion, no ice in your gin and tonic, no calamari."

Two large glasses of wine were set down in front of them. If he hadn't been driving, he would have ordered two just for himself. What had Daphne been doing in Felicia's room? Keep talking, you fool, he told himself. You don't want her settling back on that idea of Daphne's ghost.

"To good times," he said, raising his glass.

"To better times," she replied quietly.

The silence hung mid-air. His mind raced for a topic. Anything to avoid the mention of Daphne would do. "Pretty place, Fowey, isn't it? Too many people in the summer, but good for the local economy. If it weren't for summer and national holiday trade, I'd worry for our lovely village port. Hey, let's drink to the tourists who come to Fowey." Simon simply wet his lips while Felicia slowly drank from her glass. He could see her mind working under the furrowed brow.

"Simon, I was just wondering about something else from yesterday."

"Quite right, let's drink to the lucky outcome of yesterday," he said, raising his glass again. "Plenty to be happy about." She grinned, following suit. "And what about Almond? She deserves a toast at the very least. To a mare in a million." He raised the glass again.

"You're the best tonic a girl could have. I don't need a new handbag to make me feel better, not with you around."

"Let's drink to me, then – hooray."

"To my knight in shining armour." She drained her

glass. "I can think of plenty of girls who would give their best Manolo Blahnik shoes to be rescued by a handsome man galloping a horse down a beach."

"Let's drink to the girls with Manalo Blahniks. Why not?"

Felicia was giggling by now. Her cheeks were flushed. "Oops," she said, turning her glass upside down. "All gone."

"Then have some of mine," he said, pouring half his glass into hers. "I'll order more."

Two large glasses later and barely any food consumed, he ploughed Felicia and himself into the local bus that took people from town up to the car park. She was glassy-eyed, but quiet. He could only hope that when she sobered up, she wouldn't continue the subject of Daphne's ghost.

CHAPTER SEVENTEEN

ig George opened the door. "Well, well," he said to Selby. "Son George said you would be here at six, and here you are on the dot. I like a punctual girl." He planted a wet kiss on her forehead.

She wanted the family focused on her when Daphne showed up. "Do you know what that handsome son of yours did?" she asked.

"No, what?" Margaret came towards her, leaning in to give a hug.

"You might not have realised it when I was here for dinner a few weeks ago, but I'm really a city girl – no idea about sheep, cows, or goats –"

"We won't have goats here," Big George interrupted. "Stinky, destructive things."

"No, that's right. We won't have goats," Margaret said.

"Your wonderful son mended my fences. Didn't ask him to. Did it off his own bat. Isn't that the sweetest thing?"

Big George jumped in again. "And it kept them from getting in with our prized Herdwicks."

Son George came down the stairs. "You're here. I didn't hear the car drive up." He gave Selby a lingering kiss on her lips.

Cheeky bugger, she thought – he knew I couldn't pull away in front of his parents. When she tried to step back, she felt a push from behind, propelling her back into his arms. George reciprocated, wrapping his arm around Selby's shoulder.

Margaret grinned from ear to ear, happy to see her eldest being affectionate to Selby. Narrow hips or not on the girl, I need grandkids, she mused. "I'm not taking any excuses now. We've got a delicious steak and kidney pie in the oven. There's all of us here tonight. You make six. Let's go into the lounge. What's been going on with you since we last saw you?"

"Been writing," Selby replied.

"Writing what?"

"I'm writing a book on Mary Hemingway."

Sister Sarah came in from the kitchen. "Hello, Selby. It's so nice to see you again," she said as she leaned down to give her a friendly peck on the cheek.

Selby suddenly felt uneasy. Big wet kiss from the father, hug from the mother, cheeky kiss from George, friendly peck from the sister. What's he been saying, she wondered. It's all a bit too familiar compared to the last time I was here.

"Here we go, glasses for everyone," Son George said, opening the whiskey Selby had brought. "To decent prices at livestock auctions next week."

"To a successful harvest in September," his brother called out, bounding down the stairs. Advancing towards Selby, he put his hand on her waist, pulling her towards him to plant a kiss on her forehead. She felt another push from behind. Ben's surprised look settled into a satisfied grin, causing her to move quickly away.

Selby hoped no one else had noticed it appeared as if she had just made a pass at George's brother. She was certain now that Daphne was in the room, playing tricks. That proved she was, once again, invisible, and while that was a good thing, she wished she would stop being a nuisance.

When they had finished what was in their glasses, Margaret called everyone into the kitchen.

"Now, Selby, you sit between the two boys and Sarah, you and I will sit either side of your father. Son George, open that wine you ran to Tesco's to buy earlier this evening. He nearly didn't make it back in time for your arrival," Margaret said to Selby, winking as if they had just shared a secret. George shot arrows at his mother as he rooted around in the drawer for the corkscrew. "He said you gave him a lovely supper a few months ago, and that you served red wine with it. We don't drink much in this house except for weddings and funerals. Seems to go straight to all Renfolds' heads – then harsh words pass between us and before you know it, there's a puddle on the floor."

There was silence all around.

"I mean from the dog," Margaret said quickly. "Even though he's housebroken, he gets all riled up if there's a family row." Short, nervous laughs came from the table while Sarah put plates of food in front of each of them. The sheepdog sprang up, rushing for the nearest person's legs.

"Down, Ben-Ben," Big George said. "I won't have any of that when we have company."

Selby looked at George's younger brother, Ben.

"I know," he said, looking at her inquiring face. "Unfortunate, isn't it? With all the names you could choose for a sheepdog, it had to be mine."

"No, now that's not accurate, Ben, and you know it," his mother insisted. "You got the name first. Then we got the sheepdog when you were a toddler. You howled like a banshee if we didn't let the pup sleep in your room, and in the interest of some shut-eye ourselves, we let him. After that, the dog followed you around like a shadow. So, we called him Ben-Ben. Makes perfect sense, don't you think, Selby?"

Selby was about to reply when Ben-Ben began whimpering. Hackles on end, he dashed under the table, barking, knocking into everyone's legs. Big George yelled at the dog.

"Pack it in or else you're getting chucked in the kennel."

There was quiet while everyone helped themselves to gravy being passed around. When it came to Selby, she was about to pour some over her plate when she felt something touch her right leg. Ben cleared his throat, grinning at her when she turned her head to look at him incredulously. His foot was now moving up and down her calves. Daphne giggled from behind her chair. Selby moved her legs sideways out of reach and tried again to pour gravy over the pie. Daphne jostled her arm. The gravy landed on her jeans. Ben, quick off the mark, reached for a tea towel, and slowly mopped up the gooey liquid from her lap while smiling like a stupid puppy. George looked sideways, then over to his mother, and back at his brother.

"That'll do, Ben," Margaret said.

"I must have this recipe, Mrs Renfold," Selby said quickly. "It's first class. What's your secret for such crispy pastry?"

Relieved to have something to distract her from the disturbing fact that her youngest son had just been too familiar with his brother's girlfriend, she explained her theory of using lard for top quality results.

Daphne, now visible to Selby, walked around the table looking at everyone, talking over Margaret's detailed instructions. "I was always partial to a good steak and kidney pie. Is it good?" she asked. "This lot looks like they would gobble anything. When can we go? I'm getting bored just watching everyone eat. Oh, don't look so cross. You know they can't hear me. If you're annoyed at my rubbing the brother's leg, don't be. Always so serious, our Selby. Why not take a lighter view? Might perk up your love life. It was all just a bit of harmless fun. I'll fix it. Then, I'm going upstairs to use the phone to ring your mobile. And you needn't arch that eyebrow. Yes, I do know your number. I memorised it from the list on your desk in case I ever needed to ring you, and here we are. In the meantime, instead of nourishing that sour look on your face, concentrate on what you're going to say when the phone rings."

Sarah started up a conversation about the office invoices which were going out late. George took advantage of the family's discussion to turn to Selby. Looking like a Cheshire Cat, he leaned over to whisper while rubbing her leg with his foot. "Ah, I felt that just now. Very nice. We can leave this lot shortly if you like. Fancy going for a walk after dinner, some place we can be alone?"

Glancing at him sideways with a look that offered no encouragement, she wondered exactly what Daphne had done to solicit such a suggestion. I am going to kill her when we leave here, she thought before realising the futility of the threat. Her mobile started ringing its Brazilian rumba tune. Both brothers grinned as they saw her hand reach down under the table for her bag. "I'm so sorry. I thought it was turned off. I'll just get rid of whoever it is."

Selby put the phone to her ear. She heard Daphne. "I'm positively going to go stark, raving mad if we don't get out of here. I tried to go on my own, but the rules, what-ever they are, won't let me out the door without you, it appears. So, quick as you can, or I'll make more mischief."

"Oh God, Joanna, I forgot," Selby said. "Waiting outside my door now? No, I can be home in ten minutes. I hadn't planned to stay out to supper tonight. Completely forgot you were stopping by. Be right there." She turned off her phone.

"Don't beat yourself up, dear. I did corral you into stay-ing. You get your things, and hopefully we'll see you soon," Margaret said while tilting her head at George to send a message he should see her out.

"No, no. I wouldn't think of disturbing George's

supper," Selby quickly announced to the table. "I'll just slip out and please forgive me for leaving. It's just that Joanna is like a sister to me. She's driven all the way from London, hoping to break the journey to Penzance. Thank you for the delicious pie."

Daphne was standing at the door, tapping her foot. "Good God, I thought you would be an eternity in there."

When they were in the car, Daphne waited for an eruption, but none came. It wasn't until they were inside Rose Cottage that Selby spoke. "I consider your actions tonight a real betrayal, not the actions of a friend."

Daphne shook her head from side to side about to defend herself, but Selby put her hand up to stem any retort.

"Don't interrupt. Against my better judgement, I went to George's house tonight to help you out of a difficult situation. Knowing that I've done everything to dissuade George from thinking I fancied him, I came up with the idea of going to Renfolds to figure out if strangers could see you. And what do you do? You push me into both brothers' arms, rub their legs under the table, and make them think it was me doing it all. It was an embarrassing situation, and it made me cringe. You gave no thought to what will happen when George shows up here in the next few days, looking for further action. You've pissed me off in a big way. I have no interest in hearing anything more from you tonight." Selby stormed off up the stairs, banging her bedroom door.

Wincing from the tongue-lashing, Daphne grumbled, "I didn't mean to cause such a ruckus," until gushing moments later, "But happily this regrettable evening proves I am once again invisible. Hurrah."

"To speak plain, Mr Simon, it was not the idea I gave; the girl's pickled," Mrs Taylor said after putting Felicia to bed. "I got her into Miss Selby's flannel nightdress. She's out cold for the moment. What happened to the shops idea?"

He paced the room talking non-stop. "Just be grateful I was able to convince Felicia to drink up. I've had the most nerve-racking afternoon. Took me ages to convince her that she had most definitely not seen a ghost. She saw a photo of Daphne du Maurier in the window of Bookends. Then, she kept insisting she was the woman at the beach and in her room last night." He stopped speaking suddenly, worried he had sounded too matter-of-fact about Daphne, and quickly added, "Crazy, isn't it?"

Mrs Taylor thought for a moment, weighing up the pros and cons of what she was about to say. "Maybe not so crazy?"

"What?" There was no mistaking the surprise in his voice.

"The girl did see Daphne's ghost on the beach and in her room last night." She let the sentence hang mid-air for a few moments before deciding not to pussyfoot around the subject any more. "Time we speak truth, Mr Simon. I seen Daphne since my first day at Mena. Got a gift for it from my nan."

"What?" he said again.

"Long story it is, and if you'll excuse me saying, water

under the bridge for the moment. The big headache is
Daphne's dog, Mouse. He was in Felicia's room last night;
probably still is. No use me going up there to grab it 'cause
only Daphne can see the thing. It was Mouse who found
the girl in the mud. Daphne went looking for him and
then saw her."

He was dumbstruck that Mrs Taylor knew about
Daphne, but decided all the different things running
through his head would have to wait. "I don't know what
to say, but leaving aside the confusion I feel, I see now that
poor Felicia wasn't blathering nonsense. Blast, I met the
mongrel when Selby and I first found Daphne's unfinished manuscript under the bed in her room." He paused.
"Well, that's another story."

Sighing, she turned to dishes at the sink. "Know about
that too, but can we fix on this dog? We've a devil of a
problem. Daphne saw him last night on the girl's bed.
While you were in Fowey, she came over to grab the
blighter, but he wasn't here. He's been disappearing a lot
lately, and she has no idea where he goes when he goes."

"But how was Felicia able to see Daphne last night?
She's never shown herself to any friends I've had here over
the years. It's sort of an unwritten understanding between
us."

"My cousin, Rachel – she knows about the spirit world
– says sometimes there's a tear in the ether. Strange things
can happen. She's not sure if Daphne will stay visible to
everybody from now on or if things will right themselves.
Daphne needs to be invisible to get Mouse out of that
bedroom or that girl could screech again tonight. They've
gone over to Renfold's farmhouse to check things out."

"What could George Renfold possibly have to do with all this?" he asked.

"They went there at six o'clock. Daphne was to follow Miss Selby into the house to test if the family could see her. As none of them connect to the whole mess, Miss Selby thought it would be a clever way to see if Daphne is visible forever more."

"And if she is visible to them? The entire world will descend on Menabilly. Terrific."

"No disrespect intended, Mr Simon, but people don't jump to them conclusions. Daphne was to say she's a tourist needing directions if any Renfolds squeak up."

Simon's mind ran over all hypothetical situations that could occur. "Felicia won't stay passed out forever. We need to get that dog off her bed if that's where it is. I'm going over to Selby's house now to insist that something is done – tonight – before this thing gets out of hand. Can you stay while I'm gone in case Felicia wakes?"

"I'm fine for a bit, but my own house will erupt if Mr Taylor doesn't get his tea. It's past due now."

When Simon arrived at Rose Cottage, the house was dark except for a light on the first floor. In a foul humour and feeling fed up, he kept his finger on the bell, refusing to go away until someone convinced him there was a plan to get that ruddy dog out of his house.

Selby opened the door. He charged through it. "This must stop. Felicia is a nervous wreck. More to the point, and the reason I'm here, she is convinced she's seen a ghost."

"Well, she has." Daphne laughed, appearing behind Selby.

"Nothing is remotely funny about any of this. I've had a very stressful time today, trying to make Felicia believe that the woman at the beach was a tourist who just happens to look like the photo of Daphne du Maurier in the window of Bookends. In addition – and why I'm here – that the figure she saw in her room last night was a figment of her imagination. I had to ply her with wine to sidetrack her from the idea. The whole thing has left me with a sack of guilt. And – I didn't know about the dog being in her room until Mrs Taylor explained. Yes, she told me that too – that she's seen you all these years. When this whole thing is over, I'm going to have words with her for making such a fool of me. What happened at Renfolds?"

Selby looked at Daphne with disgust. "That's a rather involved story. Suffice it to say, Dame Daphne is once again invisible though not to me, sadly."

"Well, that's a relief. Nothing's ever simple with that woman, is it?"

"Stop talking about me as if I were in another room. I'm standing right here to answer for myself. I've come up with a plan to sort everything. I'll simply go over and get Mouse tonight."

Selby groaned. "Typical over-simplification. What if she wakes and sees you? You may be invisible again to other people, but still visible to Felicia. Mrs Taylor's cousin said she couldn't predict the result due to your saving her life and all that nonsense."

"Stop complicating things. The room will be dark. I'll

grab my dog and get away. Her feeling hung-over should help. Then, we can all get back to our lives, and my book."

"Never mind about your wretched book, and from now on, that wretched dog stays over here. Is that clear? I must get back in case Felicia wakes. I'm worried what will happen if she feels that dog on her bed again. Do whatever you have to do tonight. There will be no convincing her Menabilly is not haunted if she sees you again. She's not a fool."

When Simon returned to Menabilly, he popped his head around the door to check on Felicia. She was still out, mouth open, snoring away. "Going to do the same myself," he muttered. He would have to hope Daphne's plan worked.

Waiting until the middle of the night to enter Felicia's room, Daphne repeatedly called to Mouse in a whisper from behind the curtains. He ignored her. She didn't dare chance going over to the bed to feel around for him.

Felicia groaned. "What is that god-awful smell?" She turned on the light to go into the bathroom.

Daphne poked her head out quickly to look for the dog and spotted him under the bed. He was sucking on a dead mouse. Ah, that explains the smell, she thought. She stayed hidden behind the curtains.

Felicia got back into bed. "My head. Bloody cheap wine at that pub. And what is this hideous flannel thing I'm wearing?" Stripping off Selby's nightdress, she looked for the T-shirt she normally wore. "That foul smell – probably pipework or sewerage in this old heap of a place. Don't know why he lives here – it's decrepit, depressing and out in the middle of nowhere. Must get him back to London with me and away from this hideous place." She turned out the bedside table lamp.

Daphne thundered to herself – Hideous place? Old heap of a house? You dare to say that of my lovely Menabilly! Simon, back to London? Right, I'll have you out of here tonight, my girl.

She waited until Felicia fell back to sleep. Bending down, feeling around under the bed, she dragged Mouse out by the collar, holding him tightly in her arms. Then she nudged Felicia in the back, but she only moved to the other side of the mattress. More nudges a few minutes apart produced no reaction. The girl slept like the dead – this is taking too long, Daphne decided. Waiting again to hear regular breathing, she gave a bigger shove, whisking herself away behind the curtain to hide. Mouse squirmed in her arms, sneezing as he struggled to get down.

"Who's there?" Felicia called out as she turned on the light again. Getting out of bed, she walked around the room, looking in the wardrobe, and pulling up the bed skirt to look underneath.

Daphne saw Felicia's hand reach around the back of the curtains, looking for the cord. She was just about to vanish when Mouse jumped out of her arms. Felicia screamed at the top of her lungs, racing from the room, fleeing down the corridor, yelling Simon's name. Daphne stepped out from behind the curtains to grab the dog and stopped.

"You? I was never sure you really existed." Standing in

front of Daphne was a woman in a pale blue dress to the floor, her hands tucked into long, full sleeves. "Was it you she saw?"

The Blue Lady bowed her head.

"Thank you," Daphne said.

She nodded again before floating back to the bathroom.

Daphne wanted to follow to speak to her, but Felicia could come back into the room with Simon at any moment. When neither of them showed up, she crept down to listen at Simon's door.

"I'm afraid," Felicia said. "In my room, I saw a different one tonight. I'm not imagining it. There are ghosts in this house. Mrs Taylor said so."

"Mrs Taylor is a silly old goat. There are no ghosts in this –"

Felicia interrupted. "Can I get in please? Just to sleep? I'm not staying in that room tonight. Come with me to see for yourself. Then, you won't think I'm off my head. I'm not crazy."

Knowing Daphne could be in Felicia's room and possibly still visible, he did not want to agree to the request. On the other hand, the alternative was tricky. "Felicia, this is awkward."

"Please," she begged. "I won't be any trouble and will keep over on my side. Promise."

"Just for the night – just as friends," he insisted.

"Yes, as friends." Quickly getting in beside him, she nestled down under the duvet. This whole place is creepy, she thought. When I'm mistress of this house, I shall summon exorcists to get rid of whatever I just saw. Feeling his body next to her, she couldn't help but grin. Whatever it was that she had seen, she owed it thanks. This is exactly where she had been trying to get since arriving from London.

No, no, no, Daphne screamed inside her head. *That was – not – supposed to happen.*

CHAPTER EIGHTEEN

$\mathcal{D}$aphne repeatedly poked Selby in the back to wake her.

"Go away. I'm asleep and still cross with you."

"Last night was regrettable, I agree, but we've more important things to think about."

"What time is it?"

"Not too late, I hope. Get up. Things have backfired."

Selby ignored her and drifted back to sleep.

Daphne pulled the duvet off the bed. "Listen to me. That girl has her tentacles wrapped around Simon. If you don't care for him, I do."

"Right, Daphne, bloody out with it. What is it you want?"

"Felicia crawled into bed with Simon last night. I waited to wake you for as long as I could. Get up. We must do something."

Selby sat up. "Felicia in Simon's bed?"

"Yes. That's what I've been trying to tell you. I've done

something stupid. She called Menabilly an old heap and said she wanted to take Simon back to London. It just made my blood boil, so I went a bit further with our plan. I nudged her in the back a few times, and then, of course, Mouse sneezed and ruined everything." Daphne decided it was better to keep the Blue Lady to herself for the moment. "Then, she ran down to Simon's room screaming there were ghosts in the house and asking if she could get into his bed."

"Oldest trick in the book," Selby moaned. She picked the duvet back up and rolled her body in it, trying to block out Daphne's voice.

"I think she really was afraid. Simon said she could come in as a friend. He was very specific about it."

"Yah. Heard that one too. What can I do about it? If Simon wants her in his bed, friend or other, it's none of my business."

"It is your business because you're in love with him."

Selby yawned, wishing she was still asleep. Daphne was standing in front of her in some over-excited state. She unrolled herself from the duvet and put on a dressing gown. "I'm awake now, thanks to your badgering. Downstairs. Coffee."

She ignored Daphne's prattle until the entire mug of black coffee was empty. The heat from the Aga coupled with the sun streaming in through the windows made the room feel like a hot box. She opened the doors of the house to let cool air circulate.

"I'm going outdoors. I can't breathe in here. It's going to be a sweltering day," she said, throwing the dressing gown off. Once settled into a chair under the shade of a tree, she turned her attentions to Daphne.

"Right," she said. "Number one: lesson in modern etiquette for a person aged a hundred and twelve – the choice of which woman Simon has in his bed is his business. Number Two: and in my humble opinion, it is only the concern of the two people involved. In this case, that's Felicia and Simon. Yes, I do care for Simon, but I am not his mother, nor his wife, and even if I were his wife, I wouldn't..." She stopped mid-sentence. His wife. She had never really considered it. Butterflies jumped in her stomach.

"Understand this," Daphne continued, "it's not that I'm trying to force things."

"Stop talking. I need quiet." Selby wandered out of the garden into the field across the lane.

Ben Renfold had finished milking the dairy herd and had taken up the post where he perched most mornings since Selby had rubbed his leg under the table. He liked watching her come down to the kitchen before he had to get back to the farm. Lifting the binoculars to his eyes, he couldn't believe his luck. Today, she had come out in nothing but a skimpy T-shirt.

In free flow Daphne followed. "I'm trying to explain that even if you decided you didn't want him, surely you can agree, we wouldn't want him with her, don't you see?"

Selby thought about it. If I couldn't have him – the feeling surged up again – would I care whom he chose to love? Would seem a pity for him not to get a good one, but who was a good one? She didn't know Felicia. Maybe she was just the person Simon needed.

"Don't be daft. I can sense you're over-analysing the situation like you do with everything. Why can't you admit that Simon is the one? I've seen you together. You bring out the best in him. I've known him for most of his life. I can see when he's happy."

"And where does that leave me? The tool that makes the fool happy?"

Ben moved further along the hedgerow across from where Selby was standing. She was talking to someone, but he couldn't see who.

"I'm not a bad judge of these things. You're a different person since you met him. You glow when he's about. You laugh a lot more too, and if you don't mind my saying, you could do with more laughter in your life. It was one of the first things I noticed when I met you. He's the man for you. We all have one."

"You're lost in one of your romance novels."

"Oh, now I do hate that – hated hearing that when I was alive and hate it now. I was not a romance novelist. I wrote using many genres – short stories, plays, biographies and so on. Why is there this need to label people? Everyone must fit into nice, neat boxes. It's absurd."

"Right, Dame Daphne. Do you think we could dispense with the histrionics due to the early hour? Course I have feelings for Simon."

"Good Lord, call a spade a spade. Do you love him or do you not? I knew immediately I met 'Boy'. We were married soon after."

Selby didn't say anything. She couldn't imagine meeting someone and knowing in a short three months that she wanted to spend a lifetime with them. Maybe people do fall madly in love at first sight. It hadn't been her experience.

"Take my word for it. It happens – like with 'Boy' and me. Did I ever tell you the story of how we met?"

"No."

"Tommy or 'Boy' as I also called him – full proper name, Lieutenant-General Sir Frederick Arthur Montague Browning – a Grenadier like all the most handsome of men. Anyway, he read my book, *The Loving Spirit*, and was so taken with it, he wanted to meet me, the author. He sailed his boat, the Yggy I, to Fowey, and managed to get a neighbour to bring me a message asking if I wanted to go for a sail. Funny name, Yggy, isn't it? Named after Yggdrasil, The Tree of Life in Norse sagas. Had an Iggy II also in later years, but his favourite really was the Jeanne d'Arc, built right here at the old Slade boatyard."

"Stop rambling. Did you go for a sail with him or not?"

Ben was now stooped low, trying to listen to Selby from behind a hedgerow. The combine harvester in the next field was making it difficult to hear. She kept walking back and forth along the hedge, so he could only catch every few words. Go for a sail? Who's she talking to? There's no one there.

"I wasn't sure I wanted to go off in a stranger's boat, but I was curious, so I did. That began everything for us. We were married at Lanteglos church. Most of Fowey came to the dock to see us off in the boat for our honeymoon down the Helford River. I made a wedding breakfast of sausage and bacon in the galley as we pulled out of the harbour."

"Yes, all right. Get back to when you first met? How did you know from the start that he was the one?"

"Well, I didn't have to think too hard at the start of things. I was attracted to him straight off, you see. He was exceptionally handsome, but it wasn't until I did the Test that I could decide if I wanted to marry him."

"What test?"

"Lie down there, on the ground. Close your eyes," Daphne ordered.

"It's too early for games, and I'm hot. Want more coffee, and something to eat now that I'm awake for the day. You're always so bossy – always insisting people interrupt their normal routine to pay attention to you. It's very 'Tell-Him' in your vocabulary. That stunt you pulled at the Renfold house – positively evil. When you leave this existence, you may end up in hell, you know, condemned to the eternal flames of the devil's writing pool, chained to a desk as a romance novelist. So, I'd be careful if I were you. Try to build up some credits before judgement day."

Renfold? Evil? Hell? Eternal flames of the Devil? That was enough for Ben. "Not for me, this loony. And she's not getting her hands on my brother either," he whispered as he moved quietly away from the hedge. Once on the track, he ran all the way to his vehicle. He had to get home to warn George. The woman was part of a devil-cult and mentioned their family.

"Overall, I think I've led an exemplary ghostly existence. I couldn't say about when I was alive as I don't have those memories, but I very much doubt I was an evil being. Anyway, shush now. Let's get back to the Test."

Selby decided the sooner she gave in, the sooner she

could escape the harridan. She lay down in the field in the grass. "Get on with it."

Daphne sat down next to Selby and began to speak slowly in a soft, hypnotic voice:

"*Close your eyes. See yourself in ten years' time. You're standing in a garden. It's a splendid, sunny day. The scent of the roses you planted five years ago fill the air with their perfume. There's laughter around you. You look to see where it's coming from. At your feet is a small child, old enough to have just started walking. He has blond hair, blue eyes, and the sweetest smile you've ever seen. Giggles are coming from the shrubs nearby. You walk over and reach your hand in. Two little girls come running out, squealing with excitement that you've found them. You lift them up. They smell of the sun and the sea. A motor car suddenly arrives. The two girls run across the lawn to a tall man. Overjoyed at seeing them, he scoops them up, kissing them with delight. They jump down, come back to you, hugging your legs. The man walks over to you, holds you tenderly, and kisses you. Looking into your eyes, he tells you how much he has missed you though he's only been gone for the day. You feel happy, fulfilled in a way you never thought possible. You lift the baby boy at your feet, carrying him towards the house. The girls and their father follow behind. Your life is good. It's what you've always wanted: to belong, to give love, and have it returned.*"

Daphne stopped speaking for a minute before continuing.

"*Now. Tell me who the man was in the scene that I described. Tell me what you felt each time you gazed upon the children. Tell me you've never felt anything like that before. Tell me, Selby. Who was the man who arrived in the motor car? Tell me now.*"

Selby opened her eyes and was very quiet. She felt like she had been in a trance in another world. She had in fact smelled the roses, the sun, the sea, and the sweet breath of the little boy in her arms, and felt the deep surge within her body when the man had kissed her.

Jumping up, she ran for the house.

Daphne called after her. "Who was the man?"

"Simon, you idiot. Getting dressed. We're going to Menabilly."

Simon woke to a warm body curled around him. Ah, he thought, this is bliss. He had slept like a baby. Opening his eyes and seeing Felicia in his arms, he remembered her hysterical state the night before.

Though she had woken some time earlier, moving from her side of the bed next to him, Felicia pretended to sleep, hoping the moment would prove irresistible. When she felt him stir, she yawned, stretching her arms up into the air. "Good morning. Oh, I had a good sleep. I feel so much better than yesterday. There was something in my room last night though, but let's not talk about that. It's so warm and cosy right this minute." She smiled smugly.

Simon realised it was time to squelch any possible misunderstanding or expectations. "I've been meaning to talk to you about Selby. I think I've fallen for her. She doesn't know it yet, and I'm uncertain of her feelings for me. It's early days, but…"

Felicia didn't hear the rest of the sentence. Believing she needed only to get into his bed to rekindle the spark had been folly. Stupid, stupid girl, she said to herself. It had been too soon. If only she had not gone to that beach. The whole thing had upset her plans. It had torn down her image in his eyes. "Simon, get a grip," she said. "Nothing happened. We agreed we would share your bed last night as friends."

"Yes, well, anyone looking in might not describe us like that." And, frankly, he thought to himself, lying next to a drop-dead body like hers is not the easiest thing I've had to do lately. They had never had any problems in that department.

Have another go, Felicia told herself. "Doesn't it feel right though? It's like we never parted," she cooed while snuggling up against him.

"Of course, it's cosy. How could anyone cuddled up to you think otherwise? But we did part for some solid reasons. We want different things. That's not a judgement, just a fact."

"I'm not so different to you," she said, putting her leg over his.

Right, he thought. That's it. Time to get myself out of this bed before I do something I'll regret. Disentangling himself from Felicia, he threw off the duvet. As he got out of bed, he glanced back at the perfect legs on her perfect body. "Downstairs," he said, "we can continue this chat over some breakfast." Grabbing his dressing gown, he left the room.

"Is Mrs Taylor due in or can I go down in just my T-shirt?"

He popped his head back around the door to reply. "She doesn't come today. Come on. Up you get. In the kitchen now please, so I can get on with some work."

Felicia stayed where she was while considering what had just happened. Had he been about to take things to the next step a few minutes ago? If she could manoeuvre them back into position, would he back away again? He thinks he loves Selby, she told herself, but if he knew how deeply I felt about him, could it change things?

She sat at the kitchen table while he made tea and toast. "I've settled down some, you know, Simon. I'm not nearly so wild as when you lived in London. I'm much more serious about my work. Needs must – commissions are larger. I've got a rather strict routine when I'm working. When I've finished, I let my hair down."

"Sounds like the old Felicia to me."

"Don't tease me. Is that what you really think of me? That I'm some reckless party girl? I haven't felt anything for anybody since you left. That's why I came down here to be honest. I've tried other relationships. It's not the same. I'm still desperately in love with you, and I don't know what to do about it." She broke into floods of tears.

Simon went over to her, pulling her up from the chair, putting his arms around her. "Don't cry," he whispered, kissing the tears from her cheeks. "Felicia, I wish I could say we could have another go, but you and I both know, if we're honest with ourselves..." She looked up at him, and kissed him back, moving her body closer, pushing her thigh into his legs. Old feelings rose, and he pulled her closer. When he began kissing her neck, she arched her head, losing herself in the sensation she had been wanting to feel since arriving from London.

Driving into the courtyard of Menabilly, Selby saw lights on in the kitchen and walked to the back door instead of ringing the bell. She was about to rap on the window when she saw them. It was a real kiss, not just a peck on the cheek. Simon's hands were rubbing up and down Felicia's back, exposing her black bikini knickers. Selby ran for the car. It hurt. Now she knew. It hurt because she loved Simon Rashleigh.

Moving in to look through the window, Daphne screamed inside her head, *what's wrong with that boy?*

"Where are we going?" Daphne asked from the back seat of the car.

Selby pushed down on the accelerator, speeding down the drive. "Don't know – far away, not Rose Cottage."

"You've got to make a plan. We need to do something," Daphne insisted.

"Don't have to do anything – just left or right at the end of lane."

"What's left and what's right?" Daphne asked.

"Don't know. You decide."

"Me? You want me to decide where we should go? Oh, I say, now that's an easy thing. There are lots of places I'd like to go. The Dorchester, Paris."

"Just decide, left or right," Selby said in a soft voice.

Realising she had rabbited on at the wrong moment, Daphne quickly gave orders. "Follow signs for the A390 to the A38. We're going to London."

CHAPTER NINETEEN

*O*ld feelings of hurt and abandonment descended. Betrayal. Could Selby call it that? There had been no declaration of love from either of them, but Simon had given the impression he cared for her. Until she had visualised the scene Daphne had led her through – shutting her mind off, letting only her heart respond – she had not realised the depth of her feelings. In the daydream, her love for him and their children had been intense. Was it possible that Simon had not realised he was in love with Felicia? Her thoughts went around and around during the journey to London, bringing her to no conclusion. She wanted to forget the whole thing. Let it go, she told herself. You're not in too deep. She was happy in Cornwall – loved Rose Cottage, the beaches and the people who had dropped into her life – Daphne, Mrs Taylor, Merryn Penrice – and Simon. What would happen to the book?

Daphne broke the silence when they got to the

outskirts of London. "I should like to go to Hampstead Heath. Would that be okay with you?"

Selby nodded. At the exit off the M4, Daphne directed the way until asking to stop. She drifted up a small hill where she sat down. Selby followed along, commenting on the beauty of the spot.

"When we got near London, this all came back to me as if it were yesterday. The night my family buried my father, I came here to release pigeons instead of going to the grave site," Daphne explained. "I couldn't stand there watching him being lowered into earth. Pigeons flying off to freedom – that was much more him, you see. He had been a very free bird in life. Too free sometimes, my mother might have added. Strange I should think of it now. Do you mind if we stay here for a bit?"

Selby stretched out, using her handbag as a cushion behind her head. She felt tired from the drive, emotionally exhausted from the shock of seeing Simon and Felicia intimately entwined. How had she so badly miscalculated his feelings for her? Had she just run wild with expectations: the kiss at lunch at Menabilly – all the laughter while writing Daphne's book – the side glances from him – the times their eyes had met, sending butterflies fluttering in her stomach. Were these things nothing but flirtation, something he might offer any woman? When she leaned over to kiss him in the kitchen at Menabilly, the night she had taken supper over, she had dropped her defences. She had shared intimate details of her life, her relationship with her parents and Raphe. Confiding things about herself had made her feel closer to him. Now, she felt stupid. Why would it matter to him what had gone on in her life? Had she described herself as the pitiful person Raphe accused her of being, in such contrast to the self-confident Felicia who blithely ran through life on her own terms? She was like a dark shadow next to the radiant sunshine the woman projected.

It had started to drizzle when Daphne tapped Selby on the shoulder. She had left the girl alone while she walked over the heath, thinking about her father. When they were back in the car, she asked if they could go to the family house in Hampstead. "Of course, I realise it's over a hundred years now, and perhaps the house is no longer standing, but I should so like to see it again."

Driving around with Daphne directing had been a frustrating hour. The woman was intent on finding the place but didn't have an address. "Daphne," Selby finally said, "things don't look the same as when you lived here. You can't go to various spots, trying to work your way back to the house."

"I just know it's close by. I can feel it somehow. There's a garden. It's big. The house is on three floors, you see. I think there were quite a lot of bedrooms, lots of reception rooms on the ground floor – oh, and a big billiards room, a small coachman's house in the back, and a clock on it and a bell turret, and so on."

Selby pulled the car over to a leafy street for a break to eat a sandwich bought earlier at the petrol station. "Why do you want to find it? Thought you had no memories of your life except for the odd snippet."

"I should like to remember my life better. One must take the memories that shoot up and make the most of them. This house has red brick. It's large. I am small. Yes, I'm a girl sitting in the garden, reading a book. I loved reading anything I could get my hands on. I just know I want to go there."

Selby took the last bite, wiped her mouth, and drank some water. "I'm going to stretch my legs."

It was a nice neighbourhood with pretty houses which, she assumed, went for serious prices. She strolled along the street, gazing into front gardens. Beautiful rose bushes and lavender beds made one house particularly attractive. There was a blue plaque on the facade. She raced to the car. "Come and look at this."

Daphne floated along until they stood in front of the National Heritage inscription on the wall of a house. She read aloud. "Sir Gerald du Maurier 1873–1934 Actor-Manager lived here from 1916 until his death. Did he? Did I?"

"Why didn't I think of this before," Selby said. Switching on her mobile, she googled Gerald du Maurier, and read out from Wikipedia. "From the time you were nine years old, you and your two sisters lived here with your mother, actress Muriel Beaumont and your father, Gerald du Maurier."

"Of course, this is the house. I see that now. Let's have a look inside."

"I can't just barge up to the front door and ask to have a look around because my invisible friend wants to see her childhood home. Hang on, there's another site below this one. It says this house was sold recently – wow, for twenty-eight million pounds." Selby got back into the car. She watched Daphne glide up the path to the house to have a snoop. Looking back at her mobile, she read the rest of the article about property prices in London. Should she sell up in Cornwall and move back to London, she wondered? Could she continue to live at Rose Cottage or was it now ruined for her? Perhaps she should look for a different house further down the coast. On the other hand, why should she run anywhere?

"I went to look," Daphne said, reappearing at the car window. "The other side of the house is covered in scaffolding. There's no furniture in the rooms, and no one is there. Do come and see."

Reluctantly, Selby followed, though she kept looking over her shoulder, wondering if some nosy neighbour would appear to ask what she was doing.

There was a lovely big garden in the back. They peered in through the windows. "Rather grand, isn't it? I think I was happy here, but I only get a sense of past feelings, no details from childhood."

"You weren't born here. The website said you were born at twenty-four Cumberland Terrace soon after five in the evening, following a violent thunderstorm."

"Really? Would you mind if we went to have a quick look?"

Selby was tired and fed up driving around London. She could understand Daphne's excitement at seeing her old haunts, but Selby's own mental state was pulling her down.

Daphne heard the sigh and sensed the change in mood. "Look, I've been rather selfish. I've had enough sightseeing for the day. Let's cheer you up. Let's go to a play or something. Wouldn't you like that?"

"Don't know. Need a toothbrush and change of clothing if I'm not going home. Don't think I am going home."

"Right. So where are we going to stay? What about The Dorchester?"

"What is this obsession with The Dorchester? And who would pay for that anyway?"

"Why me, of course – when you sell my book, that is. I feel sure it will do well. *Rebecca* sold three million in the first twenty years of its publication. That was an enormous number of copies then."

"You're a little out of touch. *Rebecca* now sells about four thousand copies a month. It was in the papers not long back."

"Really? That seems extraordinary though it was very good. I wasn't a fan of the film. To be exact, it irritated me that they changed how Rebecca died. Maxim shoots her in the book. She doesn't hit her head. Maybe they had to change it for some cinematic reason. Thank God, I was born to be a writer. I can't imagine having to express myself visually instead of in the written word. No doubt about it, books were always me."

Selby had not meant to say what she had been thinking, but it tumbled out anyway. "Who knows what's going to happen to the one we've been writing. Simon has the other half."

"Oh, there's going to be a book, my girl. Don't worry about Simon. I know how to make his life miserable enough to get him to do almost anything. He will finish his bits."

Not wanting to dwell on Simon, Selby changed the

subject. "We're not going to a hotel. I'm ringing my godfather to ask if I can stay. Haven't seen him for a few months. He's not been well, so it will depend on if he's feeling strong enough." She pulled the car over to dial Charles Cannon's number. They chatted for a few minutes. "Lovely, CC, thank you. Yes, I heard. Sharon is the carer. I'll be with you about six o'clock. Are you sure you don't mind? I would understand if you didn't feel up to having a guest at short notice. Thank you, darling."

"So where does he live?" Daphne asked.

"Primrose Hill. He used to live in a big house when his wife was alive. The place became too much for just him. His three daughters are all married, so he moved to this flat a few years ago. I want no nonsense when we get there. He's nearly ninety-seven."

They pulled up to a smart building with three floors. Selby pressed the button of Flat 5. A buzzer sounded. They went into the entrance hall and took a lift. A woman was standing at one of the doors when they got off at the second floor. "Good evening, I'm Sharon. Let me show you where your godfather is sitting. He's had his supper. He likes it early. Then he snoozes in his chair before watching the evening news."

"How is he?" Selby asked. "It's been a few months since I've seen him."

She smiled while tapping her temple with her finger. "For a man in his late nineties, he's sharp as a tack. He's excited about your visit."

Daphne followed on behind, looking at everything,

thrilled to be in a new place. Paintings of historical naval battles hung on wide striped, cream and brown wallpaper in the entrance hall. A crescent-shaped table fitted snugly against the wall with an ornate mirror hanging above. Paintings in the sitting room were portraits she assumed had hung on larger walls of the former, more spacious residence Selby had mentioned. Lamps on the various tables cast a warm glow over an elderly gentleman sitting on a green, velvet settee near the fire. He held an ivory cane with a silver top across his lap. Daphne strolled around the room, looking at everything, stopping to peer at photographs in silver frames that covered a round table.

"Hello, CC," Selby said, leaning down to kiss him.

"What a pleasant surprise. Gosh, I've missed you. I'm so happy you rang up. Have you had supper? No, I can read that look." He turned to speak to Sharon. "Be a darling, old thing, and make something for her. Scrambled eggs and smoked salmon, I think. Oh, and could you bring a whiskey for me and a glass of bubbly for my goddaughter, please? Now," he said to Selby, "let's hear everything. Dear girl, you sounded upset on the phone. It's been about a year, I think, since you broke off with that ghastly man, hasn't it? What's gone on?"

"I feel a bit silly barging in here, interrupting a peaceful evening. Oh, CC, let's not talk about me. How have you been? Sharon seems nice. Have you got everything you want? Tell me if there's something you crave, and I'll run out tomorrow to get it. Hope pistachio ice cream is in the freezer. Can't imagine it not being close by for your nightly splurges. Remember when we both caught each other coming around the corner one night, making our way to the kitchen? I was about fourteen, I think."

CC threw his head back and laughed. "Ran right into each other, didn't we? But we managed to devour the entire thing between us. Oh, yes, it's firmly planted in my memory. Now, enough of bygone days – out with it – what's your life like on the Cornish Riviera?"

She let out a long sigh. "I'm happy there. Love my cottage, the sea air. The writing is going well. It's what happened this morning, really. It's changed everything – where I thought my life might be heading – what I wanted. When I realised I'd fallen in love with someone, I went over to his house to tell him how I felt, but when I got there, I –"

"He's your godfather?" Daphne suddenly blurted out. She was waving a silver frame in the air behind the settee where CC was sitting. "Yes, I see it now, of course."

Selby moved to another chair so that CC wouldn't see the frame suspended mid-air. She gave Daphne a withering look and continued to explain to Charles what had happened. "Let me start again. There's this man who lives near me. I thought he was interested in me. When I realised I also felt something for him, I went to his house this morning to tell him. I found him kissing another woman."

"Well, he's either a rogue in which case you should have nothing more to do with him, or it was a kiss of another kind and meant nothing. Kisses are not always indications of love."

"This kiss was mouth on mouth, bodies pressed closely together. I couldn't go in after seeing them."

"Ah, yes, I see how that would have been very awkward. Barging in on an intimate moment between two people is bad enough. When one of them is someone for whom you have deep feelings, it's worse."

Daphne chuckled. Selby shot her another look

"I'm not a schoolgirl any more, Charles. I'm not going to chase after a man if I don't have clear signals my feelings will be reciprocated. Raphe – he said some awful things when he left. Said I was boring, only wrote about pathetic creatures like myself. How did I read him so wrong?"

"You know what I thought," CC exclaimed.

"Yes, I did, but I assumed you were being protective of me."

"I was. The man was a bore of the first order, only interested in himself. He brought nothing to the table. Oh, maybe something that looked sophisticated to you at the time, but no warmth, no humour. Good Lord, who can live without humour."

"Too true." Daphne snorted out a laugh.

Selby ignored her. "It took me ages to get my confidence back after Raphe. I went around like an angry bull most of the time. Don't think I was a pleasure to be around. The move to Cornwall, my cottage there – I wish you could see it. It's a perfect place for me – the views from the windows, the atmosphere – most of the time," she said, glancing in Daphne's direction. "And I'm happy to get up each day. The blues have gone, thank God. I met this man quite by accident. We have so much in common. We have fun together. Everything seemed to fit, and then this morning, everything collapsed. I was ready to tell him

how I felt. Now, I just can't. I won't. It would be humili-
ating after what I saw."

"Yes, I can see that, but I've known you all your life. I
understand why you'd prefer not to take chances with
your feelings, but that's the thing about love. It can't be
experienced within barriers we erect."

"I don't want to give all of myself to someone unless
they're ready to make a commitment. I've come to realise I
want marriage and children."

CC was listening to his adored Selby whom he had
always considered a fourth daughter. She had been a
delight once settled into the love of his family. Except for
this predicament with the man, Cornwall seemed to have
done her good. She no longer spoke in abbreviated
sentences. This alone was a triumph. The child psychologist had mentioned her speech pattern could revert in the
future. Fewer words meant exposing less of herself, he
had explained. Selby gave only what was necessary to
communicate unless she trusted you.

Daphne could wait no longer. "I've got to speak to you.
Make an excuse or I'll start causing a ruckus."

There was nothing Selby could do but to break off the
conversation and excuse herself.

"Of course," CC said. "You'd like to freshen up,
wouldn't you? Sharon will be in the kitchen, but it's not
such a big place that you can't find the spare room. Down
that hall, second room on the right. It's got an en suite
bathroom, darling, so go and help yourself to anything.
Then we'll continue our chat."

When Selby got into the bedroom, she turned sharply
on Daphne, but kept her voice down. "What the bloody

hell are you doing? You see how frail he is. Just shut up. Go somewhere else. This is not the time.

"He's Charles Cannon," Daphne whispered.

"Yes?"

"Just before I met Tommy, Charles Cannon and I were involved."

"What?"

"We'd known each other for years. One day, it just turned into a romance. Then, I met Tommy. I'm sorry to say I broke Charles's heart. Think he took it rather badly, but he didn't give up. He kept ringing me, you see, trying to woo me back until the formal engagement was announced in the papers."

"Bloody hell," Selby said. "How can this be happening?"

"Don't ask me to start explaining my world. Mrs Taylor is always saying there's a reason for things, but I couldn't tell you what it might be, but it's all true. I'm the one who can't believe it. That I should see Charles after all these years. What a darling he always was."

Selby was getting annoyed. "What can I do about any of that now? You're to stay quiet and let me have my visit with him. I won't have that dear man upset."

Daphne thought for a moment. "Selby, couldn't we tell him that I'm here?"

"No," she replied with a furious look. "We could not tell him the ghost of an old girlfriend is in the room, and then introduce you like it was an everyday, natural thing to do. He could have a heart attack. Out of the question, and you and I will have a serious parting of the ways if you don't behave." Selby was about to open the door to the bathroom when she turned back at the last moment. Pointing her finger at the object of her temper, she whispered, "On second thoughts, you stay in here, and not a sound. Do you hear me?"

Daphne did not reply and had no intention of staying in the bedroom. If necessity required, she would go invisible and play havoc with Selby. Teach that girl to forbid me to go somewhere, she thought.

Selby washed her hands, combed her hair, and tidied herself up before returning to the sitting room.

"Ah, good, here you are," CC said. "I've been thinking about your predicament. How hard would you say you've fallen for this chap?"

"Completely," she sighed. "But I didn't really know it until I took the Test."

"No, no, don't say that," Daphne yelled. "Don't go into that!"

Selby was furious Daphne had come back to the room. She continued explaining to Charles how she had closed her eyes. How she had pictured a future with the man and their children. How it had been the visualisation that had caused her to realise the depth of her love. "It surprised me that I was so out of touch with my emotions. I didn't know how I felt until I imagined him in someone else's arms."

"How extraordinary you should say that," he exclaimed. "I once in my life made the same examination. It was my mother who told me to close my eyes and create a similar scene. There was only one woman who could have filled that picture with the love I felt for her, but when I tried to get her to close her eyes to the same end, she said it was no use her taking the Test as I wasn't the chap. She humoured me, nevertheless, and let me lead her through the scenes as my mother had done for me, but in the end, it was clearly not meant to be. Broke me up quite badly for a while.

The lights in the room suddenly went off.

"Darling girl, go and ask Sharon if she can look at the fuse box, please. An electrical short of some kind, I expect."

From outside the room, Selby waved frantically at Daphne to come out. She ignored her, and sat down next to Charles, staring at him. Sharon came past her with a tumbler of whiskey and a glass of champagne. She noticed the darkened room, "A fuse has gone? I'll see to it. Can you take this tray in, please? Food is coming in a minute." Selby went back to the sitting room with the drinks just as the lights went on. She handed Charles his glass and sat in a chair opposite.

"Come over here next to me," he said. "I'm feeling a bit tired. It's less effort to speak if you're closer."

Selby sat down right on top of Daphne.

"Humph. Well, that's insulting. As if one were nothing," she exclaimed before floating across the room. Selby arched her eyebrow in confirmation.

"That's it. Good," Charles said. "Now, about love – true love won't be denied. Infatuation, lust, and other such things come and go, but true love stays forever, even after disappointment. Of course, it's important that it be reciprocated, but don't forget that one person always loves more than the other. Don't ask me why. They just do. I'm not suggesting you enter a relationship, knowing your affections will not be returned, but men and women show their love differently. One thing I know for certain is that you should not just walk away if you truly love this man. Go and fight for him. Tell him how you feel. If nothing comes of it, pull yourself back up, putting the rest down to learning more about life."

"I can't just barge into his house and say, 'I love you' in front of her. I'd make a terrible fool of myself."

"Of course not, it needs careful consideration. You'll find a way. Give it some thought. Sleep on it. You need some distance. It was only this morning that you realised you loved him or perhaps only this morning that you allowed yourself to admit it?"

Sharon arrived with supper and set the tray on a stand before topping up Selby's glass and leaving.

"Let's hear news about the girls," she said. "I haven't heard from them in a while though I guess you know Joanna came down to Rose Cottage to help me with curtains right after I moved in. Then she met me at the storage place to choose what would fit the cottage. You were so kind to let me have what I needed. Your lovely furniture and paintings have made it look so wonderful. I cherish everything." Selby said.

Charles patted her hand, telling her she was like a daughter, loved by the entire family as if she had been born into it. They chatted about the grandchildren and the latest family gossip until Sharon appeared at the door again.

"I'm going to my room, Mr Cannon, until you need me, if that's all right. Can I get you anything further?" she asked him.

"No, that's all splendid. Thank you, Sharon."

Suddenly feeling ravenous, Selby tucked into the food while they chatted. By the time she had finished eating, she could see he was fading. "CC, it's late. Should we finish the catching up tomorrow? The food and the bubbly have done me wonders. I feel better just being here with you. I'll take the tray to the kitchen, tidy up, and put out the lights. It's just so lovely to see you. So sweet of you not to mind my barging in, emptying my heart."

"Dear girl, what are godfathers for anyway?"

"You've been a father to me. Don't know how I would have made it through all these years without you, Miranda, and the girls. How I love you," she said. Standing to offer her arm as he steadied himself on his cane, she walked him to his room. How fragile he feels, she thought, as she kissed him goodnight.

He paused before going in. "Don't let life live you, my darling. Get what you want by asking for it. Have courage. Love is the only thing that matters. Believe you deserve it."

As she walked back to the sitting room, she heard Sharon enter her godfather's room to ready him for bed. She was grateful he had someone nice around him.

"Don't speak," she said to Daphne when she went to collect the tray from the sitting room.

"I did love him very much, you know, but when I met Tommy...well."

"Not interested," Selby said before going to her room and closing the door.

Daphne drifted into Charles's bedroom during the night. A small table lamp had been left on in the corner of the room. She sat on the bed, gazing at him.

"Still handsome," she said softly. "You were a fine-looking man. Don't think I didn't notice all the women who stared at you when we entered a room. I felt quite chuffed being the one on your arm. What a splendid time we had, didn't we? I don't know how you managed it, what with the Crash, but you always seem to have enough to take us some place nice. Gosh, we would've caused a scandal with your being fourteen years younger. Neither of us thought much about that at the time, but just as well we kept things a secret. Quite naturally I died before you. It's not so bad, you know – dying. One minute you are – the next, you aren't. Can't remember a thing about it." She wandered about his bedroom, looking at all the photos scattered around.

"This must be your wife," she said, peering down at one of the frames. "Pretty woman – people always said charming things about her. How like you one of the girls is in this photograph. We were lucky, weren't we? We didn't have years together, but I wouldn't have traded it for the world. I can't deny I didn't think about you over the years. All a long time ago now, wasn't it?" Walking back over to Charles, putting her hand upon his head, she leaned down to kiss his cheek. "Sleep, dear boy. Sleep," she whispered.

In the morning when Selby woke, the noise of London traffic reminded her that she was at CC's house. Feeling safe, and better than the night before, she relaxed. He had always been able to offer perspective. His love took care of anything else needed. She got up to go to the loo. When she was getting back into bed, she heard a soft tapping on the door.

"Yes?"

Sharon opened the door.

"I heard you get up just now, so I thought it would be fine to knock. I didn't want to disturb you earlier." She paused, reaching into her pocket for a tissue to blow her nose. "It's difficult news. I'm so sorry. Mr Cannon died sometime during the night."

"No," Selby cried out. Putting her head face down into the pillow, she wept.

CHAPTER TWENTY

Self-disgust was all Simon had felt after allowing Felicia to tempt him into nearly seducing her in the kitchen. What had he been thinking? He had finally pushed her away. Lost his temper. Said hurtful things. After a long hack on Almond, he had apologised. Then, he had hidden in his study for days, working on his book until this morning when she knocked on the door.

"Sorry to disturb you, but I've been asked by some friends to join their house party for the weekend. You're busy writing, and I'm feeling recovered enough to make the drive to Penzance, and well, I think a change of scene wouldn't hurt. I'm going up to get my things together now."

"Look, Felicia, no hard feelings – can we agree on that? We've known one another a long time." They gave each other a hug.

Upstairs in the bedroom, Felicia packed and washed her hair, deciding to arrive in Penzance looking polished and smart. Slipping on a summer skirt and blouse, she laced up some trainers before sitting down at the dressing table. She wondered about the romance Simon hoped for with Selby. "She's nothing special," she said. "Mousy hair, no conversation – perhaps it won't stick? I'll stop by on my way back to London just to check. After all, she may not want him."

She leaned down to plug in the hair dryer and froze when she looked back in the mirror. Behind her, there was a woman dressed in blue – the same apparition she has seen the other night. Jumping up off the stool, she turned to face it. The Blue Lady pointed to the door of the room. Felicia was glued to the spot, petrified to move. The woman raised both arms and whirled around and around, sending a wind and an eerie noise throughout the room. The curtains swayed from side to side. The girl dashed to the bed, grabbed her case, and flew down the stairs. Once out the front door and into her car, she peeled down the drive as fast as she could.

Watching from an upstairs window, the Blue Lady smiled. Felicia Barrett was leaving Menabilly forever.

Simon had been ringing Rose Cottage all afternoon. Where is everyone, he wondered? Hitting the redial button on the phone, he was secretly relieved no one was answering. Having missed so many sessions for Daphne's book, he doubted he was in anyone's good graces. When he arrived at Selby's house, only Mrs Taylor's car was parked outside. He rang the bell.

"Oh. It's you," she said, opening the door and walking back into the kitchen.

"I've been ringing all day. There's been no answer."

"I'm only just arriving. She's not here."

"Where is she?"

"Gone to London, she said on the phone. Ashamed is what you should feel," Mrs Taylor said, moving the mop across the floor. "Move out the way. Don't walk in the wet bits."

"Why ashamed?" he asked.

"Because leading that poor girl along is what you've been doing. It's not right, and know it's not my place to say, but it's not right."

"I don't understand."

"Don't be a booba. If you can't figure out for yourself why a woman would feel let down by seeing the man she loved dolly-moppin' and kissing someone else, then I've got no time for you. Now scat. I've work to do."

"Loved? What woman saw who doing what? Mrs Taylor, I really don't know what you're going on about. If you're referring to Felicia, she left today in rather a hurry after I explained there was no future for us. I guess she just couldn't face me again. Apparently, she's been going through a rough patch, trying to figure out her life."

"And you'll go through a rough patch if you don't leave. I'm busy. I want no sight of you today. Shame."

"Can you start over," Simon pleaded.

Mrs Taylor stopped mopping the floor and sat down. "Miss Selby went to Menabilly, seen you kissing that woman, and left for London right after."

His face and neck coloured when he thought back to

Felicia and the kitchen. It hadn't been his finest hour. More importantly, what would Selby have thought when she had seen them together. I've lost her, he told himself. "Stupid man," he called out before looking at Mrs Taylor. "How did you find out about all this?"

"Never you mind. I'm here because Miss Selby asked me to look after things while she's gone. Don't know anything else except she sounded low."

He covered his face with his hands. "This is a complete misunderstanding. Felicia was crying. I tried to comfort her, but things got a little carried away."

"Giss on," was all Mrs Taylor said as she bent down to ring the water from the mop. She was getting increasingly annoyed at the man whom she had looked after since childhood. "Don't say no more. Nan always said dirty linen ought not to get aired in public. Anyways, you're blubbing to the wrong person, boy. Get yourself together or you're going to make a mess of your life. You're going to lose someone who may just be the one."

Leaning his back against the wall, he ruffled his hair back and forth with his fingers. "How does anybody know that, for God's sake? Of course, I'm interested in Selby."

"Interested? What the bleddy hell does 'interested' mean? I'm interested in the cod on ice at the fishmonger if I'm making a fish pie. Interested in having an umbrella if it's going to lash down. You need a better word, boy. What kind of interest? Enough to spend the rest of your life with her?

"We haven't had that kind of conversation. I don't know how she feels."

"Saints alive, you've got strange ideas. Leave her feel-

ings to herself. I'm asking you about yours. Not so complicated in my village – a look here, a look there, a sweet
word. For bleddy sakes, you spent the last three months
with the woman holed up with a ghost writing a book,
didn't you?"

Simon didn't say anything.

She took the bucket of dirty water outdoors. When she
returned, she pointed a finger at him. "Can't see no other
way. Nope, you gotta take the Test. Sit yourself down and
close them eyes."

"I'm not in the mood for silly games, Mrs Taylor. I'm
upset. What am I going to do for God's sake?

With the mop in hand as a weapon, she bellowed.
"You're going to sit over there in one of them chairs or else
I'll give you a basting on those chacks, boy."

Simon had never seen Mrs Taylor is such a mood,
bullying him, making him feel like a schoolboy again. He
sat down.

She hiked herself up on the stool at the counter,
concentrating on what Daphne had told her to say.

"Now, the eyes – shut 'em," she ordered. "Picture a
garden filled with roses with such strong perfume, it'd
knock the smell out of a fish and chip shop."

Simon opened one eye. Mrs Taylor turned her head
sharply, glaring at him. He quickly closed it again. She
continued, lowering her voice, speaking very slowly.

"Lost my train now – yes, it's a pretty garden, it is. It's
got the roses. That's right. It's also a sunny day, mind. Sea
air going right up the nostrils. A woman is holding two
cheldern in her arms and a boy toddler is crawling at her
feet. You've been gone, see? Like to the shops – only now

you're back. You get out of the car. You watch them cheldern running amuck before they see you and tear across. You hoick them up and kiss them from head to toe. Their hair smells of summer hay in hot Cornish sun. Scooping both, one under each arm, you're carrying them back to their mum. Oh, she's a fine-looking woman. Dark hair past her waist, eyes the colour of them bluebells over the county in May. After you put them girls down, you take hold of the woman, pulling her close. You kiss – a long one. You're happy to see her, see. Your heart's on a trapeze in your chest when you look in her eyes. You toss the toddler boy up high to the sky. He likes this. Oh, how he does love his da. These are your cheldern – yours and hers. The girls have the colour of her eyes – the boy, your dimples in his cheeks. You take the woman's hand and make for the house. You're happy to be alive, lad. You love the woman, the cheldern. You couldn't live without them. You know life wouldn't be worth living if you didn't see them in morning light and at night when sun leaves the clifftops."

Mrs Taylor stopped speaking and waited a few seconds.

"Open your eyes, then. Tell me. Who be the woman?"

Simon felt he had been in a dream. His heart still raced from the kiss he had given the woman, the joy experienced when he held the children, their children. He had never allowed himself to imagine such scenes.

"Who?" she asked again.

"You know who," he said quietly, looking up at her, "and I'm worried I may have lost her forever. Where is she? Where in London?"

"I've no knowledge of that, but be warned, Daphne's with her," she said before scuttling out of the room to put the mop away.

He called down the hall. "What did you say?"

"You heard me."

"I thought Daphne was confined to houses where she lived?"

"Never you mind all that. Just get this into that head of yours – she's got your interest at heart like always." Mrs Taylor came back in with the hoover, slightly out of breath. "Daphne did not take to Felicia. We've been plotting how to get rid of her, only things backfired a bit. Daphne upset that iron."

"I'm surrounded by snooping harridans," Simon cried, slapping his forehead with the palm of his hand. "She could've burned the house down. Mind you, that would've killed her just as much as me, in a manner of speaking, if you see what I mean."

"'Tis all true. She belongs to be there."

"Why is Daphne with Selby?"

"Don't know."

Simon got up and walked to the front door.

"Where are you going?"

"I'm going home to think, Mrs Taylor. Home to Menabilly to decide the rest of my life."

"Proper job," she mumbled when she heard his car start up. "Did a proper job."

Hours crawling along in dense traffic gave Selby time to

think during the drive back to Cornwall. She could sense Daphne's presence, but heard nothing from her. The options kept going around in her head. Should she go to Menabilly, just barge in, ask to speak to him? Felicia's presence would make it awkward. Should she ring to say she would like to see him? Ask him to come to Rose Cottage where they could have privacy? Perhaps a letter would be better. Why was she pussyfooting around the obvious? He agreed Felicia could stay on at his house because he liked having her there. The kiss she had seen was not a platonic one. Call a spade, a spade, she insisted. You don't wrap yourself around someone in that kind of embrace if you feel love for someone else.

The other option carried risks. If she declared her feelings only to discover he didn't feel the same, could she take another disappointment like the one with Raphe? The hurt? The betrayal? She wasn't sure. Signs appearing for Bristol meant she had a few hours more to mull things over. Perhaps she should avoid seeing him altogether. Shut him out of her life. Her godfather's words swirled around in her head – "Don't let life live you. Tell him how you feel. Love is the only thing that matters."

CC's funeral had been a solemn affair. She couldn't bear to think how much she would miss his love and wise counsel. The reception after the church service today had been in his flat. Looking at the settee where they had sat talking had brought tears to her eyes. She took comfort from the slide show on a laptop in the sitting room. One of the girls had compiled a selection of photographs of CC throughout his life. Many of them included her.

In was dark when she finally arrived at Rose Cottage.

Weary from the long journey, she longed to dive under the duvet to shut out the world. Mrs Taylor opened the door. "How are you, Miss Selby? Seen the lights of the car. It's been a hard time, hasn't it? Sorry about your godfather."

"Thank you, and for looking after things, Mrs Taylor. I hope it hasn't caused any problems."

"If the husband gets his three-squares, all is well. I've come and gone during the week, but when you rang this morning, I nipped back for when you arrived." She took a breath, letting out a long sigh. "I know it's a lot to take in, just getting out of the car and all, but Mr Simon is in the sitting room. He rode Almond over earlier this evening and parked her in the field."

Selby suddenly panicked. Knowing what she must do, hoping she wouldn't regret her decision, she thought she should just get it over and say her bit. "Courage," she muttered under her breath.

Mrs Taylor went on, "Wasn't anything I could do about him here. He insisted, and said he wasn't leaving 'til he got to speak to you." She shuffled along slowly back to the kitchen.

Taking deep breaths, Selby put her things down in the hall. When she walked into the sitting room, Simon stood up.

"I'm sorry to be here – taking you by surprise...um, under the circumstances," he stuttered. "When Mrs Taylor told me that you were returning tonight... It's only decent that I explain. What you saw last week at Menabilly...um, Felicia and me. I'm not proud of it. Nothing happened. I know it didn't look good."

She realised in that moment from the look on his face

that she had made the wrong decision. Cutting him off, coming over to where he was standing, she put her fingers gently over his lips. "None of that matters now, Simon. Love is what's important. Love is what I feel for you with all my heart." She kissed him tenderly.

Holding her face, he kissed her back. "It's how I feel about you, Selby," he whispered. "Nearly drowning the other day, everything came into focus. The entire time I was in the sea on Almond with Felicia, I kept thinking – what if I never get to see Selby again. That's the truth, but I didn't know how you felt about me. Since Mrs Taylor told me you had seen Felicia and me kissing in the kitchen, I've been crazed, worrying I might've lost you. I couldn't bear to think of going through life without you."

Mrs Taylor thought that whatever happened in the sitting room, food would be needed by one person or both. She opened the fridge to take out the chicken casserole she had made earlier. Once it was in the oven, she stood on the stepladder to reach some plates to warm. When she got down and turned around, Daphne was there.

"Bleddy hell, saints alive. I nearly dropped the crockery," she called out. "Wasson? It's been over an hour since Selby got back. Wondered where you got to. You're always creeping up."

"Never mind all that. I've so much to tell. We had quite a time in London. You know, I was never able to go anywhere except where I'd had a connection – and the most remarkable thing – Selby's godfather, the man who just died – I knew him when I was alive. He was an old beau of mine, the most extraordinary coincidence."

"Giss on, I've never believed in them," Mrs Taylor said, shaking her head. "Before he passed, did you speak with him? Did you tell him it was you standing before him? It was a long time ago, and you didn't come back in spirit form as a young woman."

"Humph, I don't think I've changed that much that I would've looked a stranger, thank you very much."

"Humph yourself, and I see we've arrived back in one of our moods. What did he say?"

"Oh, the queen bee wouldn't let me show myself to him. Pity, it could have been quite an exciting conversation, but she would've thrown a real fit. Insisted it might give him a heart attack, and then the darling man popped off anyway during the night. Did you miss us?"

"Course I didn't miss you," Mrs Taylor said, whipping a tea towel in the air towards Daphne. "I've had enough to be getting on with here. Mr Simon's worn a path in the carpet about Miss Selby. He's in the sitting room now, speaking with her."

They crept around the corner, peering into the room. Simon and Selby were sitting on the sofa in each other's arms. The two women put their thumbs up. Feeling this was a time to make herself scarce, Mrs Taylor returned to the kitchen. She felt a certain satisfaction for helping the love match take form.

Her partner in crime felt no such compunction to disappear. Instead, Daphne glided into the room with a grin on her face. "Whilst this is a cosy picture, what about my book?"

Simon and Selby laughed at the predictability of the question.

"Just talking about it, amongst other more important matters," Simon said, gazing with affection at Selby. "Reluctantly, we've admitted *Pistol Meadow* has been a more enjoyable experience than working on our own books."

Daphne clapped her hands. "Splendid news. When can we look forward to getting back to it?"

"We've made a plan to begin tomorrow at Menabilly. It's easier to be in one place. Deadlines or no deadlines, we're putting our work aside to get *Pistol Meadow* finished as soon as possible."

"Very satisfactory," Daphne said before vanishing. It was not the moment to linger. When she reappeared in the kitchen, there was an odd sensation in the atmosphere. She complained to Mrs Taylor of feeling peculiar.

"Didn't think ghosts felt anything. What sort of peculiar?"

"I'm not altogether sure, just different. It's coming in waves. I noticed it in the car on the way back from London – feel light in the head, you see."

"Not been drinking, have you?" the housekeeper teased. "I could do with a medicinal nip myself right now. It's been nerve-racking around here lately."

"Why don't you reach in amongst the washing-up stuff, and take out that tipple you keep there," Daphne remarked casually.

"Oh, you are a blackguard – always spying on people. You'll be counting the times I pick my nose next." Mrs

Taylor reached under the sink to bring out a small shape wrapped in a tea towel. "Just a wee bit," she said, tilting the bottle back for a mouthful of brandy.

"Better?"

"Much."

"There it is again," Daphne said faintly. "What's happening?"

Fortifying herself further with the bottle in her hand, Mrs Taylor examined Daphne. "I do see a little something different." She peered closely. Pointing her index finger, she traced it around Daphne's form. "Can't see that print on your shirt like I'm used to seeing it two days a week all these years. I'd be feeling gawky by now, wearing the same thing twenty-four seven. Can't see your features like I'm used to seeing them neither. Could be it's your time?"

"What does that mean? It sounds a very open-ended, non-scientific pronouncement."

Mrs Taylor sat down in the chair, feeling a bit light-headed herself. "Science got nothin' to do with it. It's not a given that spirits stay attached to this earthly plane forever if they didn't go when they should've done, see. My grandmother used to tell a story – two soldiers from centuries ago, every night at the stroke of twelve, they fought each other in a garden near that beautiful house. What's it called? You know," she said to Daphne.

"A faint hint of any kind would be?"

"You know, the beautiful, big, grand mansion near Liskeard – locals call it Bride's Dream 'cause it fits everyone's picture of a perfect wedding. That's why I can't remember the proper name. Let me think." She took another few sips. "Got it. Boconnoc. It seemed them soldiers died in battle near there. When the well went dry, builders dug around, and found skeletons. After a proper burial at the local church, no one ever saw the ghosts again."

"I don't know how that applies to me, assuming mine was a proper burial. I can't remember it for obvious reasons."

"Cremated – you were cremated. I remember reading about it. Mr Taylor and I married the same day."

"An odd pairing of memories, but I appreciate the information."

"Yup, your ashes were scattered off the cliffs at Kilmarth. Read that too in the paper." No one spoke for a few minutes until Mrs Taylor started up again about her grandmother. "Course, then there's that other story she told about a pirate who hid gold at the top of a cliff near Polruan. Locals said he haunted the coastal path. Young lovers who went up there, swore they saw him. One summer's eve, a girl with a broken heart ran up to the spot, ready to throw herself off the cliffs. The pirate ghost appeared. He told her he'd show her where the treasure was if she didn't jump. The girl agreed and found the gold. After he'd done what he'd been hanging around for, no one ever saw him again."

"I still see no correlation between these tales and me."

"I'm just saying – it could be your time. Them soldiers waited to leave 'til they was buried proper-like – the pirate to do a good deed. Why have you stayed attached here anyway?"

Daphne considered the question. "I'm not quite sure, though I was thinking about it the other day. I've taken for granted I am where I'm supposed to be for whatever reason. I've never liked over-analysing things, being more interested in the why of people's actions, you see – very 'Tell-Him' otherwise."

"But you must've wondered why you didn't see others like yourself though I'd not be thrilled to hear there were more like you about the place – unlikely in any case," Mrs Taylor said with affection.

"Yes, I've wondered about all that, and why we're on the subject, I've something quite remarkable to tell you. You know the night I was in Felicia's room, the night she ended up in Simon's bed?"

"Shush, don't bring all that up again, not with how well things are going out there," she scolded, nodding in the direction of the sitting room.

"Don't be silly, you old goat. They can't hear us. As I was saying – I was hiding behind the curtains, holding Mouse in my arms. He sneezed. Felicia sprang out of bed to search the room. I saw her hand reach around the back of the curtains, looking for the pull. I knew I was done for and was getting ready to vanish when the girl ran screaming from the room down to Simon."

"She is a dobeck, isn't she," Mrs Taylor exclaimed with conviction. "So, she could still see you?"

"Could you draw a breath for one second, so I can finish? Stepping out from behind the curtain, I saw her."

"I thought she went running from the room?"

"I saw the Blue Lady, you nincompoop. She was standing there in front of me as clear as day."

Mrs Taylor reached down for the bottle again. "No.

Really? Well, I never," she whispered, leaning in closer to hear every word.

"Yes," Daphne said, "and I spoke to her. 'Was it you?' I asked, meaning had Felicia seen her. Blue Lady nodded her head. She was dressed in a distinctly bluey-grey, long, floaty dress with quite full sleeves that fell into points at knee-length. Then, she drifted away to the bathroom."

"Is that it? Didn't you ask who she was? Why she was here?"

"I wanted to ask her lots of questions, but I also needed to see what was going on with that hysterical girl. So, I stood outside Simon's room eavesdropping which is when I heard him say she could get into his bed. The rest you know."

"Wonder what her story is? Why she's stayed at Mena for so many years?"

"Why she's been another Menabilly spirit, I've no more idea about her than I do about myself. Don't think I haven't given my situation thought over the years because I have, but I was often busy with the young Simon. He seemed to be the reason holding me here, yet we're not related in any way. Of course, he lived at Menabilly, which has always had a special place in my heart, an all-consuming passion in a way.

"The house called to me, you know, from an early age. It's a memory even death hasn't dulled. I'd read about it as a young person. One day I convinced my sister Angela to come for a walk to see if we could find it. We finally arrived at the start of the drive to the house, some three miles of it, but it began to get dark, so we had to turn back. I didn't forget though. I couldn't. In the spring, I made my way back again. It was hidden from view, overgrown with bramble, like it hadn't been lived in for ages. For fifteen years I visited the house like that, even climbed in through windows sometimes. I suppose it was trespassing, don't you know. I'd make my way into the garden and just walk around for hours. Eventually, I was able to let it. When the lease expired, I moved to Kilmarth where I died, but it was to Menabilly I returned in my present state. It had a terrific pull. I couldn't deny it."

"So, what got you here to Miss Selby's house?" asked Mrs Taylor.

"That's a bit of a puzzle, having only lived here a brief time when alive. Of course, we had the encounter while she was locked in the bathroom at Menabilly. When I heard her mention Rose Cottage, it resonated. I wished myself there after Simon and I had that silly tiff. You, know – in an 'I'll show him' kind of way. Then, eventually I got to know Selby. She can be a hard nut to crack, but being with her was a bit of fresh air for me. She's not unlike me in quite a few ways. I watched Selby and Simon when he was here one afternoon skinning a rabbit, knowing instinctively they belonged together. Since then I like to think I've had a hand in where things have ended up tonight."

"Ahem." Mrs Taylor cleared her throat and raised an eyebrow.

"Yes, all right then, and you too. I've felt tenderly towards him since he first found me – a sweet, little seven-year-old thing in pyjamas. It's funny to think back on that now – eyes on stalks, shaking with fear at the very existence of me in the middle of the night in a secret room behind the linen cupboard. I've wanted to see him settled with someone to whom he could give love. Really, he's like a son. I get so distressed that I can't retrieve memories of my own family from my lifetime, but Selby looked me up on her phone. It said I had three children of my own apparently, and grandchildren, and they were all very important to me. I should so like to remember them."

"Perhaps you stayed to see the boy settled then. And what about that book you slave-drive them two about every second of the day? You're teasy as an adder when you don't get what you want when you want it."

"That's the most ridiculous statement anyone could make about a – a – a spirit. That was the word I was looking for. Anyone in spirit form must take what is and lump the rest as they've no control over anything."

"Dumping shoes out of drawers and opening gates to let sheep escape hardly sounds helpless to me," the housekeeper insisted while she got up to check the casserole in the oven.

"You're right about the other thing, you know. What drove me to distraction all these years was Merryn's story. It was bubbling over. I had to get it out of my system. That's why I hid their manuscripts and caused a ruckus. I needed to disrupt their own work. Somehow, I had to get them united. I rationalised that my selfishness would reward them when they saw how perfect they were for each other."

"You took a risk. They could've hated each other's guts."

"Not a chance. I saw it right from the start. They were both taken with each other."

"Pretty don't make for an easy twenty-four hours all your life, my nan used to say."

"No, that's perfectly correct. I would've had to revise my plan if I hadn't seen all the right signs further down the line, but I did, and here we are. *Pistol Meadow* is almost finished. Leaving it unwritten was a tortuous affair. I don't believe any writer could settle into a tranquil eternal rest, knowing they had left their best work hanging mid-air. I couldn't have, quite obviously." Daphne stopped talking. And all the other stories, she suddenly thought. What will happen to them? She had not had the courage to look for them after Constance had died.

CHAPTER TWENTY-ONE

*S*elby could not quite believe they had finished *Pistol Meadow* in three months. The decision to submit the book for publication, using a pseudonym, had spurred them on. Day and night, they had written, edited, and argued. "That's a very satisfying ending," she said yawning, and flexing stiff back muscles. "I feel we've written something worth reading."

"What do you mean – we've – written?" Daphne scowled, a smile twitching at the corners of her mouth. "And of course it's worth reading."

Having moved her laptop to Menabilly, Selby and Simon had hardly slept until Merryn's story had been told. The three of them sat back to admire the bulky manuscript representing Daphne du Maurier's last book. Though the writing had finished a few weeks before, they had each read the entire thing one last time before agreeing they were happy with it.

"This calls for a celebration," Simon said, jumping up,

striding around the room, and stretching his arms up towards the ceiling. "How about champagne?"

Daphne looked at the two people in front of her, wondering why she could barely hear what they were saying. Their voices faded in and out. Then suddenly, as if a dial had been turned to full volume, she heard Selby say, "Yes, we deserve champagne."

"Of course, you both did excellent jobs, getting *Pistol Meadow* written for me. Thank you, dear ones. It's taken a lot out of me though. I feel a bit thin on juice this evening."

"The manuscript is going off to Selby's publisher tomorrow morning," Simon remarked as he eased the cork out of a bottle to pour into a glass for Selby. "And we all know what the wait is like. Right then." He held his glass up with one hand while clutching a small package behind his back. "The first toast goes to you, Dame Daphne –"

Selby cleared her throat and crooked a finger at him. "Not Dame – abhors it," she whispered into his ear when he leaned down.

"Let's start over," Simon said, holding the glass in the air once again. "The world may know you as a famous author, but to us, you are our dearest and beloved Daphne – quick-witted, terribly amusing, impossibly tyrannical from time to time, calculating – often. Along with Merryn Penrice and Richard Penvose whom, I might add, are not both at the bottom of the sea where we thought they were headed in chapter twelve, we thank you. Not only did your book bring us together, but it was one hell of an adventure. If I could, I'd throw my arms around you."

Daphne snorted a laugh. "Thank heaven for the laws of the Universe."

"We've got a surprise," Simon continued as he placed something wrapped in coloured paper and gold ribbon on the table in front of her.

"I say, this makes up for not being able to share in the bubbles you're drinking."

She unwrapped the package, revealing a navy leather-bound book with silver-edged pages. Turning it over, she gasped. On the front, embossed in silver script were the words, *Pistol Meadow*.

"We had it privately printed as a present, just this one copy for you," he explained. "Even though we're confident it will be published, we wanted to mark the occasion. You've waited long enough."

Daphne held the book, turning it over in her hands before opening it and lifting the thin tissue covering the title page. At the top, printed in bold italic script, *Pistol Meadow*, and lower down the page, Daphne du Maurier. It was hard to take it all in, but the sense of pride and relief was overwhelming. Of course, she had had the thrill of many published books during her lifetime, but this was different. It would be the only copy of *Pistol Meadow* that would bear her name as the author.

"It's lovely, thank you. I'm quite at a loss for words."

"Refreshing reply," Selby teased.

The room was quiet. Everyone was thinking about the journey shared that had led to this point. Challenging, Selby thought, but worth it.

A bonus worth cherishing, Simon reflected as he glanced at Selby.

What now, Daphne wondered, reaching into her sleeve for a handkerchief.

"Simon and I thought of taking a few weeks break while we wait to hear back. We're going to the South of France."

"Now there's a place I adored. Loved travelling most places overall, really – just couldn't get enough of it. Oh, don't worry. I understand. I've no plans to join you. I shall stay here to annoy Mrs Taylor," Daphne said as she disappeared.

Simon sat down on the sofa next to Selby. "I think she was truly touched, don't you? That escape looked a bit rushed. She's really a sentimental old thing."

"What's it going to be like going back to our own work?"

"It doesn't matter to me what I write if you're by my side," Simon said, pulling her closer.

"If we're leaving tomorrow, I've got to pack and speak to Mrs Taylor to make sure she's fine about looking after Rose Cottage."

"To think she's known about Daphne all these years and never let on. Ha, I believe she's thoroughly enjoyed pulling her little jokes on me over the years. I'm glad they'll have each other while we're in France."

"Simon, what would you think of the idea of going to Tuscany as well? We would already be halfway there. I would love you to meet Viviana and Carlo."

He thought carefully about what he was about to say, wondering if he had the right to offer an opinion. "You may say it's not my business, but would it be awkward to be in the same town as your parents and not stop in to at least say hello? How will they feel if they discover we're staying with their old housekeeper?"

Selby stiffened. Feelings of worry and anxiety from the past sank down into the pit of her stomach. Did she want the happiness she had only just found tarnished by the sense of abandonment she felt when she was around her parents? "My parents and I – a difficult relationship, especially Mother. Think I've mentioned. Don't want to drag you into the middle. Complicated. Feel uncomfortable."

They sat silently for some time. The abbreviated sentences had emerged. It was something he noticed when she was stressed. It saddened him to think she had suffered pain in her life, but she had to make the decisions concerning her parents. He stroked her head, kissing the top, hoping to reassure her.

"You're right," she finally said. "It could be awkward. I don't want you thrust into my difficult memories and ghosts of the past. We won't go."

"Fine with me," he whispered. He considered that Selby might never be free to receive or give her love unconditionally until she made peace with her parents, whatever form that took.

She began rifling around in her handbag, looking for something. "I went to Italy earlier this summer. Stayed at Viviana's, not with my parents. It was hot as hell in the middle of the night. I went outside to the small fountain in the square for some air. My father showed up – a bit of serendipity I guess. He was drunk, weaving across the cobblestones. Maybe seeing him in that vulnerable state knocked him off that pedestal I'd put him on. The worse part about my whole history with my parents is that we had had such loving, happy times when we lived in Cornwall. If I'd never known what real love felt like, I may not have suffered so, but I had those seven years to compare. I don't know what got into me that night at the fountain, but I told him how it felt growing up in a home without love, ignored by parents whose careers dominated their every thought. Well, never mind, there were a lot of things I said. Left the next evening to come back to Cornwall. The reason I'm telling you all this..." She stopped speaking to search the bottom of her bag, and then in frustration, dumped the contents on the sofa, eventually lifting an envelope from the pile of stuff. "This came a few weeks ago. It's a letter from my father."

She removed the letter from the envelope and ran her eyes over the first page before reading it out.

Dearest of Sweet Peas,
Got quite a shock when I sobered up and remembered what you let burst the night I saw you here. Burst is the right word, for it was obvious you've been holding these painful memories in for many...

Tears rolled down Selby's face. She handed the letter to Simon to read to himself.

...for many years. I could see that. Your words keep resounding in my head. I've done no work since. My problem, I know.

The worst part for me is that you told me your pain has been going on for so long. It was right there in front of me, but I never stopped long enough to see it. Makes me realise

I'm a shit of the first order, but really that's all too easy, the name-calling. Doesn't excuse anything. What you said – it's made me see what a terrible father I've been. Self-centred. Major ego. Terrible human being. And in case you think this is the drink speaking, I haven't had one since sobering up after that night. Intend to keep it that way.

This abuse that I – we've – dealt you. It wasn't with intent. When someone first said they liked my work, I was cock-a-hoop. There are thousands of artists, many much better than I am who never get a look-in. My early torments, the years after you were born were full of worry of how I would provide for you and Celia. When the money got good, I couldn't help it. Keep producing while they like the stuff, I told myself. That sounds denigrating. I don't mean it that way, but artistic types create bodies of work from passion within their soul, never knowing if it's any good. Look, I'm also not going to discount that enormous ego of mine. Yes, it felt good hearing the applause; yes, it relieved the worry of not having to wonder how or if I could pay a bill or buy food.

And then there's Celia. I could never believe that she had settled on little old me. She's smart, beautiful, talented – much more talented than I am. It just took longer for people to spot it. I was always trying to measure up to what I thought may have been the wonder she saw in me. Not sure now what it was, something intangible maybe. Love, maybe. Can't speak about that now. Not sure she's ever coming back.

Why I'm writing this letter...let's cut to the chase before I digress further. I want to know if there's any hope for us – you and me – not now, but sometime in the future. I realise I will have to earn your trust. That you may never show me any love would be a just punishment, the result of my own stupid, heartless behaviour.

I've thought long and hard about how I could repair our relationship. I say our, and I'm speaking of yours and mine. The only answer I can come up with is time. Over time, maybe something will shift. For anything to have a decent chance, I've decided to move back to the UK. I hope you can find it in your heart to see me occasionally, and that we can take things slowly to see what happens. Please don't panic when I tell you that I'm looking for a house in Cornwall. I'll make sure it's at the other end of the county, so that you don't feel obligated or pressured.

I am the pathetic, truly ashamed father who loves you so, Sweet Pea.

Simon handed the letter back to Selby. "That's quite a raw, emotional gut-spilling."

"You understand now why I couldn't go to Tuscany to see them, don't you?" Putting the letter back in her bag, she pushed it to the bottom where it could rot for all she cared. She had no intention of replying.

"It's what you think that's important," Simon told her. "I will support whatever you want to do about any of this whenever or never." But how I hope you don't just hide it under the carpet, he thought. Wounds like this fester, and I'll not allow anything to ruin what we have. We'll see if the old boy manages the move to Cornwall. Then, I'll find a way.

~

Mrs Taylor made a pot of tea, taking out mugs and swirling around hot water from the kettle to warm them before pouring it. "What a dobeck I am. Look what I done! I forget you're what you are sometimes. Took out two mugs, didn't I. It's so quiet around here with them two gone to France, it's making me feel giddy."

Daphne laughed. "In complete agreement, but your constant chatter hardly qualifies as quiet. You haven't enough to do. Why don't you take advantage of their absence and do a spring clean or something?"

"I'm not a creature who likes changing its mind, and I have that down for the next two months. Can't rush it 'cause I'm not getting any younger."

"Ah yes, you'll be joining me soon."

"Don't rush me to my grave. When it's my time, I'll go, but I had an idea the other day. Let's go up to that awful nest of yours and give it a good going over. Been wanting to get my hands on it for years."

"Leave things as they are. Dust is not a thing I particularly notice."

"I could make some lovely new drapes. Get the bed righted again and take one of Mrs Rashleigh's old bed covers in there."

"You would make curtains for my room? It has been frightfully depressing watching them disintegrate over the years. Oh, you old boot, I would like that."

Upstairs in Daphne's room, the housekeeper dragged the moth-eaten curtains down off their fixings and opened the window to chuck them onto the grass. Then, she put all the books on the bed, dusted each one, and put them back onto clean shelves. She polished the few bits of furniture in the room and pushed the bed out to hoover underneath.

"Heaven's above, what's all this?" she cried out.

Daphne was looking at some old fabrics that Mrs Taylor had brought from the sewing room as possible curtain material. "What's what?" she asked, without looking up.

"Them boxes there," Mrs Taylor said, pointing to the space where the bed had been.

Both women leaned down to look more closely. A box with dried up brown tape across the top was covered in cobwebs and dead spiders. Mrs Taylor got down on her hands and knees to haul it out.

"There's more under there, but the stuffing in the mattress is in bits," she said, letting out a series of small sneezes followed by one good, big one. "Bleddy hell, it's dusty down there. I'm going to need something to get them others free of the wadding." When she came back, she pushed the others out with a mop handle, and beat the tops with the dust rag in her hands. "They got your name on them. There's a blue envelope here with a 'D' on it. That's you, I suppose." She handed it to Daphne who read it to herself.

It's been two years since you went away. I come to this room every day, hoping you have returned. On the day that you left, after having discovered no print appeared on the page when you typed, I put your notebooks into boxes and sealed them. Their content would only torture, and you've been such a dear friend that I wanted to spare you. I've hidden them in the room, should you feel strong enough sometime to look for them. Also, the shelves are down in the linen cupboard in the hope that if you do return one day, Simon and you might meet.

Farewell for now, my friend.

It was signed 'C' which must be for Constance, Daphne thought as she sat down, unable to speak. What a joy it had been to meet Constance Rashleigh. What a difference it had made to her existence. Daphne had found the letter on top of her typewriter when she had returned to Menabilly after Constance had died.

"Shall I open them?" Mrs Taylor asked, breaking the silence.

"No. I remember now – that letter – I've read it before."

"But what's in all them boxes?"

"I'm sorry, but I can't," Daphne said in an agitated state before fleeing the room.

Mrs Taylor closed the boxes back up and picked up the fabric that Daphne had chosen for curtains. There would be time this afternoon when she got home to run them up. Perhaps new curtains would make a difference. She had never seen Daphne so upset.

Coming down the drive to Menabilly in the morning, she noticed Daphne's window was open.

"A glorious morning," Daphne said when Mrs Taylor walked into her room.

"It's a morning to put up new curtains. That's what it is."

"You've made them already? You are a marvel."

The housekeeper went about getting them fixed to the curtain rail. "There now, see. What do you think?"

"I think they are perfectly marvellous. Thank you."

Both women stood looking at the clean and tidy room, admiring the beautiful floral pattern of the curtains. Neither spoke of the boxes.

"Now, I'm fetching a bed cover that will show up proud with my handiwork, and then you'll have a cosy nest in here." When she came back into the room, she could barely see Daphne. "Wasson?" she asked. "You're looking thin, my girl. Standing in the light by the window, I can barely make you out."

"It's been like this for some time now," Daphne explained. "Last night I thought I was going to evaporate. Listen, about the boxes –"

"Now, now, I'm no snoop. There's no need. I could see it was hard on you. Them boxes can stay there 'til eternity, and I'll not breathe a word."

"That's just it, you see. I've been thinking – what if I do just evaporate? Those boxes are full of my old notebooks with outlines for new stories – written during my lifetime, you see. Simon's mother taped them closed and hid them, hoping to spare me from ever having to read all the plot ideas I'd come up with, but would never be able to write. I went a bit crazy when I discovered I couldn't get words to appear on paper. I left Menabilly for a while."

Mrs Taylor quickly added, "Always wondered about that, but I remember saying to myself that you must just be holed up in this room. Weren't my place to wonder really. Then, I heard your typewriter start up again one day. All these years, I thought you was crafting them stories up here until you spilled the beans a while back."

"I walked the floors all night, considering what to do with the boxes. I've decided, but I'm going to need your help." Daphne's eyes met Mrs Taylor's. "Can you make a bonfire in the garden? I want to burn them."

After Mrs Taylor left for the day, Daphne wandered from room to room at Menabilly. Somehow, she was suddenly able to remember her life there – her husband, her two daughters, her son, her grandchildren, and the love she had felt for them. All her memories were now within reach to cherish. She had been lucky in life, she decided – a lovely family and the freedom to write. Living in the best county had been a bonus. No matter to what exotic place she had travelled, it was to Cornwall she had always longed to return. She curled up on the sofa in the sitting room, wishing there was a fire lit in the grate. It had always been her favourite place to be in the evening.

"Daphne."

She turned her head to look behind her. Wishful thinking, old thing, she said to herself. It was lonely without Simon and Selby. The sound of wood crackling in the grate made her glance back at the fireplace. It glowed, radiating warmth she could feel.

"Daphne."

"Is someone here?" she asked.

"It's Charles, Daphne. Charles Cannon."

She could see the outline of a shape taking form in front of her. "Charles?" she repeated as she got up from the sofa. He was becoming visible. It was most certainly him, not as an old man, but as she remembered him when they first met. "How can this be?"

"What about a glass of champagne?" he asked.

"How I'd love that, but alas, the ability to enjoy such things long ago left me."

"Try this," he said, handing her a fluted glass filled with golden liquid, bubbles whizzing up and down.

She held the glass to her lips and took a sip. "Ah. My, how I've wanted to do that for the longest time. However did you manage it, Charles? How do you manage to be here for that matter?"

"I wouldn't know how to explain, not understanding it all. I just know that I'm here. I've come for you, Daphne."

"Come for me? Why?"

"Because it's time, dearest of girls. You're to come with me, but not for a little while yet. We have some time. Let's sit by the fire for a while, shall we, and enjoy ourselves."

They sat down side by side on the small sofa, the light from the fire flickering on their faces. Daphne looked at him and smiled. "I did love you so, dear Charles, but when I met Tommy, that was it. There was no going back. I'm sorry if I hurt you."

"Broke the heart in two, that's a fact, but I had a very happy life with a wonderful woman, the mother of three loving daughters who gave us six grandchildren, but I never stopped loving you, Daphne. To my dying day, I thought about you."

"Shall I tell you something? I was there in your flat, Charles. When Selby came to see you recently, the night you died."

"Really? Are such things possible?"

"Well, we're both sitting here, aren't we?"

He laughed. "I suppose so."

"You were very good with her – with Selby. You said all the right things. She came home and told Simon she loved him. Of course, I knew he had fallen for her. It was in his face the first time he looked at her. I wanted someone good for him, don't you know. I'd grown impossibly fond of him over time. Maybe that's why I stayed here after I died, and because I couldn't let my book remain unfinished. It had become an obsession, like this house."

"It's a lovely house. Another glass, Daphne?"

"Yes please. What's it like, Charles? Where we're going, I mean."

"Whatever I said would be inadequate. Plus, I haven't your flare for description. Questions like the one you pose do not enter the mind.

"What do you think about all day, then?"

"There are no dilemmas, so there's no angst, no problems to solve."

"Doesn't sound terribly entertaining. Not sure I want to evaporate, if that's the right word, into nothing, floating for eternity and so on."

"Let me try again. One word to describe the overriding, all-encompassing feeling that dominates would be love in its most perfect form."

"You're just an old romantic. Ah well, it will be what it will be. I realise there may no longer be a choice. It has been a very fortunate extra run, one might say, so I can't complain. Charles, I've got to do a few things if we're leaving. I won't be long." She glided up the stairs and along to a bedroom at the end of the corridor.

When the door opened, she was standing there. "Do you know?" Daphne asked. "That someone has come for me, I mean?"

Blue Lady bowed her head.

"Would you like to come along as well? I could ask."

Shaking her head from side to side, tears fell from Blue Lady's eyes.

"You will have good reason, like I had, no doubt. Though I will miss Menabilly, it's time for me to leave. I see that now. All things righted and accomplished as a soldier might say. One thing more – the people in this house are good people. I think you know that?"

Blue Lady nodded.

"Watch over them when you can, and the house. Let no harm come to any of them or Menabilly," she said solemnly. "If it's within your abilities, of course."

Daphne looked around the house one last time, walking through each room, remembering. Then, she entered her bedroom behind the linen cupboard to gather up some things to take downstairs to Simon's study.

"I'm ready, Charles," she said, returning to the sitting room. "Think I've been ready for some time. Now, lacking in purpose, I find it hard to concentrate. No, wait. I have forgotten something important. May I?

"Of course."

When she returned, she asked, "How do we do this?"

"You just take my hand, dear girl, and leave the rest to the Universe."

Daphne put her right hand into his. In her left, she held a blue leather-bound book with silver-edged pages to her heart.

CHAPTER TWENTY-TWO

S imon drove over the Tamar Bridge, looking down at the sailing boats anchored in the harbour. This is always the point in any journey home when my heart sings, he thought to himself. On the other side of the bridge was Cornwall and his cherished Menabilly. He loved the house as much as Daphne loved it, and even after all those years, it amused him to recall how Menabilly had brought together a young boy, forlorn at the loss of his mother, and a ghost. He smiled – his ghost.

"Won't be long now," he said, looking over at Selby. Her brown face and body were the result of lunches in the sun, long walks on the beach, and swims in the Mediterranean. He reviewed the plan in his head. When we get to Menabilly – it's got to be on Menabilly soil.

She breathed in the smell of a Cornish summer as they made their way through the lush countryside. Cows and sheep grazed at the end of a warm day. Crops, now high, were nearly ready for harvest. She was happy to come home to Rose Cottage – the place she felt she belonged – the bonus that it was haunted by the most amusing and wittiest of ghosts.

Would Daphne ever have felt the kind of panic that had overwhelmed last night, keeping her awake until dawn? Suddenly, she had been unable to picture her future life. Loving Simon, that was easy. Her passion for writing – that was worrying her. It was not possible to live without it, but would she continue to produce manuscripts about women who – as Raphe crudely put it – were emotionally crippled? The motivation for these books had come, she now believed, from the lack of love and sense of abandonment during her childhood. Did she want to begin life with Simon, dwelling in the negative world of couples trapped in dysfunctional relationships? How she wished she could write something like *Pistol Meadow*, but she was no Daphne du Maurier.

"You know, I think I could be blindfolded, dropped anywhere within a five-mile radius and find my way home," Simon said as they drove through the gates of Menabilly. "Can you smell it? It's very distinctive – that earthy aroma of rich dark soil, the slightly musky scent of tall oaks and beech above. Listen – thrush, blackbird – singing in profusion. Swallows and house martins catching an evening meal. Let's get out here for a few minutes, to watch the sun go down."

Selby smiled. She knew there would always be that special place in his heart reserved only for Menabilly. They walked for a while without speaking.

In the middle of the field, he stopped and turned towards her. "With my feet on this soil on the land where I was born in the county of my soul, this is where I wanted to be – to ask – if – you will spend your life with me."

Listening to the sounds of the countryside at dusk, Selby had been in a reverie of her own. It took her a moment to realise what had just happened. She giggled like a schoolgirl. "Simon Rashleigh, did you just ask me to marry you?"

"I did."

"And I do," she replied without hesitation. It had been that simple, and all that she had needed to say. Knowing it was the right decision from the moment she had taken the Test – when she had watched the children running across the lawn – when he had kissed her, holding her tenderly. She had felt the peace, the sense of being cherished and loved.

"Phew. I don't know what I would've done if you'd said no," he suddenly blurted out before asking, "Shall we go tell the old snoops the news?"

The lights were on in the house when they drove into the courtyard. They found Mrs Taylor in the kitchen. "Good trip away? Oh my, but you're both brown. There's been rain here. Crops needed it, mind. Not staying long, but I knew you'd be hungry when you got home. Some supper's in the warming oven."

"Thank you, Mrs Taylor, but before you disappear,

there's something we want to tell you and Daphne."
Taking Selby's hand, he stepped out into the hall.
"Daphne. Come quick. We have something to tell you," he
bellowed. Waiting in the hall, he looked towards the stairs
that would bring her flying down from her bedroom
behind the linen cupboard.

Mrs Taylor came up behind, putting her hand on his
back. "She's gone, boy."

"Where?" Selby asked.

"I've had no sight of her for the last week."

"Maybe she's at my house," Selby suggested.

"Not there neither. I've been at both houses doing a
spring clean. I've had no sight of her. 'Twas her time, see.
She knew something weren't right before you left for
France. Told her Nan spoke of when spirits have been left
behind – that it's not a thing forever. She was fading in
spirit. I've made my peace with her moving on. Nothing
easy about it, but I've done it."

They went back into the kitchen in a daze and sat
down at the table. No one spoke. Mrs Taylor made a pot of
tea. When it was ready, she poured it into three cups.

"Daphne can't be gone," Simon said. "I wanted to tell
her that Selby and I are getting married."

"Great news, that is. Best news I've heard for a long
time, and overjoyed she would be to hear it," the housekeeper exclaimed.

"Yes, but she's not here to share in the celebration," he
said quietly.

"Giss on, she saw how things were developing. What
she wanted for you was someone like Miss Selby. I

couldn't say for sure now, but I sense she knows somehow that all is well – and saints alive, I almost forgot – left you both something – on your desks where you wrote her book. Here's a letter I was to give you." Mrs Taylor fished into the deep pocket of her apron.

Simon opened the envelope and Selby read over his shoulder,

Dear Ones,

That I am now able to put words on paper makes me believe that change is in the wind. If I move along to the next great adventure, no tears please, no sadness. Everything must evolve. I shall be no exception. I've left something for you both on the table in the study. Mrs Taylor kept me from destroying them. It took a while, but the more I thought about things, the more certain I became that you will know what's to be done. Any decision you make will be fine with me. I have had the good fortune of remembering my lovely family recently, and although I had a huge love for them – you, Simon, have had a special place in my heart in my more recent existence; and you, Selby, have been the best bit of fresh air a woman of a hundred and twelve could have had. Enjoy your lives together, dear children.

Adieu,
   Daphne

While Simon and Selby rushed into the study, Mrs Taylor pulled a handkerchief from her pocket for a good squall. It's no use, she thought, I be lonely here without that woman. She busied herself checking the supper in the Aga. Opening the oven door, she reached in with a long wooden spoon to give the casserole a quick stir. Something nudged her leg, and she looked down knowing that her imagination was likely to play up for a while until she got used to Daphne's absence. When she felt it again, she suddenly wondered. "That you, Mouse?" She felt him jump up on her apron. Then he raced around everywhere, sniffing and knocking over baskets and the bin. She heard his toenails scamper along the stone floor outside the kitchen, and then up the stairs. Mrs Taylor followed to the top floor and down the corridor to the last room. She opened the door and switched on the lights. There stood Blue Lady with a white dog in her arms.

"Well, I never. You? Daphne told me, but I never seen you myself before. And Mouse? You're visible. Is this where he's been hiding all these days gone when Daphne looked over hill and dale for him? He's to stay with you, I see."

Blue Lady's smile answered the question.

"All right then, I'll leave you two. Happy to make your acquaintance in a manner of speaking." Mrs Taylor closed off the light and shut the door. It would not be the same as having Daphne around, but it was comforting to know there was a friendly presence in the house.

Boxes were spread over a long table in the study. A blue

envelope marked with a 'D' lay open on top of one of them. Simon opened it. "This is my mother's writing," he said. They read the letter that Constance Rashleigh had left for Daphne to find if she ever returned to Menabilly. "Daphne told me Mother had taken down the shelves in the linen cupboard."

"Are these the boxes your mother writes about?" Selby asked.

"I've no idea." He tore the tape from the tops of all the cartons. Inside, pale-blue notebooks lay stacked in bundles bound up with red ribbons. They untied each and divided them up.

After a while, Simon spoke. "Selby, these are outlines of plots for stories not yet written. I don't recognise any of them. There must be two dozen or more in each group." He stopped talking, suddenly realising he would never see his Daphne again. He had never really known Menabilly without her. Selby could see from Simon's face what he was thinking. She reached for his hand.

"Darling Simon, we shall fill this house with laughter and happiness. You don't think Daphne left these for us without good reason, do you? We will honour this legacy and write the stories she's left behind."

He walked to the bookcase. It was full of books written by the famous author. Tracing a finger over the spines, he saw favourites, some that Daphne had read to him as a boy.

"Write Daphne's stories without her? I'm sure I couldn't reproduce her kind of narrative."

It suddenly became clear to her what path lay ahead for her – for them. "That's just it. We can write these

books in our own style, together, here at Menabilly."
Taking his face in her hands, she explained that she
couldn't go back to writing the same kinds of books she
had always produced. The writing of *Pistol Meadow* had
been so different, so exciting in comparison. "What adventures we will have. Believe me. Believe in us."

Looking down at the beautiful, blue eyes staring up at
him, he took a deep breath for the first time since hearing
that Daphne was gone. He wrapped Selby in his arms and
smiled. "How did I get so lucky that you got locked in a
bathroom and needed rescuing?"

Feeling a new sense of peace, Daphne watches the two
lovers. She is freer now that she is not so earthly bound.
She is no longer visible; nor can she speak to the living.
Her presence can be sensed by some who allow such
thoughts into their heads. Most will not, dismissing a
shiver up the back or down a leg as silly business. She
knows otherwise and has always believed that those who
lived before leave something behind of themselves in
houses they have loved. For her, Menabilly had been
everything. She had loved its grace, its simplicity, how the
light sparkled off the Cornish granite. It had held her in
storms and opened its arms in good times, letting in the
light that reflected from the sea.

Caught in a dream of long ago, Daphne closes her
eyes, and stands in the garden one last time. She sees
herself as a young woman, her baby son is at her feet and
her two little girls run to their father across the lawn.
Though he's only been gone for the day, Tommy takes her

in his arms and kisses her tenderly. A wind blows up the Cornish coast, bringing a sudden downpour from which they shelter under a Cedar of Lebanon. From here, she has the best view of her belovèd Menabilly, the one she will hold for eternity.

AUTHOR'S NOTE

The idea for Daphne's Ghost came to me while visiting Menabilly for a Cornish charity event, although descriptions in this book of the interior are entirely fictitious. The Rashleigh family live at Menabilly today, but Simon Rashleigh, the fictional character in *Daphne's Ghost*, is a figment of my imagination and bears no resemblance to any member of the Rashleigh family, living or dead. Most importantly, I must emphasise that the existence of *any* ghosts at Menabilly is a complete invention on my part, as are the locations of some beaches and other places in Cornwall.

I have also taken liberties with Mrs Taylor's Cornish slang, as only some people in Cornwall use the charming colloquialisms more prevalent in times past.

Finally, the Daphne du Maurier ghostly character in the book is, of course, an imaginary one. I took inspiration from interviews she gave during her lifetime to capture the intonation, vocabulary and phrasing she might use. Also referenced were her letters and books. I hope I've caught something of her personality – *though what she would be like in spirit form is anyone's guess.*

D L Baylis is a former journalist who lives in Cornwall.

ACKNOWLEDGEMENTS

Gratitude in abundance goes to those family and friends who were early readers of *Daphne's Ghost,* especially Joan Lazar, Bruce Kroog, Gail Adler, Jemima Fox, Clare Baker, Delia Roche-Kelly, and most especially, Lisa Forrell and Jane Stonborough. I would like to thank Ian Jenner, Sue and Barney Taylor, and Rachel Keith, for all their support.

I am indebted to Richard Rashleigh for allowing the use of his family name for a fictionalised character, and also for permission to place the location of the story at Menabilly.

Of overarching importance has been the wise counsel and knowledge of editor, Maria Moloney. I am so very grateful for all her input, and contributions.

Credit and appreciation goes to Jane Stonborough for creating the recipe, and to Annabella Salvalaggio for the Italian translations.

Thank you to Matt Buckett at Ink-Pot Graphics for the design of the book cover.

GLOSSARY

MRS TAYLOR – CORNISH VERNACULAR

Aye? – Yes? What was that?

Backalong – in former times

Better fit would be – it would be better if

Bobber lip – bruised and swollen lip

Cakey – soft, feeble-minded

Catchpit – a place in the home where everything is dropped

Chacking – thirsty

Cheldern – children

Crib – a mid-morning break for a snack

Dobeck – somebody stupid

Dreckly – at some point, but not immediately

Gawky – stupid

Giss on – don't talk rubbish

Leave the door abroad – leave the door open

Mind – remember

Mutt – sulk

My Lover – an affectionate greeting that is unisex

Oggy – a Cornish pasty

Party – a young woman

Screech – to cry loudly

Squall – to cry

Teasy – bad-tempered

Upcountry – anywhere in England, except Cornwall or the Isles of Scilly

Wasson – what's going on?

DAPHNE – HER OWN MADE-UP VOCABULARY

Hard-chair – to be cross with someone

See-Me – pleased with oneself

Tell-Him – mundane and tedious

Boy or Tommy – Daphne du Maurier's husband whose full name was Lieutenant-General Sir Frederick Arthur Montague "Boy" Browning (1896–1965)

GLOSSARY OF ITALIAN PHRASES

Delizios
Delicious

Tutto
Everything

Carissima
My darling girl

Si, Bellezza, e vero
Yes, beautiful girl, it's true

Adesso, carissima, qual è il problema? Dimmi.
Now, my dear, what's the problem? Tell me.

Coscienza sporca
Guilty conscience

Buongiorno, amore, come stai?
Good morning, my love. How are you?

Si, e vero
Yes, it's true.

Caffe latte, fette biscottate, brioche con marmellata et con crema
Coffee with milk, rusk, brioche with marmalade and cream.

Panino

An Italian sandwich

Et allora, ascoltami

And now, tell me.

Come se niente fosse

Like nothing has happened

Che idiota

What an idiot

Usi il cervello, cretino

Use your head, idiot

Idiota

Idiot

E solo cena, sciocca. Calmati!

It's just dinner, stupid girl. Calm yourself!

MRS TAYLOR'S CORNISH FISH PIE

Serves 4

Ingredients

FISH

200g Undyed smoked haddock fillet, skinned and cut into small pieces

200g Cod fillet, skinned and cut into small pieces

200g Salmon fillet, skinned and cut into small pieces

OR replace the salmon with lobster or scallops, also in small pieces

Parsley – a small bunch chopped fairly fine

SAUCE

50g Unsalted butter

50g Plain white flour

600ml Whole milk, heated

50g Cheese, half sharp-cheddar and half Parmesan, freshly grated

1 tbsp Mustard, English or Dijon to taste

1 tsp Worcestershire sauce

Squeeze of lemon

Salt and freshly ground black pepper

MASHED POTATO TOPPING

900g Floury potatoes, King Edward or Desiree, peeled and sliced

70g unsalted butter, cut into pieces

50g Whole milk, heated

30g Parmesan cheese, freshly grated for final topping

Salt

Hand held electric beater

METHOD

Pre-heat the oven to 190C/gas mark 5

Butter a large pie dish

SAUCE

Prepare the roux by melting the butter until gently bubbling, then stir in the flour, whisking until very smooth and cooked through. Lower the heat and add the warm milk from a jug, whisking constantly until smooth. Bring to a simmer for a few minutes until you have a smooth sauce. Off the heat, add the seasonings and whisk again. Stir in the chopped parsley. Check seasoning and adjust as necessary.

Slowly fold the raw fish into the hot sauce, stirring gently but constantly for a few minutes, until the fish has literally just cooked.

Carefully pour the mixture into the buttered dish and leave to cool.

MASHED POTATOES

Bring a large pan of water, with salt, to a boil. Add the sliced potatoes and cook. Test with a knife to check if properly soft. Drain well and set back on heat to dry out a bit. Off the heat, beat with electric beater, adding pieces of butter until there are no visible chunks. Then add milk slowly, beating all the while until smooth and fluffy. Do not add more milk than needed. Add salt, NOT Parmesan, which is a final topping.

If making in advance: place cling film over the mash in the pan and set aside to cool.

Spread the mashed potato over the fish mixture. Use the tines of a fork to make a nice pattern.

Bake the fish pie in the centre of a hot oven for 30 minutes.

Remove and sprinkle the Parmesan over the top and bake for 10 more minutes. The potatoes should be golden brown. If not, place them under a hot grill quickly, watching scrupulously.

With thanks to Jane Stonborough for this recipe.

Lightning Source UK Ltd.
Milton Keynes UK
UKHW041844010419

340295UK00001B/60/P